KILLER

Jason checked his watch and reached into his pocket. 'I'm really late.' He pulled out his wallet and fished out a twenty, enough to cover both their drinks. Then he looked at Aria. 'So,' he started.

'So,' Aria echoed. And then she leaned forward, grabbed his hand, and kissed him the way she'd wanted him to kiss her years ago. His lips tasted like lime juice and vodka. Jason pulled her close, kneading his hands in her hair. After a moment, they broke apart, grinning. Aria thought she might faint.

'So I'll see you later,' Jason said.

'Definitely,' Aria breathed. Jason strode across the room, opened the door, and was gone.

'Oh my God,' Aria whispered, turning back to the bar. A huge part of her wanted to climb up on the bar stool and scream to the whole room what just happened.

Her phone began to bleat. Aria jumped and stared at it. *One new text message*, the little window said. The sender was *Caller Unknown*.

A draft wafted from the back of the room, making the candle flames bow to the right. It was as if an unseen back door had just opened and shut.

One new text message. Aria ran her hands through her hair. Slowly, she pressed read.

Enjoy your gimlets? Well, sorry, darling, but the fantasy's over. Big Brother is hiding something from you. And trust me . . . you don't want to know what it is. – A

By Sara Shepard

KILLER

SARA SHEPARD

www.atombooks.net

ATOM

First published in the United States in 2009 by HarperTeen
an imprint of HarperCollins Publishers
This paperback edition published in 2011 by Atom
Reprinted 2011

A CIP catalogue record for this book
is available from the British Library.

ISBN 978-1-907410-84-0

Typeset in Sabon by M Rules
Printed and bound in Great Britain by
Clays Ltd, St Ives plc

Atom
An imprint of
Little, Brown Book Group
100 Victoria Embankment
London EC4Y 0DY

An Hachette UK Company
www.hachette.co.uk

www.atombooks.net

To Riley

Liars ought to have good memories.

– ALGERNON SYDNEY

If Memory Serves . . .

What if, all of a sudden, you could remember every single second of your entire life? And not just the major events everyone remembers – little things, too. Like that you and your best friend first bonded over hating the smell of rubber cement in third-grade art class. Or that the very first time you saw your eighth-grade crush, he was walking through the school courtyard, palming a soccer ball in one hand and an iPod Touch in the other.

But with every blessing comes a curse. With your spanking-new flawless memory, you'd also have to remember every fight with your BFF. You'd relive each time your soccer-loving crush sat next to someone else at lunch. With 20/20 memory, the past could suddenly get a whole lot uglier. Someone who seems like an ally now? Look again – could be they weren't as nice as you thought. A friend you remember as always having your back? Oops! On closer inspection, not so much.

If four pretty girls in Rosewood were suddenly given perfect memories, they might know better who to trust and who to stay away from. Then again, maybe their pasts would make even less sense than before.

Memory's a fickle thing. And sometimes we're doomed to repeat the things we've forgotten.

There it was. The big Victorian house at the corner of the cul-de-sac, the one with the rose trellises along the fence and the tiered teak deck in the back. Only a select few had ever been inside, but everyone knew who lived there. She was the most popular girl in school. A girl who set trends, inspired passionate crushes, and made or broke reputations. A girl who every guy wanted to date and every girl wanted to be.

Alison DiLaurentis, of course.

It was a peaceful early September Saturday morning in Rosewood, Pennsylvania, an idyllic Main Line town about twenty miles from Philadelphia. Mr Cavanaugh, who lived across the street from Alison's family, strolled out to his yard to get the newspaper. The tawny golden retriever that belonged to the Vanderwaals a few doors down loped around the fenced-in backyard, barking at squirrels. Not a flower or a leaf was out of place ... except for the four sixth-grade girls who all happened to be stealthily creeping into the DiLaurentises' backyard at the same time.

Emily Fields hid among the tall tomato plants, tugging nervously on the strings of her Rosewood Long Course Swimming sweatshirt. She'd never trespassed on anyone's property, let alone the backyard of the prettiest, most popular girl in school. Aria Montgomery ducked behind an oak tree, picking at the embroidery on the tunic her dad had brought back from yet *another* last-minute art history conference in Germany. Hanna Marin abandoned her bike by a boulder near the family's shed, devising her plan of attack. Spencer Hastings crossed from her neighboring backyard and crouched behind a carefully pruned raspberry bush, inhaling the berries' slightly sweet, slightly tangy smell.

Quietly, each girl stared into the DiLaurentises' rear bay window. Shadows passed through the kitchen. There was a shout from the upstairs bathroom. A tree branch snapped. Someone coughed.

The girls realized they weren't alone at exactly the same moment. Spencer noticed Emily fumbling by the woods. Emily spied Hanna squatting by the rock. Hanna glimpsed Aria behind the tree. Everyone marched to the center of Ali's backyard and gathered in a tight circle.

'What are you guys doing here?' Spencer demanded. She'd known Emily, Hanna, and Aria since the Rosewood Public Library first-grade reading contest – Spencer had won, but all of them had participated. They weren't friends. Emily was the type of girl who blushed when a teacher called on her in class. Hanna, who was now tugging at the waistband of her slightly too-small black Paper Denim jeans, never seemed comfortable with herself. And Aria – well, it looked like Aria was wearing lederhosen today. Spencer was pretty sure Aria's only friends were imaginary.

'Uh, nothing,' Hanna shot back.

'Yeah, nothing,' Aria said, looking suspiciously at all of them. Emily shrugged.

'What are *you* doing?' Hanna asked Spencer.

Spencer sighed. It was obvious they were here for the same reason. Two afternoons ago, Rosewood Day, the elite prep school they attended, had announced the kickoff of its much-anticipated Time Capsule game. Each year, Principal Appleton cut a bright blue Rosewood Day flag into many pieces, upperclassmen hid them around town, and the teachers posted scavenger hunt-style clues to the whereabouts of each piece in the upper- and lower-school lobbies. Whoever found a piece got to decorate it however he or she wanted, and once every piece was found, the staff sewed the flag

3

together again, held a big assembly honoring the winners, and buried it in a Time Capsule behind the soccer fields. Students who found Time Capsule pieces were legends – their legacies lived on for*ever*.

It was hard to stand out at a school like Rosewood Day, and it was even harder to snag a piece of the Time Capsule flag. Only one loophole gave everyone a glimmer of hope: the stealing clause, which stated that it was legal to steal a piece from someone, right up until the piece's time of burial. Two days ago, a certain beautiful somebody had bragged that one of the pieces was as good as hers. Now, four nobodies were hoping to take advantage of the stealing clause when she least expected it.

The thought of stealing Alison's piece was intoxicating. On one hand, it was a chance to get close to her. On the other, it was an opportunity to show the prettiest girl at Rosewood Day that she might not always get everything she wanted. Alison DiLaurentis definitely deserved a reality check.

Spencer glared at the three other girls. 'I was here first. That flag's mine.'

'*I* was here before you,' Hanna whispered. 'I saw you come out of your house only a few minutes ago.'

Aria stomped her purple suede boot, gawking at Hanna. 'You just got here too. I was here before *both* of you.'

Hanna squared her shoulders and looked at Aria's messy braids and chunky layered necklaces. 'And who's going to believe you?'

'Guys.' Emily jutted her pointy chin toward the DiLaurentis house and held a finger to her lips. There were voices coming from the kitchen.

'Don't.' It sounded like Ali. The girls tensed.

'*Don't*,' imitated a second high-pitched voice.

4

'Stop it!' Ali screeched.

'*Stop it!*' the second voice echoed.

Emily winced. Her older sister, Carolyn, used to squeakily imitate Emily's voice the same exact way, and Emily *hated* it. She wondered if the second voice belonged to Ali's older brother, Jason, a junior at Rosewood Day.

'Enough!' called a deeper voice. There was a wall-shaking *thud* and shattering glass. Seconds later, the patio door opened, and Jason stormed out, his sweatshirt flapping open, his shoes untied, and his cheeks flushed.

'Shit,' Spencer whispered. The girls scurried behind the bushes. Jason walked diagonally across the yard toward the woods, then stopped, noticing something to his left. An enraged expression slowly slithered across his face.

The girls followed his gaze. Jason was looking into Spencer's backyard. Spencer's sister, Melissa, and her new boyfriend, Ian Thomas, were sitting on the edge of the family's hot tub. When they saw Jason staring, Ian and Melissa dropped hands. A few pregnant seconds crept by. Two days before, right after Ali bragged about the flag she was about to find, Ian and Jason had gotten in a fight over Ali in front of the entire sixth-grade class. Maybe the fight hadn't ended.

Jason pivoted stiffly and marched into the woods. The patio door slammed again, and the girls ducked. Ali stood on the deck, looking around. Her long blond hair rippled down her shoulders, and her deep pink T-shirt made her skin look extra glowing and fresh.

'You can come out,' Ali yelled.

Emily widened her brown eyes. Aria ducked down further. Spencer and Hanna clamped their mouths shut.

'Seriously.' Ali walked down the deck steps, balancing perfectly on her wedge heels. She was the only sixth grader ballsy enough to wear high heels to class – Rosewood Day didn't technically allow them until high school. 'I *know* someone's there. But if you've come for my flag, it's gone. Someone already stole it.'

Spencer pushed through the bushes, unable to contain her curiosity. 'What? Who?'

Aria emerged next. Emily and Hanna followed. Someone *else* had gotten to Ali before they did?

Ali sighed, plopping down on the stone bench next to the family's small koi pond. The girls hesitated, but Ali gestured them over. Up close, she smelled like vanilla hand soap and had the longest eyelashes any of them had ever seen. Ali slid off her wedges and sank her petite feet into the soft green grass. Her toenails were painted bright red.

'I don't know who,' Ali answered. 'One minute, the piece was in my bag. The next minute, it was gone. I'd decorated it already and everything. I drew this really cool manga frog, the Chanel logo, and a girl playing field hockey. And I worked *forever* on the Louis Vuitton initials and pattern, copying the design straight from my mom's handbag. I got it *perfect*.' She pouted at them, her sapphire blue eyes round. 'The loser who took it is going to ruin it, I just know it.'

The girls murmured their condolences, each suddenly grateful that she hadn't been the one to steal Ali's flag – then *she* would be the loser she was complaining about.

'Ali?'

Everyone whipped around. Mrs DiLaurentis stepped onto the deck. She looked as if she was on her way to a fancy brunch, dressed in a gray Diane von Furstenberg wrap dress and heels. Her gaze lingered on the girls for a moment, confused. It wasn't as if they'd ever been in Ali's backyard before. 'We're going now, okay?'

'Okay,' Ali said, smiling sweetly and waving. 'Bye!'

Mrs DiLaurentis paused, as if she wanted to say something else. Ali turned around, ignoring her. She pointed to Spencer. 'You're Spencer, right?'

Spencer nodded sheepishly. Ali looked searchingly at the others. 'Aria,' Aria reminded Ali. Hanna and Emily introduced themselves too, and Ali nodded perfunctorily. It was a total Ali move – she obviously knew their names, but she was subtly saying that in the grand hierarchy of the Rosewood Day sixth-grade class, their names didn't matter. They didn't know whether to be humiliated or flattered – after all, Ali was asking their names *now*.

'So where were you when your flag was stolen?' Spencer asked, grappling for a question to keep Ali's attention.

Ali blinked dazedly. 'Uh, the mall.' She brought her pinkie finger to her mouth and started to chew.

'What store?' Hanna pressed. 'Tiffany? Sephora?' Maybe Ali would be impressed that Hanna knew the names of the mall's upscale shops.

'Maybe,' Ali murmured. Her gaze shifted to the woods. It seemed like she was looking for something – or some*one*. Behind them, the patio door slammed. Mrs DiLaurentis had gone back inside the house.

'You know, the stealing clause shouldn't even be permitted,' Aria said, rolling her eyes. 'It's just ... *mean.*'

Ali pushed her hair behind her ears, shrugging. An upstairs light in the DiLaurentis house snapped off.

'So where had Jason hidden the piece, anyway?' Emily tried.

Ali snapped out of her funk and stiffened. 'Huh?'

Emily flinched, worried she'd accidentally said something upsetting. 'You said a few days ago that Jason had told you where he'd hidden his piece. That's the one you found,

7

right?' Really, Emily was more interested in the *thud* she'd heard inside the house minutes ago. Had Ali and Jason been fighting? Did Jason imitate Ali's voice a lot? But she didn't dare ask.

'Oh.' Ali spun the silver ring she always wore on her right pointer finger faster and faster. 'Right. Yeah. That's the piece I found.' She swiveled to face the street. The champagne-colored Mercedes the girls often saw picking Ali up after school slowly emerged down the driveway and rolled to the corner. It paused at the stop sign, put on its blinker, and turned right.

Then Ali let out a breath and regarded the girls almost unfamiliarly, as if she was surprised they were there. 'So ... bye,' she said. She turned and marched back into the house. Moments later, the same upstairs light that had just gone dark snapped on again.

The wind chimes on the DiLaurentises' back porch clanged together. A chipmunk skittered across the lawn. At first, the girls were too baffled to move. When it was clear Ali wasn't coming back, everyone said awkward good-byes and went their separate ways. Emily cut through Spencer's yard and followed the trail to the road, trying to see the bright side – she was thankful Ali had even spoken to them at all. Aria started for the woods, annoyed she'd come. Spencer trudged back to her house, embarrassed that Ali had snubbed her as much as the others. Ian and Melissa had gone inside, probably to make out on her family's living room couch – *eww*. And Hanna retrieved her bike from behind the rock in Ali's front yard, noticing a sputtering black car sitting at the curb right in front of Ali's house. She squinted, perplexed. Had she seen it before? Shrugging, she turned away, biking around the cul-de-sac and down the road.

Each girl felt the same heavy, hopeless sense of humiliation. Who did they think they were, trying to steal a Time Capsule piece from the most popular girl at Rosewood Day? Why had they even *dared* to believe they could do it? Ali had probably gone inside, called her BFFs Naomi Zeigler and Riley Wolfe, and laughed about the losers who'd just shown up in her backyard. For a fleeting moment, it had seemed like Ali was going to give Hanna, Aria, Emily, and Spencer a chance at friendship, but now, that chance was most definitely gone.

Or ... was it?

The following Monday, a rumor swirled that Ali's piece of the flag had been stolen. There was a second rumor, too: Ali had gotten into a vicious fight with Naomi and Riley. No one knew what the argument was about. No one knew how it had started. All anyone knew was that the most coveted clique in sixth grade was now missing a few members.

When Ali made conversation with Spencer, Hanna, Emily, and Aria at the Rosewood Day Charity Drive the following Saturday, the four girls thought it was just a nasty prank. But Ali remembered their names. She complimented the way Spencer had flawlessly spelled *knickknacks* and *chandeliers*. She ogled Hanna's brand-new boots from Anthropologie and the peacock-feather earrings Aria's dad had brought her from Morocco. She marveled at how Emily could easily lift a whole box of last season's winter coats. Before the girls knew it, Ali had invited them to her house for a sleepover. Which led to another sleepover, and then another. By the end of September, when the Time Capsule game ended and everyone turned in their decorated pieces of the flag, a new rumor was swirling around school: Ali had four new best friends.

They sat together at the Time Capsule burial ceremony in

9

the Rosewood Day auditorium, watching as Principal Appleton called each person who'd found a piece of the flag to the stage. When Appleton announced that one of the pieces previously found by Alison DiLaurentis had never been turned in and would now be considered invalid, the girls squeezed Ali's hands hard. *It isn't fair*, they whispered. *That piece was yours. You worked so hard on it.*

But the girl at the end of the row, one of Ali's brand-new best friends, was shaking so badly she had to hold her knees steady with the heels of her palms. Aria knew where Ali's piece of the flag was. Sometimes, after the five-way prebedtime phone call with her new best friends ended, Aria's gaze would lock on the shoe box on the very top shelf of her closet, a hollow, sour pain quickly forming in the pit of her stomach. It was better that she hadn't told anyone that she had Ali's flag piece, though. And it was better that she hadn't turned it in. For once, her life was going great. She had friends. She had people to sit next to at lunch, people to hang out with on the weekends. The best thing to do was forget about what had happened that day ... forever.

But maybe Aria shouldn't have forgotten so quickly. Maybe she should've pulled the box down, taken the lid off, and given Ali's long-lost piece a thorough look. This was Rosewood, and everything meant *something*. What Aria might have found on that flag might have given her a clue about something that was coming in Ali's not-so-distant future.

Her murder.

10

1
The Girl Who Cried 'Dead Body'

Spencer Hastings shivered in the frigid, late-evening air, ducking to avoid a thorny briar branch. 'This way,' she called over her shoulder, pushing into the woods behind her family's large, converted farmhouse. 'This was where we saw him.'

Her old best friends Aria Montgomery, Emily Fields, and Hanna Marin followed quickly behind. All of the girls teetered haphazardly in their high heels, holding the hems of their party dresses – it was Saturday night, and before this, they'd been at a Rosewood Day benefit at Spencer's house. Emily was whimpering, her face streaked with tears. Aria's teeth were chattering, the way they always did when she was afraid. Hanna wasn't making any sounds, but her eyes were huge and she was brandishing a large silver candlestick she'd grabbed from the Hastingses' dining room. Officer Darren Wilden, the town's youngest cop, trailed after them, beaming a flashlight at the wrought-iron fence that separated Spencer's yard from the one that had once belonged to Alison DiLaurentis.

'He's in this clearing, right down this trail,' Spencer called.

It had started to snow, first wispy flurries, but harder now – fat, wet flakes. To Spencer's left was her family's barn, the very last place Spencer and her friends had seen Ali alive three and a half years ago. To her right was the half-dug hole where Ali's body had been found in September. Straight ahead was the clearing where she'd just discovered the dead body of Ian Thomas, her sister's old boyfriend, Ali's secret love, and Ali's killer.

Well, *maybe* Ali's killer.

Spencer had been so relieved when the cops arrested Ian for Ali's murder. It all made sense: the last day of seventh grade, Ali had given him an ultimatum that either he break up with Melissa, Spencer's sister, or Ali was going to tell the world they were together. Fed up with her games, Ian had met up with Ali that night. His fury and frustration had gotten the best of him … and he'd killed her. Spencer had even seen Ali and Ian in the woods the night she died, a traumatic memory she had suppressed for three and a half long years.

But the day before Ian's trial was set to start, Ian had broken his house arrest and sneaked onto Spencer's patio, begging her not to testify against him. Someone *else* had killed Ali, he insisted, and he was on the verge of uncovering a disturbing, mind-blowing secret that would prove his innocence.

The problem was, Ian never got to tell Spencer what the big secret was – he vanished before the opening statements of his trial last Friday. As the entire Rosewood Police Department sprang into action, combing the county to find out where he might have gone, everything Spencer thought was true was thrown into question. Had Ian done it … or hadn't he? *Had* Spencer seen him out there with Ali … or had she seen someone else? Then, just minutes ago at the party, someone by the name of Ian_T had sent Spencer a text. *Meet me in the woods where she died*, it said. *I have something to show you.*

Spencer had run through the woods, anxious to figure it all out. When she came to a clearing, she looked down and screamed. Ian was lying there, bloated and blue, his eyes glassy and lifeless. Aria, Hanna, and Emily had shown up just then, and moments later they'd all received the same exact text message from the new A. *He had to go.*

They'd run back into Spencer's to find Wilden, but he hadn't been anywhere in the house. When Spencer went out to the circular driveway to check one more time, Wilden was suddenly *there*, standing near the valet-parked cars. When he saw her, he gave her a startled look, as if she'd caught him doing something illicit. Before Spencer could demand where Wilden had been, the others ran up in hysterics, breathlessly urging him to follow them into the woods. And now, here they were.

Spencer stopped, recognizing a familiar gnarled tree. There was the old stump. There was the tamped-down grass. The air had an eerie static, oxygenless quality. 'This is it,' she called over her shoulder. She looked down at the ground, bracing herself for what she was about to see.

'Oh my God,' Spencer whispered.

Ian's body was ... gone.

She took a dizzy step back, clutching her hand to her head. She blinked hard and looked again. Ian's body had been here a half hour ago, but now the spot was bare except for a fine layer of snow. But ... how was that *possible*?

Emily clapped her hands over her mouth and made a gurgling sound. 'Spencer,' she whispered urgently.

Aria let out a cross between a moan and a shriek. 'Where is he?' she cried, looking around the woods frantically. 'He was just *here*.'

13

Hanna's face was pale. She didn't say a word.

Behind them was an eerie, high-pitched squawking sound. Everyone jumped, and Hanna gripped the candlestick tightly. It was only Wilden's walkie-talkie, which was attached to his belt. He gazed at the girls' expressions, and then at the empty spot on the ground.

'Maybe you have the wrong place,' Wilden said.

Spencer shook her head, feeling pressure rising up into her chest. 'No. He was *here*.' She staggered crookedly down the shallow slope and knelt on the half-thawed grass. Some of it seemed flattened, as if something weighty had recently been lying there. She reached out her fingers to touch the ground, but then pulled back, afraid. She couldn't bring herself to touch a place where a dead body had just been.

'Maybe Ian was hurt, not dead.' Wilden fidgeted with one of the metal snaps on his jacket. 'Maybe he ran away after you left.'

Spencer widened her eyes, daring to consider the possibility.

Emily shook her head fast. 'There was no way he was just *hurt*.'

'He was definitely dead,' Hanna agreed shakily. 'He was ... blue.'

'Maybe someone moved the body,' Aria piped up. 'We've been gone from the woods for over a half hour. That would've given someone time.'

'There *was* someone else out here,' Hanna whispered. 'They stood over me when I fell.'

Spencer whirled around and stared at her. 'What?' Sure, the last half hour had been crazed, but Hanna should have said something.

Emily gaped at Hanna too. 'Did you see who it was?'

Hanna gulped loudly. 'Whoever it was had a hood on. I

14

think it was a guy, but I guess I don't know. Maybe he dragged Ian's body somewhere else.'

'Maybe it was A,' Spencer said, her heart thudding in her chest. She reached into her jacket pocket, pulled out her Sidekick, and showed A's menacing text to Wilden. *He had to go.*

Wilden glanced at Spencer's phone, then handed it back to her. His mouth was taut. 'I don't know how many ways I have to say this. Mona is dead. This A is a copycat. Ian escaping is hardly a secret – the whole country knows about it.'

Spencer exchanged an uneasy glance with the others. This past fall, Mona Vanderwaal, a classmate and Hanna's best friend, had sent the girls twisted, torturous messages signed A. Mona had ruined their lives in countless ways, and she'd even plotted to kill them, hitting Hanna with her SUV and almost pushing Spencer off the cliff at Floating Man Quarry. After Mona slipped off the cliff herself, they thought they were safe ... but last week they began receiving sinister messages from a *new* A. Originally, they thought the A notes were from Ian, as they'd started getting them only after he'd been released from prison on temporary bail. But Wilden was skeptical. He kept telling them that was impossible – Ian didn't have access to a cell phone, nor could he have freely skulked around while under house arrest, watching the girls' every move.

'A is real,' Emily protested, shaking her head desperately. 'What if A is Ian's killer? And what if A dragged Ian away?'

'Maybe A is Ali's killer too,' Hanna added, still holding the candlestick tightly.

Wilden licked his lips, looking unsettled. Big flakes of snow were landing on the top of his head, but he didn't wipe them away. 'Girls, you're getting hysterical. *Ian* is Ali's killer.

15

You of all people should know that. We arrested him on the evidence *you* gave us.'

'What if Ian was framed?' Spencer pressed. 'What if A killed Ali and Ian found out?' *And what if that's something the cops are covering up?* she almost added. It was a theory Ian had suggested.

Wilden traced his fingers around the Rosewood PD badge embroidered on his coat. 'Did Ian feed you that load of crap during his visit to your porch on Thursday, Spencer?'

Spencer's stomach dropped. 'How did you know?'

Wilden glared at her. 'I just got a phone call from the station. We got a tip. Someone saw you two talking.'

'*Who?*'

'It was anonymous.'

Spencer felt dizzy. She looked at her friends – she'd told them and only them that she and Ian had secretly met – but they looked clueless and shocked. There was only one other person who knew she and Ian had met. *A.*

'Why didn't you come to us as soon as it happened?' Wilden leaned closer to Spencer. His breath smelled like coffee. 'We would've dragged Ian back to jail. He never would've escaped.'

'A threatened me,' Spencer protested. She searched through her phone's inbox and showed Wilden that note from A, too. *If poor little Miss Not-So-Perfect suddenly vanished, would anyone even care?*

Wilden rocked back and forth on his heels. He stared hard at the ground where Ian had been not an hour ago and sighed. 'Look, I'll go back to the house and get a team together. But you can't blame everything on A.'

Spencer glanced at the walkie on his hip. 'Why don't you radio them from here?' she pressured. 'You can have them meet you in the woods and start looking right now.'

16

An uncomfortable look came over Wilden's face, as if he hadn't anticipated this question. 'Just let me do my job, girls. We have to follow ... procedure.'

'Procedure?' Emily echoed.

'Oh my God,' Aria breathed. 'He doesn't believe us.'

'I believe you, I believe you.' Wilden ducked around a few low-hanging branches. 'But the best thing you girls can do is go home and get some rest. I'll handle this from here.'

The wind gusted, fluttering the ends of the gray wool scarf Spencer had looped around her neck before running out here. A sliver of moon peeked out from the fog. In seconds, none of them could see Wilden's flashlight anymore. Was it just Spencer's imagination, or had he seemed eager to get away from them? Was he just worried about Ian's body being somewhere in the woods ... or was it because of something else?

She turned and stared hard at the empty ravine, willing Ian's body to return from wherever it had gone. She'd never forget how one eye bugged open, and the other seemed glued shut. His neck was twisted at an unnatural angle. And he'd still been wearing his platinum Rosewood Day class ring on his right hand, its blue stone glinting in the moonlight.

The other girls were looking at the empty space too. Then, there was a *crack*, far off in the woods. Hanna grabbed Spencer's arm. Emily let out an *eep*. They all froze, waiting. Spencer could hear her heart thudding in her ears.

'I want to go home,' Emily cried.

Everyone immediately nodded – they'd all been thinking the same thing. Until the Rosewood police started searching, they weren't safe out here alone.

They followed their footsteps back to Spencer's house. Once they were out of the ravine, Spencer spotted the thin golden beam of Wilden's flashlight far ahead, bouncing off

17

the tree trunks. She stopped, her heart jumping to her throat all over again. 'Guys,' she whispered, pointing.

Wilden's flashlight snapped off fast, as if he sensed they had seen him. His footsteps grew more and more muffled and distant, until the sound vanished altogether. He wasn't heading back toward Spencer's house to get a search team, like he'd said he was going to do. No, he was quickly creeping deeper into the woods ... in exactly the opposite direction.

2

What Goes Around Comes Around

The following morning, Aria sat at the yellow Formica table in her father's tiny kitchen in Old Hollis, the college town next to Rosewood, eating a bowl of Kashi GoLean doused in soy milk and attempting to read the *Philadelphia Sentinel*. Her father, Byron, had already completed the crossword puzzle, and there were inky smudges on the pages.

Meredith, Byron's ex-student and current fiancée, was in the living room, which was right next to the kitchen. She'd lit a few sticks of patchouli incense, making the whole apartment smell like a head shop. The soothing strains of crashing waves and cawing seagulls tinkled from the living room TV. *'Take a cleansing breath through your nose at the start of each contraction,'* a woman's voice instructed. *'When you breathe out, chant the sounds* hee, hee, hee. *Let's try it together.'*

'Hee, hee, hee,' Meredith chanted.

Aria stifled a groan. Meredith was five months pregnant, and she'd been watching Lamaze videos for the last hour, which meant Aria had learned about breathing techniques, birthing balls, and the evils of epidurals by osmosis.

After a mostly sleepless night, Aria had called her father early that morning and asked if she could stay with them for a while. Then, before her mother, Ella, woke up, Aria packed some things in her floral-upholstered duffel from Norway and left. Aria wanted to avoid a confrontation. She knew her mother would be puzzled that Aria was choosing to live with her dad and his marriage-wrecking girlfriend, especially since Ella and Aria had finally repaired their relationship after Mona Vanderwaal (as A) had nearly destroyed it forever. Plus, Aria hated to lie, and it wasn't like she could tell Ella the truth about why she was here. *Your new boyfriend is kind of into me, and he's convinced I want him, too*, she imagined saying. Ella would probably never speak to her again.

Meredith turned up the TV volume – apparently she couldn't hear over her own *hee* breathing. More waves crashed. A gong sounded. '*You and your partner will learn ways to lessen the pain of natural childbirth and hasten the labor process*,' the woman instructor said. '*Some techniques include water immersion, visualization exercises, and letting your partner bring you to orgasm.*'

'Oh my God.' Aria clapped her hands over her ears. It was a wonder she hadn't spontaneously gone deaf.

She looked down at the paper again. A headline was splashed across the front page. *Where Is Ian Thomas?* it asked.

Good question, Aria thought.

The events of last night throbbed in her mind. How could Ian's dead body be in the woods one minute and gone the next? Had someone killed him and dragged his body away when they'd gone inside to find Wilden? Had Ian's killer silenced him because he'd uncovered the huge secret he'd told Spencer about?

Or maybe Wilden was right – Ian was injured, not dead, and had crawled away when they ran back to the house. But if that was what happened, then Ian was still ... *out there*. She shivered. Ian despised Aria and her friends for getting him arrested. He might want revenge.

Aria snapped on the little TV on the kitchen counter, eager for a distraction. Channel 6 was showing the cobbled-together reenactment of Ali's murder – Aria had already seen it twice. She pressed the remote. On the next channel, the Rosewood chief of police was talking to some reporters. He wore a heavy, fur-lined navy blue jacket, and there were pine trees behind him. It looked as if he was giving an interview from the edge of Spencer's woods. There was a big caption at the bottom of the screen that said, *Ian Thomas Dead?* Aria leaned forward, her heart speeding up.

'There are unsubstantiated reports that Mr Thomas's dead body was seen in these woods last night,' the chief was saying. 'We have a great team assembled, and we began searching the woods at ten A.M. this morning. However, with all this snow ...'

Kashi burbled in Aria's stomach. She grabbed her cell phone off the little kitchen table and dialed Emily's number. She answered immediately. 'Are you watching the news?' Aria barked, in lieu of a hello.

'I just turned it on,' Emily answered, her voice worried.

'Why do you think they waited until this morning to start searching? Wilden said he was going to get a squad together last night.'

'Wilden also said something about procedure,' Emily suggested in a small voice. 'Maybe it has something to do with that.'

Aria snorted. 'Wilden never seemed to care about procedure before.'

21

'Wait, what are you saying?' Emily sounded incredulous.

Aria picked at a place mat one of Meredith's friends had woven out of hemp. Almost twelve hours had passed since they'd seen Ian's body, and a lot could happen in those woods between then and now. Someone could have cleared away evidence ... or planted false leads. But the police – Wilden – had been careless with this entire case. Wilden hadn't even had a suspect for Ali's murder until Aria, Spencer, and the others handed them Ian's head on a platter. He'd also somehow missed both when Ian broke out to visit Spencer and when he escaped on the day of his trial. According to Hanna, Wilden wanted Ian to fry as much as they did, but he hadn't done a very good job of keeping him under lock and key.

'I don't know,' Aria finally answered. 'But it *is* weird they're just getting around to it now.'

'Have you gotten any more A notes?' Emily asked.

Aria stiffened. 'No. You?'

'No, but I keep thinking I'm going to get one at any minute.'

'Who do you think the new A is?' Aria asked. She had no theories whatsoever. Was it someone who wanted Ian dead, Ian himself, or someone else entirely? Wilden believed the texts were pranks from some random person in a whole other state. But A had taken incriminating photos of Aria and Xavier together last week, meaning A was here in Rosewood. A also knew about Ian's body in the woods – all of them had gotten a note urging them to go find him. Why was A so desperate to show them Ian's body – to scare them? To warn them? And when Hanna fell, she'd seen someone looming over her. What was the likelihood that someone else *happened* to be in those woods the exact same time as Ian's body? There had to be a connection.

'I don't know,' Emily concluded. 'But I don't want to find out.'

'Maybe A is gone,' Aria said, in the most hopeful voice she could manage.

Emily sighed and said she had to go. Aria got up, poured a glass of acai berry juice Meredith had bought at the health food store, and rubbed her temples. Could Wilden have delayed the search on purpose? If so, *why*? He'd seemed so fidgety and uncomfortable last night, and then he'd walked off in the opposite direction of Spencer's house. Maybe *he* was hiding something. Or maybe Emily was right – the delay was due to procedure. He was just a cop dutifully playing by the rules.

It still baffled Aria that Wilden had become a cop, let alone a dutiful one. Wilden had been in Jason DiLaurentis and Ian's year at Rosewood Day, and back then he'd been a troublemaker. The year Aria was in sixth and they were in eleventh, she often sneaked into the Upper School during her free periods to spy on Jason – she'd had such a painful crush on him, and sought him out every chance she got. For just a moment, she would gaze through the window of the wood-shop cottage as he sanded his homemade bookends, or swoon at his muscular legs as he ran up and down the soccer practice fields. Aria was always careful never to let anyone see her.

But once, someone did.

It was about a week into the school year. Aria had been watching Jason checking out books at the library from the hallway when she heard a *click* behind her. There was Darren Wilden, his ear pressed to the door of one of the lockers, slowly turning the dial. The locker opened, and Aria saw a heart-shaped mirror on the inside of the door and a box of Always maxi pads on the upper shelf. Wilden's hand closed

23

around a twenty-dollar bill wedged between two textbooks. Aria frowned, slowly processing what Wilden was doing.

Wilden stood up and noticed her. He stared back, unapologetic. 'You're not supposed to be here,' he sneered. 'But I won't tell ... this time.'

When Aria looked at the TV again, there was a commercial on for a local furniture outlet store called The Dump. She stared at her phone on the table, realizing there was another phone call she had to make. It was almost eleven – Ella would certainly be awake.

She dialed the number to her house. The phone rang once, then twice. There was a *click*, and someone said, 'Hello?'

Aria's words got stuck in her throat. It was Xavier, her mother's new boyfriend. Xavier sounded chipper and comfortable, completely at ease with answering the Montgomerys' phone. Had he stayed overnight last night after the benefit? *Ew.*

'Hello?' Xavier said again.

Aria felt tongue-tied and skeeved out. When Xavier had approached Aria at the Rosewood Day benefit last night and asked if they could talk, Aria had assumed that he was going to apologize for kissing her a few days before. Only, apparently, in Xavier-speak, 'talk' meant 'grope'.

After a few seconds of silence, Xavier breathed out. 'Is this Aria?' he said, his voice slimy. Aria made a small squeak. 'There's no need to hide,' he teased. 'I thought we had an understanding.'

Aria hung up fast. The only understanding she and Xavier had was that if she warned Ella what kind of person Xavier was, Xavier would tell Ella that Aria had liked Xavier for a nanosecond. And that would ruin Aria and Ella's relationship for good.

'Aria?'

Aria jumped and looked up. Her father, Byron, was standing above her, wearing a ratty Hollis T-shirt and sporting his typical just-rolled-out-of-bed hairstyle.

He sat down at the table next to her. Meredith, wearing a sari-style maternity dress and Birkenstocks, waddled in and leaned against the counter. 'We wanted to talk to you,' Byron said.

Aria folded her hands in her lap. They both looked so serious.

'First off, we're going to have a baby shower for Meredith Wednesday night,' Byron said. 'It's going to be a little thing with some of our friends.'

Aria blinked. They had *joint* friends? That seemed impossible. Meredith was in her twenties, barely out of college. And Byron was ... old.

'You can bring a friend if you want,' Meredith added. 'And don't worry about getting me a gift. I totally don't expect it.'

Aria wondered if Meredith was registered at Sunshine, the eco baby store in Rosewood that sold organic baby booties made out of recycled soda bottles for a hundred dollars.

'And as for where this shower is going to be ...' Byron tugged at the cuffs of his white cable-knit sweater. 'We're going to have it at our new house.'

The words took a moment to sink in. Aria opened her mouth, then shut it fast.

'We didn't want to tell you until we were sure,' Byron rushed on. 'But our loan went through today, and we're closing on it tomorrow. We want to move right away, and we'd love it if you'd join us there.'

'A ... house,' Aria repeated. She wasn't sure whether to laugh or cry. Here in this student-friendly, shabby-chic, drippy little 650-square-foot apartment in Old Hollis, Byron

25

and Meredith's relationship seemed sort of ... pretend. A house, on the other hand, was grown-up. Real.

'Where is it?' Aria finally asked.

Meredith ran her fingers along the pink spiderweb tattoo on the inside of her wrist. 'On Coventry Lane. It's really beautiful, Aria – I think you'll love it. There's a spiral staircase leading to a big loft bedroom in the attic. That can be yours, if you want. The light up there is great for painting.'

Aria stared at a small stain on Byron's sweater. Coventry Lane had a familiar ring to it, but she wasn't sure why.

'You can start moving your stuff over anytime after tomorrow,' Byron said, eyeing Aria warily, as if he wasn't sure how she was going to react.

She turned absently to the TV. The news was showing Ian's mug shot. Then, Ian's mother came on the screen, looking pale and sleepless. 'We haven't heard from Ian since Thursday night,' Mrs Thomas cried. 'If anyone knows what has happened to him, please come forward.'

'Wait,' Aria said slowly, a thought congealing in her mind. 'Isn't Coventry Lane in the neighborhood right behind Spencer's house?'

'That's right!' Byron brightened. 'You'll be closer to her.'

Aria shook her head. Her dad didn't get it. 'That's *Ian Thomas's* old street.'

Byron and Meredith glanced at each other, their faces paling. 'It ... *is?*' Byron asked.

Aria's heart thumped. This was one of the reasons she loved her dad – he was so hopelessly oblivious to gossip. At the same time, how on earth could he not know this?

Great. Not only would she be right next to the woods where they'd found Ian's body, but where Ali had died, too. And what if Ian was still alive, stalking those very woods?

She faced her father. 'Don't you think that street's going to have some seriously bad karma?'

Byron crossed his arms over his chest. 'I'm sorry, Aria. But we got an amazing deal on a house, one we couldn't pass up. It has tons of space, and I'm sure you'll find it more comfortable than living in ... this.' He waved his arms around, pointing specifically to the apartment's one tiny bathroom, which they had to share.

Aria glared at the bird-faced totem pole in the corner of the kitchen that Meredith had dragged home from a flea market about a month ago. It wasn't like she could go back to her mom's. Xavier's teasing voice rattled through her head. *There's no need to hide. I thought we had an understanding.*

'Okay. I'll move on Tuesday,' Aria mumbled. She gathered her books and cell phone and retreated to her tiny bedroom at the back of Meredith's studio, feeling exhausted and defeated.

As she dropped her stuff on her bed, something outside the window caught her eye. The studio was at the back of the apartment, facing an alleyway and a dilapidated wooden garage. A filmy shadow moved behind the garage's murky windows. Then a pair of unblinking eyes peered through the glass, straight at Aria.

Aria shrieked and pressed herself against the back wall, her heart rocketing. But in a flash, the eyes vanished, as if they'd never been there at all.

3

Fly Me To The Moon

Sunday evening, Emily Fields curled her legs underneath her in a cozy booth at Penelope's, a homey diner not far from her house. Her new boyfriend, Isaac, sat across the booth, the two slices of peanut butter-laden bread he'd ordered in front of him. He was demonstrating how to make his world-famous, life-changing peanut butter sandwich.

'The trick,' Isaac said, 'is to use *honey* instead of jelly.' He picked up a bear-shaped bottle from the middle of the table. The bear made a farting noise as Isaac squeezed honey onto one of the slices. 'I promise this will take *all* of your stress away.' He handed her the sandwich. Emily took a big bite, chewed, and smiled.

'Gooh,' she said, her mouth full. Isaac squeezed her hand, and Emily swooned. Isaac had soft, expressive blue eyes, and there was something about his mouth that made him look like he was smiling even when he wasn't. If Emily didn't know him, she'd assume he was too good-looking to be going out with someone like her.

Isaac pointed at the television over the diner counter. 'Hey, isn't that your friend's house?'

Emily turned in time to see Mrs McClellan, Spencer's neighbor from down the street, paused in front of the Hastings estate, her white standard poodle on a retractable leash. 'I haven't been able to sleep since Saturday,' she was saying. 'The idea that there's a dead body *lying there* in the woods behind my house is too much to bear. I just hope they find it fast.'

Emily slid down in her seat, acid rising to her throat. She was happy the police were searching for Ian, but she didn't want to hear about it right now.

A cop from the Rosewood police force appeared next. 'The Rosewood PD has produced all the necessary warrants, and they've started their search of the woods today.' Flashbulbs popped in the cop's face. 'We are taking this matter seriously and moving as fast as we can.'

The reporters began bombarding the cop with questions. 'Why did the officer on the scene delay the search?' 'Is there something the cops are covering up?' 'Is it true that Ian broke house arrest earlier in the week and met with one of the girls who found his body?'

Emily bit her pinkie nail, surprised that the press had found out that Ian had staked out Spencer on her back patio. Who told them that? Wilden? One of the other cops? A?

The cop raised his hand, silencing them. 'Like I just explained, Officer Wilden did not delay the search. We had to obtain the proper permits to get access to those woods – they're private property. As for Mr Thomas breaking house arrest, that's not something I'm prepared to comment on right now.'

The waitress made a *tsk* sound and flipped channels to another newscast. *Rosewood Reacts*, said the big yellow caption. There was a girl on the screen. Emily immediately recognized her raven black hair and wraparound Gucci sunglasses. *Jenna Cavanaugh*.

Emily's stomach flipped. *Jenna Cavanaugh*. The girl Emily and her friends had accidentally blinded in sixth grade. The girl who'd told Aria, just over two months ago, that Ali had troubling 'sibling' problems with her brother, Jason, problems Emily didn't even want to *think* about.

She jumped up from the table. 'Let's go,' she blurted out, averting her eyes from the TV.

Isaac stood too, looking concerned. 'I'll have them turn the TV off.'

Emily shook her head. 'I want to leave.'

'Okay, okay,' Isaac said gently, pulling out a few limp bills and setting them on his coffee cup. Emily staggered for the front door. When she reached the little area by the hostess stand, she felt Isaac's hand close over hers.

'I'm sorry,' she said guiltily, her eyes filling with tears. 'You didn't even get to eat your sandwich.'

Isaac touched her arm. 'Don't worry about it. I can't imagine what you're going through.'

Emily leaned her head into his shoulder. Whenever she shut her eyes, she pictured Ian's prone and swollen body. She'd never seen a dead person before, not at a funeral, not in a hospital bed, and certainly not in the woods, murdered. She wished she could delete the memory with the press of a button, as easily as trashing unwanted spam from her e-mail inbox. Being with Isaac was the only thing that took some of her pain and fear away.

'I bet you didn't bargain for this when you asked me to be your girlfriend, huh?' she mumbled.

'Please,' Isaac said softly, kissing her forehead. 'I'd help you through anything.'

The coffeemaker at the counter burbled. Outside the

window, a grumbling snowplow barreled down the street. For the millionth time, Emily thought about how lucky she was to have found someone as wonderful as Isaac. He had accepted her even after she told him that she'd fallen in love with Ali in seventh grade, and then with Maya St Germain this fall. He'd patiently listened when she explained how her family struggled with her sexuality, sending her to Tree Tops, a gay-away program. He'd held her hand when she told him that she still thought about Ali constantly, even though Ali had kept a lot of secrets from them. And now he was helping her through this.

It was growing dark outside, and the air smelled like the diner's scrambled eggs and coffee. They walked hand in hand to Emily's mom's Volvo station wagon, which was parallel-parked at the curb. Big drifts of snow were piled on the sidewalk, and a couple of kids were sledding down a tiny hill behind the vacant lot across the street.

As they reached the car, a person wearing a heavy gray jacket with the furry hood tight over his head barreled toward them. His eyes blazed. 'Is this your car?' He pointed at the Volvo.

Emily stopped, startled. 'Y-yeah …'

'Look what you did!' The guy stomped through the snow and pointed at a BMW parked in front of the Volvo. There was a ding right under the license plate. 'You parked here after me,' the guy growled. 'Did you even look before you pulled in?'

'I-'m sorry,' Emily stammered. She couldn't recall bumping anything when she parked, but she *had* been in a daze all day.

Isaac faced the guy. 'It might have been there before. Maybe you just didn't notice it.'

'It *wasn't*,' the guy sneered. As he staggered closer to them, his hood fell off. He had tousled blond hair, piercing blue eyes, and a familiar, heart-shaped face. Emily sucked in her stomach. It was Ali's brother, Jason DiLaurentis.

She waited, sure Jason would recognize her too – Emily had been at Ali's house practically every day in sixth and seventh grade, and Jason had also just *seen* her at Ian's trial on Friday. But Jason's face was red, and his eyes weren't looking directly at anything; it seemed like he had worked himself into an enraged trance. Emily sniffed the air in front of him, wondering if he was drunk. But she couldn't smell alcohol on his breath.

'Are you guys even old enough to drive?' Jason roared. He took another threatening step toward Emily.

Isaac stepped between them, shielding Emily from him. 'Whoa. You don't need to yell.'

Jason's nostrils flared. He clenched his fists, and for a moment, Emily thought he was going to throw a punch. Then, a couple stepped out of the diner onto the street, and Jason turned his head. He let out a frustrated groan, smacked the trunk of his car hard, wheeled around, and climbed into the driver's seat. The BMW growled to life, and Jason peeled away into traffic, cutting off an oncoming car. Horns honked. Tires squealed. Emily watched the taillights disappear around a corner, her hands pressed to the sides of her face.

Isaac faced Emily. 'Are you okay?'

Emily nodded mutely, too stunned to speak.

'What was his deal? It was hardly a dent. I don't even remember you bumping him.'

Emily swallowed hard. 'That was Alison DiLaurentis's brother.' Just saying the words out loud made her burst into scared, troubled tears. Isaac hesitated for a moment, and then he wrapped his arms around Emily, holding her close.

'*Shhh*,' he whispered. 'Let's get you in the car. I'll drive.'

Emily handed him the keys and got into the passenger seat. Isaac pulled out of the spot and started down the road. Tears rolled down Emily's cheeks faster and faster. She wasn't even sure what she was crying about – Jason's odd outburst, yes, but also just *seeing* Jason in front of her. He looked so startlingly like Ali.

Isaac looked over again, his face crumpling. 'Hey,' he said softly. He turned onto a road that led to a row of office buildings, pulled into a dark, empty parking lot, and shifted into park. 'It's okay.' He stroked Emily's arm.

They sat there for a while, saying nothing. The only sound was the Volvo's rattling heater. After a while, Emily wiped her eyes, leaned forward, and kissed him, so happy he was here. He kissed her back, and they paused, looking longingly at each other. Emily dove back in, kissing more hungrily. Suddenly, all her problems blew away, like ashes in a breeze.

The car's windows fogged up. Wordlessly, Isaac picked up the bottom hem of his long-sleeved T-shirt and pulled it over his head. His chest was smooth and muscular, and he had a small, shiny scar on the inside of his right arm. Emily reached out and touched it. 'What's that from?'

'Falling off a BMX ramp in second grade,' he answered.

He tilted his head and nudged toward Emily's long-sleeved T-shirt. She lifted her arms. Isaac pulled it off. Though the heat was on full blast, Emily's arms were still covered in goose bumps. She looked down, embarrassed at the navy sports bra she'd dug out of her drawer that morning. It was printed with moons, stars, and planets. If only she'd put on something a little more feminine and sexy – but then, it wasn't as if she'd planned on taking her clothes off.

Isaac pointed at her belly button. 'You have an outie.'

Emily covered it up. 'Everyone makes fun of it.' Mostly, she meant Ali, who had caught a peek at Emily's belly button once when they were changing at the Rosewood Country Club. 'I thought only chubby boys had belly buttons like those,' she'd teased. Emily had worn one-piece bathing suits ever since.

Isaac pried her hands away. 'I think it's great.' His fingers grazed the bottom edge of the bra, sliding his hand inside. Emily's heart pounded. Isaac leaned into her, kissing her neck. His bare skin touched hers. He tugged at her sports bra, urging her to pull it off. Emily yanked it over her head, and a goofy smile appeared on Isaac's face. Emily giggled, amused at how *serious* they were being. Yet, she didn't feel self-conscious. This felt ... right.

They embraced tightly, pressing their warm bodies together. 'Are you sure you're okay?' Isaac murmured.

'I think so,' Emily said into his shoulder. 'I'm sorry my life seems so crazy.'

'Don't apologize.' Isaac caressed her hair with his hands. 'Like I said, I'd help you through anything. I ... love you.'

Emily leaned back, agape. Isaac had such a sincere and vulnerable look on his face, and Emily wondered if she was the first person he'd ever said he loved. She felt so grateful to have him in her life. He was the only person who made her feel even remotely safe.

'I love you too,' she decided.

They embraced again, tighter this time. But after a few blissful seconds, Jason's twisted, furious face swam into Emily's mind. She squeezed her eyes tight, and her stomach swirled with dread.

Calm down, said a little voice inside her. There was probably a logical explanation for Jason's outburst. Everyone was devastated by Ali's death and Ian's disappearance, and it wasn't unusual for someone – especially a family member – to go a little crazy out of grief.

But a second voice prodded at her, too. *That's not the whole story,* the voice said, *and you know it.*

4
That Boy Is Mine

Later that night, Hanna Marin sat at a gleaming white café table at the Pinkberry at the King James Mall. Her soon-to-be stepsister Kate Randall, Naomi Zeigler, and Riley Wolfe surrounded her, little cups of frozen yogurt in front of each of them. A snappy Japanese pop song thudded out of the speakers, and a line of girls from St Augustus Prep stood at the counter, musing over the choices.

'Don't you think Pinkberry is a *much* better hangout than Rive Gauche?' Hanna said, referring to the French-style bistro at the other end of the mall. She gestured out the door, into the mall atrium. 'We're right across from Armani Exchange *and* Cartier. We can ogle hot guys *and* gorgeous diamonds without getting up.'

She dipped her spoon into her cup of Pinkberry and shoved an enormous bite in her mouth, letting out a little *mmm* to emphasize how good an idea she thought this was. Then she fed a little bite to Dot, her miniature Doberman, whom she'd brought along in her brand-new Juicy Couture doggie carrier. The Pinkberry workers kept shooting daggers in Hanna's direction. Some lame rule said that dogs weren't allowed in here, but surely they meant *dirty* dogs, like labs and Saint Bernards and hideous little shih tzus. Dot was the cleanest dog in Rosewood. Hanna gave him weekly bubble baths in lavender-scented dog shampoo imported from Paris.

Riley twirled a piece of coppery hair around her fingers. 'But you can't sneak wine here like you can at Rive Gauche.'

'Yes, but you can't bring *dogs* to Rive Gauche,' Hanna said, cupping Dot's little face in her hands. She gave him another tiny bite of Pinkberry.

Naomi took a bite of yogurt and immediately reapplied a coat of Guerlain KissKiss lipstick. 'And the lighting in here is so … unflattering.' She peered into the round mirrors that lined Pinkberry's walls. 'I feel like my pores are magnified.'

Hanna slammed her Pinkberry cup on the table, making the little plastic spoon jump. 'Okay, I didn't want to resort to this, but before we broke up, Lucas told me that Rive Gauche has rats in the kitchen. Do you really want to hang out somewhere with a rodent problem? There could be rat poop in your *frites*.'

'Or do you not want to hang out there because of a *Lucas* problem?' Naomi snickered, tossing her pale blond hair over her bony shoulder. Kate giggled and raised the cup of mint tea she'd bought earlier at Starbucks in a toast. Who drank mint tea besides old ladies, anyway? *Freak*.

Hanna glowered at her quasi-stepsister's turned head, unable to read her. Earlier the week before, Kate and Hanna had almost bonded, sharing some secrets over breakfast. Kate alluded that she had a 'gynecological problem' but didn't explain what it was, and Hanna confessed to bingeing and purging. But when A started hinting to Hanna that Kate was less of a new BFF and more of an evil stepsis, Hanna fretted that trusting Kate had been a huge mistake. So at the

Rosewood Day benefit, Hanna blurted out to the entire school that Kate had herpes. If Hanna hadn't, she was certain that Kate would have spilled Hanna's secret instead.

Naomi and Riley had recognized the herpes incident as a big power play immediately, calling both Hanna and Kate this Sunday morning to see if they wanted to go to the King James like it never even happened. Kate seemed to brush it off, too, turning to Hanna in the car on the way to the mall and saying in a cool and unbothered voice, 'Let's just forget about last night, okay?'

Unfortunately, not *everyone* saw the herpes trick as the queen bee move it really was. Right after Hanna said it, Lucas, Hanna's then-boyfriend, said it was over between them – he didn't want to be with someone who was so obsessed with popularity. And when Hanna's dad had found out, he mandated that Hanna must spend every spare minute with Kate so they could bond. So far, he was taking the punishment seriously. This morning, when Kate wanted to go to Wawa for a Diet Coke, Hanna went along. Then, when Hanna wanted to take a Bikram yoga class, Kate ran upstairs and changed into her Lululemon yoga capris. And this afternoon, the press had shown up to Hanna's door to ask her questions about Ian breaking house arrest last week to meet with Spencer. 'What were they talking about?' the reporters crowed. 'Why didn't you tell the police Ian had busted out?' 'Are you girls keeping something from us?' As Hanna explained that she *hadn't* known that Ian showed up on Spencer's porch until long after Ian had escaped, Kate was right there at her side, applying a fresh coat of Smashbox lip gloss in case the reporters needed an extra Rosewood girl's opinion. No matter that she'd only been a Rosewood girl for a week and a half. She'd moved into Hanna's house after Hanna's mother took a high-paying job in Singapore. Kate's mother, Isabel, and Hanna's father had moved into the house too, and the two planned to marry. *Yecch.*

Now, a pitying smile formed on Kate's lips. 'Do you want to talk about Lucas?' She touched Hanna's hand.

'There's nothing to talk about,' Hanna snapped, drawing her hand away. She wasn't about to open up to Kate – that was *so* last week. She was sad about Lucas and had already started to miss him, but maybe they weren't right for each other.

'But you seem pretty upset yourself, Kate,' Hanna shot back, matching Kate's sweetie-pie voice. 'You haven't heard from Eric, huh? Poor thing. Are you heartbroken?'

Kate lowered her eyes. Eric Kahn, Noel's hot older brother, was interested in Kate . . . well, he had been until the herpes remark, anyway.

'It's probably for the best,' Hanna said airily. 'I heard Eric's a big player. And he only likes girls with big boobs.'

'Kate's boobs are fine,' Riley jumped in quickly.

Naomi wrinkled her nose. 'I never heard Eric was a player.'

Hanna balled up her napkin, annoyed that Naomi and Riley were so quick to jump to Kate's defense. 'You guys don't have the same kind of inside info that I do, I guess.'

They all turned back to their Pinkberries, saying nothing. Suddenly, a flash of blond hair in the atrium caught Hanna's eye, and she whirled around. A group of girls in their twenties passed, swinging Saks shopping bags. They were all brunettes.

Hanna had been seeing a lot of phantom flashes of blond hair lately, and was constantly haunted by the eerie feeling that it could be Mona Vanderwaal, her old best friend. Mona had died almost two months earlier, but Hanna still thought of her many times a day – all the sleepovers they'd had, all the shopping trips they'd gone on, all the drunken nights at Mona's house, giggling over boys who had crushes on them. Now that Mona was gone, there was a huge hole in Hanna's life. At the same time, she felt like an idiot. Mona hadn't really been her friend – Mona had been A. She'd ruined Hanna's relationships, aired her dirty laundry, and tortured her for months. And BFFs *definitely* didn't hit BFFs with Daddy's SUV.

After the shoppers passed, Hanna noticed a familiar dark-haired figure just outside Pinkberry, talking on a cell phone. She squinted. It was Officer Wilden.

'Just calm down,' Wilden murmured into the phone, his voice urgent and distressed. His brow furrowed as he listened to the person on the other end. 'Okay, okay. Sit tight. I'll be there soon.'

Hanna frowned. Had he found out something about Ian's body? She also wanted to ask him about the spooky hooded figure she'd seen in the woods the night of the party. Whoever it was had loomed over Hanna so threateningly, and, after a moment, the person had raised a finger to his lips and whispered *shhh*. Why would someone shush Hanna unless he'd done something awful – and didn't want to be seen? Hanna wondered if the person had something to do with Ian's death. Maybe he was A too.

Hanna started to stand, but before she could push her chair away from the table, Wilden jogged off. She sank back into her seat, figuring he was just busy and flustered. Unlike Spencer, Hanna didn't think Wilden was hiding anything. Wilden had dated Hanna's mom before she moved to Singapore to take a new job, and Hanna felt that she knew Wilden a little more intimately than the others. Okay, so finding him fresh from her shower wrapped in her favorite

Pottery Barn towel was more *awkward* than intimate, but he was essentially a good guy who was looking out for them, right? If he thought A was a copycat, maybe A really was. Why would he mislead them?

Still, Hanna wasn't taking any chances. With that in mind, she pulled her brand-new iPhone out of its calf leather Dior case and turned back to the girls. 'So. I changed cell numbers, but I'm not giving it out to just anyone. You guys have to promise not to pass it around. If you do, I'll know.' She eyed them seriously.

'We promise,' Riley said, eagerly pulling out her BlackBerry. Hanna sent them each a text with her new number. Really, she should've thought about getting a new phone number much sooner – it was a perfect way to A-proof her life. Besides, getting rid of her old number was a way of freeing herself from everything that had happened last semester. Voilà! All those shitty memories were gone for good.

'So anyway,' Kate said loudly after the girls finished texting, bringing the attention back to herself. 'Back to Eric. I'm over him. There are plenty of other cute guys right under our noses.'

She jutted her chin in the direction of the atrium. A group of Rosewood Day lacrosse players, including Noel Kahn, Mason Byers, and Aria's younger brother, Mike, were lingering by the fountain. Mike was gesticulating wildly with his hands as he told a story. He was too far away for them to hear what he was saying, but the other lacrosse boys were hanging on his every word.

'*Lax* boys?' Hanna made a face. 'Tell me you're joking.' She and Mona once made a pact never to date anyone on the lacrosse team. They did everything together, from studying to working out at Philly Sports Club, the grimy gym at the back of the King James, to eating nasty Chick-fil-A. Hanna and Mona used to joke that they also secretly had group sleepovers and styled each other's hair.

Kate took another sip of her mint tea. 'Some of them are seriously hot.'

'Like who?' Hanna challenged.

Kate watched the boys as they passed M.A.C., David Yurman, and Lush, the store that sold a million different types of handmade candles and soaps. 'Him.' She pointed at one of the boys on the end.

'Who, Noel?' Hanna shrugged. Noel Kahn was okay, if you liked rich boys who had no inner censor and were obsessed with jokes about testicles, third nipples, and animals having sex.

Kate chewed on the stirrer in her mint tea. 'Not Noel. The other one. With the dark hair.'

Hanna blinked. '*Mike?*'

'He's gorgeous, isn't he?'

Hanna's eyes boggled. Mike, *gorgeous*? He was loud and annoying and uncouth. Okay, so maybe he wasn't a total dog – he had the same blue-black hair, lanky body, and ice blue eyes as Aria did. But … *still*.

Suddenly, a possessive feeling began to course through Hanna's veins. The thing was, Mike had been following Hanna around like a lost puppy for years. One weekend in sixth grade when Hanna, Ali, and the others were sleeping over at Aria's house, Hanna had gotten up in the middle of the night to use the bathroom. In the dark hall, a pair of hands reached out and groped her boobs. Hanna yelped, and Mike, then in fifth grade, stepped back. 'Sorry. I thought you were Ali,' he said. After a pause, he leaned in and kissed Hanna anyway. Hanna let him, secretly flattered – she was chubby, ugly, and lame back then, and it wasn't like she had

42

tons of guys fighting over her. Mike was technically her first kiss.

Hanna faced Kate. She felt like a pot bubbling over. 'Hate to break it to you, sweetie, but Mike likes me. Haven't you noticed the way he ogles me at Steam every morning?'

Kate ran her fingers through her chestnut hair. 'I'm at Steam every morning, too, Han. It's hard to know who he's looking at.'

'It's true,' Naomi interjected, brushing some wisps of her growing-out severe blond haircut. 'Mike looks at *all* of us.'

'Yeah,' Riley said.

Hanna pressed her French-manicured nails into her thigh. What the hell was going on here? Why were those two so solidly on Team Kate? *Hanna* was the queen bee.

'We'll just have to see about that,' Hanna said, puffing up her chest. Kate cocked her head, as if to say, *Oh yeah?*

Then Kate rose. 'You know, girls, I suddenly got a major craving for some red wine. Wanna swing by Rive Gauche?'

Naomi and Riley's eyes lit up. 'Totally,' they both said in unison, and stood up too.

Hanna let out an indignant squeak, and everyone stopped. Kate stuck out her lip in a faux-concerned pout. 'Oh, Han! Are you really ... *upset* about Lucas? I seriously thought you didn't care.'

'No,' Hanna snapped, her voice irritatingly shaky. 'I don't care about him. I ... I just don't want to go somewhere with rats.'

'Don't worry,' Kate said gently. 'I won't tell your dad if you don't want to come along.'

She slung her Michael Kors bag over her shoulder. Naomi and Riley looked back and forth from Hanna to Kate, trying to decide what to do. Finally, Naomi shrugged, fiddling with her blond hair. 'Red wine *does* sound really good.' She

43

glanced at Hanna. 'Sorry.' And Riley followed behind saying nothing. *Traitors*, Hanna thought.

'Watch out for rat tails in your wineglasses,' Hanna yelled after them. But the girls didn't turn, traipsing into the court-yard, linking elbows and laughing. Hanna watched them for a moment, her cheeks blazing with fury, and then turned back to Dot, took a few deep breaths, and wrapped her cash-mere poncho around her shoulders.

Kate might have won the queen bee battle today, but the war was far from over. She was the fabulous Hanna Marin, after all. That silly little bitch had no idea who she was deal-ing with.

5

Take A Chance On Me

Early Monday evening, Spencer and Andrew Campbell sat in her family's sunroom, their AP econ notes spread before them. A lock of Andrew's long blond hair fell into his eyes as he leaned over the textbook and pointed to a drawing of a man. 'This is Alfred Marshall.' He covered up the paragraph under his picture. 'Quick. What was his philosophy?'

Spencer pressed her fingers to her temples. She could add columns of numbers in her head and supply seven synonyms for the word *assiduous*, but when it came to AP econ, her brain went ... mushy. But she had to learn this. Her teacher, Mr McAdam, said Spencer would be out of his class unless she aced this semester – he was still pissed that she'd stolen her older sister's AP econ paper and hadn't confessed to it until after she'd won the prestigious Golden Orchid essay prize. So now Andrew, who *did* naturally get econ, was her tutor.

Suddenly, Spencer brightened. 'The theory of supply and demand,' she recited.

'Very good.' Andrew beamed. He flipped a page of the book, his fingers accidentally brushing against hers. Spencer's heart quickened, but then Andrew pulled away fast.

Spencer had never been so confused. The house was empty right now – Spencer's parents and her sister, Melissa, had all gone out to dinner, not inviting Spencer along, as usual – which meant Andrew could make a move if he wanted. He'd certainly seemed interested in kissing her Saturday night at the Rosewood Day benefit, but since then ... nothing. True, Spencer had been preoccupied with Ian's Disappearing Body late on Saturday, and on Sunday she'd made a quick trip to Florida to attend her grandmother's funeral. She and Andrew had been friendly in class today, but Andrew didn't mention what had happened at the party, and Spencer certainly wasn't going to bring it up first. Spencer had been so anxious before Andrew came over that she'd dusted every one of her trophies for spelling bees, drama club, and field hockey MVPs just for something to do. Maybe Saturday's kiss had been just a kiss, nothing more. And anyway, Andrew had been her nemesis for years – they'd been competing for the top spot in the class ever since their kindergarten teacher held a contest to see who could make the best paper bag puppet. She couldn't seriously *like* him.

But she wasn't fooling anyone.

A bright light shone through the sunroom's floor-to-ceiling windows, and Spencer jumped. When Spencer returned from Florida last night, there were four media vans on her front lawn and a camera crew near the family's converted barn apartment at the back of the property. Now, a police officer and a German shepherd from the K-9 unit were prowling around the pine trees at the corner of the lot with an enormous flashlight, puzzling over something. Spencer had a feeling they'd found the bag of Ali memories the girls' grief counselor, Marion, had urged them to bury last week. A reporter would probably ring her doorbell any minute, asking her what the objects meant.

A fearful, nervous feeling throbbed deep in her bones. Last night, she hadn't been able to sleep a wink, terrified that not one but *two* people had now died in the woods behind her house, just steps from her bedroom. Every time she heard a twig snap or a *whoosh* of the wind, she sat up in horror, certain Ian's killer was still roaming the woods. She couldn't help but think that the murderer had killed him because he'd gotten too close to the truth. What if *Spencer* was too close to the truth too, simply from the vague hints that Ian had given her when they talked on the porch – that the cops were covering something up and that there was an even *bigger* secret about Ali's murder that all of Rosewood had yet to uncover?

Andrew cleared his throat, gesturing to Spencer's nails, which were digging into the surface of the desk. 'Are you okay?'

'Uh-huh,' Spencer snapped. 'I'm fine.'

Andrew pointed to the cops out the window. 'Think of it this way. At least you have twenty-four-hour police protection.'

Spencer swallowed hard. That was probably a good thing – Spencer needed all the protection she could get. She glanced at her econ notes, shoving her fears down deep. 'Back to studying?'

'Of course,' Andrew said, suddenly businesslike. He turned to his notes.

Spencer felt a mix of disappointment and apprehension. 'Or we don't *have* to study,' she blurted, hoping Andrew got her drift.

Andrew paused. '*I* don't want to study.' His voice cracked.

Spencer touched his hand. Slowly, he inched toward her. She moved closer too. After a few long moments, their lips touched. It was a thrilling relief. She wrapped her arms

47

around Andrew. He smelled like a mix of a woodstove and the pineapple-shaped, citrus-smelling air freshener that dangled from the rearview mirror of his Mini Cooper. They broke apart, then kissed again, longer this time. Spencer's heart thudded fast.

Then, Spencer's phone let out a loud *ping*. As she reached for it, her heart sped up, worried it was from A. But the e-mail was titled *News About Your Mom Match!*

'Oh my God,' Spencer whispered.

Andrew leaned over to look. 'I was just about to ask you if anything happened with that.'

Last week, Nana Hastings had willed her 'natural-born grandchildren' Melissa and Spencer's cousins two million dollars each. Spencer, on the other hand, got nothing. Melissa had raised a theory about why – perhaps Spencer had been adopted.

As much as Spencer wanted to believe it was just another one of Melissa's ploys to humiliate her – they were constantly trying to one-up each other, with Melissa usually winning – the idea nagged at her. Was *that* why her parents treated Spencer like shit and Melissa like gold, barely acknowledging Spencer's accomplishments, reneging on their promise to let Spencer live in the backyard barn for her junior and senior years, and even canceling Spencer's credit cards? Was *that* why Melissa looked like a clone of her mother, and Spencer didn't?

She'd confessed the theory to Andrew, and Andrew told Spencer about a biological mom-matching service a friend had used. Curious, Spencer registered her personal information – things like her birth date, the hospital where she was born, and the color of her eyes and other genetic traits. When she received an e-mail at the Rosewood Day benefit on Saturday that the site had matched her data with that of a potential mother, she hadn't known what to think. It had to be a mistake. Certainly they'd contact the woman and she'd say Spencer couldn't possibly be her child.

With trembling hands, Spencer opened the e-mail. *Hello Spencer, My name is Olivia Caldwell. I'm so excited, because I think we're a match. If you're up for it, I would love to meet you. With sincere fondness, O.*

Spencer stared at it for a long time, her hand clapped to her mouth. *Olivia Caldwell.* Could *that* be her real mother's name? Andrew poked her in the side. 'Are you going to respond?'

'I don't know,' Spencer said uneasily, wincing as a police car outside turned on its shrill, piercing siren. She gazed at her Sidekick screen so hard, the letters began to blur. 'I mean … it's hard to believe this is even real. How could my parents keep this from me? It means my whole life has been … a lie.' Lately, she'd discovered that so much of her life – especially the stuff with Ali – was built on lies. She wasn't sure if she could stomach anything more.

'Why don't we see if we can prove it?' Andrew stood up and offered his hand. 'Maybe there's something in this house that explains it beyond a shadow of a doubt.'

Spencer considered for a moment. 'All right,' she conceded slowly. It was probably a good time to snoop around – her parents and sister wouldn't be home for hours. She clasped Andrew's hand and led him into her father's office. The room smelled like cognac and cigars – her dad sometimes entertained his law clients at home – and when she flipped the switch on the wall, a bunch of soft lights flickered on above her father's massive Warhol print of a banana.

She sank down in the Aeron chair at her dad's tiger maple desk and gazed at the computer screen. There was a slide show of family pictures as the screen saver. First was a photo

49

of Melissa graduating from the University of Pennsylvania, the cap's tassel in her eyes. Then there was a photo of Melissa standing on the stoop of her brand-new Philadelphia brownstone their parents had bought for her when she got into the Wharton School. Then, a photo of Spencer popped up on the screen. It was a snapshot of Ali, Spencer, and the others crowded on a giant inner tube in the middle of a lake. Ali's brother, Jason, was swimming next to them, his longish hair sopping wet. This had been taken at Ali's family's lake house in the Poconos. By the looks of how young everyone was, it must have been one of the first times Ali had invited them there, a few weeks after they'd become friends.

Spencer sat back, startled to see herself in the family montage. After Spencer admitted she'd cheated to win the Golden Orchid, her parents had pretty much disowned her. And it was eerie to see such an early photo of Ali. Nothing bad had happened between Ali, Spencer, and the others yet – not The Jenna Thing, not Ali's clandestine relationship with Ian, not the secrets Spencer and the others tried to keep from Ali, not the secrets Ali kept from them. If only it had remained that way forever.

Spencer shuddered, trying to shake her jumble of uneasy feelings. 'My dad used to keep everything in file cabinets,' she explained, wiggling the mouse to make the screen saver disappear. 'But my mom's such a neat freak and hates piles of papers, so she made him scan everything. If there's something about me being adopted, it's on this computer.'

Her dad had a few Internet Explorer windows open from the last time he'd been on the computer. One was the front page of the *Philadelphia Sentinel*. The top headline was *Search for Thomas's Body Rages On*. Right below it was an opinion piece that said *Rosewood PD Should Be Hanged for*

Negligence. Below that was yet another story that read, *Kansas Teenager Receives Text from* A.

Spencer scowled and minimized the screen.

She gazed at the folder icons on the right side of the desktop. '*Taxes,*' she read out loud. '*Old. Work. Stuff.*' She groaned. 'My mom would kill him if she knew he organized the files like this.'

'What about that one?' Andrew pointed at the screen. '*Spencer, College.*'

Spencer frowned and clicked on it. There was only one PDF file inside the folder. The little hourglass icon whirled as the PDF slowly loaded on the screen. She and Andrew leaned forward. It was a recent statement from a savings account.

'Whoa.' Andrew pointed to the total. There was a two, and more than a few zeroes. Spencer noticed the name on the account. *Spencer Hastings.* Her eyes widened. Maybe her parents hadn't cut her off entirely.

She shut the PDF and kept looking. They opened a few more documents, but most of the files were spreadsheets Spencer didn't understand. There were tons of folders that had no classifications whatsoever. Spencer fluffed the feathery end of the quill pen her father had purchased at a 1776-themed auction at Christie's. 'Going through this will take forever.'

'Just copy the hard drive onto a disc and go through it all later,' Andrew suggested. He opened a big box of blank CDs on her dad's bookshelf and popped one into her dad's hard drive. Spencer looked at him nervously. She didn't want to add breaking into her dad's computer to the long list of grievances her parents had against her.

'Your dad will never know,' Andrew said, noting her look. 'I promise.' He clicked a few directives on the screen. 'This'll take a few minutes to run,' he said.

Spencer gazed at the rotating hourglass on the monitor, a nervous chill rushing through her. It was very possible that the truth about her past was on this computer. It had probably been right under her nose for years, and she hadn't had the slightest idea.

She pulled out her phone and opened the e-mail from Olivia Caldwell again. *I would love to meet you. With sincere fondness.* Suddenly, Spencer's brain turned over, and she felt clear-eyed and sure. What were the odds that a woman had given up a baby on the very same day Spencer was born at the very same hospital? A woman with emerald green eyes and dirty blond hair? What if this wasn't a theory ... but the truth?

Spencer looked at Andrew. 'It wouldn't *kill* me to meet with her, I guess.'

A surprised and excited smile appeared on Andrew's face. Spencer turned back to her Sidekick and hit reply, a giddy feeling spreading in her stomach. Squeezing Andrew's hand, she took a deep breath, composed her message, and hit send. Just like that, the e-mail was gone.

6

Strangers Not On A Train

The following morning, Aria's brother, Mike, turned up the stereo in the family's Subaru Outback. Aria winced as Led Zeppelin's 'Black Dog' snarled out of the speakers. 'Can you turn it down a little?' she whined.

Mike kept bobbing his head. 'It's best to listen to Zeppelin at maximum volume. That's what Noel and I do. Did you know the guys in the band were serious badasses? Jimmy Page rode his motorcycle down hotel hallways. Robert Plant threw TVs out windows onto the Sunset Strip.'

'Nope, can't say I knew that,' Aria said dryly. Today, Aria had the unfortunate chore of driving Mike to school. Mike usually rode with his Typical Rosewood mentor, Noel Kahn, but Noel's Range Rover was in the shop getting an even larger stereo installed. God forbid Mike take the bus.

Mike absentmindedly fiddled with the yellow rubber Rosewood Day lacrosse bracelet he wore nonstop on his right wrist. 'So why are you living with Dad again?'

'I thought I should spend equal time with Ella and Byron,' Aria mumbled. She made a left-hand turn onto the long drive that led to the school, narrowly missing a fat squirrel darting across the road. 'And we should get to know Meredith, don't you think?'

'But she's a puke machine.' Mike made a face.

'She's not that bad. And they're moving into that bigger house today.' Aria had overheard Byron breaking the news to Ella on the phone the night before, and she assumed Ella had told Mike and Xavier. 'I'll have a whole floor to myself.'

Mike gave her a suspicious look, but Aria stuck to her story.

Aria's cell phone, which was nestled in her yak-fur bag, beeped. She glanced at it nervously. She hadn't received a text from whoever this new A was since they'd discovered Ian's body Saturday night, but like Emily had said the other day, Aria had the distinct feeling that she was going to get a text from A any second.

Taking a deep breath, she reached into her purse. The text was from Emily. *Pull around back. School is mobbed with news vans again.*

Aria groaned. The news vans had clogged up the school's front drive the day before, too. Every media outlet in the tri-state area had sunk their teeth into the Ian Dead Body story. On the 7 A.M. news, reporters had canvassed the Rosewood Starbucks, random mothers waiting with their kids at school bus stops, and some people in the local DMV line, asking if they thought the cops had bungled the case. Most people said yes. Many were outraged that the police might be hiding something about Ali's murder. Some of the more tabloidy newspapers concocted elaborate conspiracy theories – that Ian had used a body double in the woods, or that Ali had a long-lost cross-dressing cousin who was responsible not only for her murder, but also a string of killings in Connecticut.

Aria craned her neck over the line of Audis and BMWs that jammed the driveway to the school. Sure enough, there were five news vans parked in the bus lane, blocking traffic.

'Sweet!' Mike exclaimed, his eyes on the vans too. 'Let me off here. That Cynthia Hewley's hot. Think she'd do me?' Cynthia Hewley was the curvy blond reporter relentlessly covering Ian's trial. *Every* guy at Rosewood Day hoped she'd do him.

Aria didn't stop the car. 'What would Savannah say about that?' She poked Mike's arm. 'Or have you forgotten you have a girlfriend?'

Mike flicked a toggle on his navy duffel coat. 'I kind of don't anymore.'

'*What?*' Aria had met Savannah at the Rosewood Day benefit, and thrillingly, she'd been normal and nice. Aria had always worried that Mike's first real girlfriend would be a skanky, brainless Barbie on loan from Turbulence, the local strip club.

Mike shrugged. 'If you must know, she broke up with me.'

'What did you do?' Aria demanded. Then she held up her hand, silencing him. 'Actually, don't tell me.' Mike had probably suggested Savannah start wearing crotchless panties or begged her to hook up with a girl and let him watch.

Aria drove around to the back of the school, past the soccer fields and the art barn. As she pulled into one of the last spaces in the back lot, she noticed a flapping sign on one of the lot's tall, metal floodlights. TIME CAPSULE, THE WINTER EDITION, STARTS TODAY! HERE'S YOUR CHANCE TO BE IMMORTALIZED! said big block letters.

'You're *kidding* me,' Aria whispered. The school held the Time Capsule contest every year, although Aria had missed the last three because her family had been living in Reykjavík, Iceland. The game usually took place in the fall, but Rosewood Day had been tactful enough to suspend it this year after construction workers found Alison DiLaurentis's dead body in the half-dug hole in her old backyard. But Rosewood wouldn't dare skip out on their most venerable tradition entirely. What would the donors think?

Mike sat up straighter, spying the sign. '*Nice.* I have the perfect idea of how to decorate it.' He rubbed his palms together eagerly.

Aria rolled her eyes. 'Are you going to draw unicorns on it? Write a poem about your bromance with Noel?'

Mike raised his nose in the air. 'It's way better than that. But if I told you, I'd have to kill you.' He waved to Noel Kahn, who was climbing out of James Freed's Hummer, and dashed out of the car without saying good-bye.

Aria sighed, peering again at the Time Capsule sign. In sixth grade, the first year Aria had been able to play, Time Capsule had been a huge deal. But when Aria, Spencer, and the others had sneaked into Ali's yard hoping to steal her piece, everything had gone so wrong. Aria pictured the shoe box at the back of her closet. She hadn't been brave enough to look inside it for years. Maybe Ali's piece of the flag had decomposed by now, just like her body.

'Ms Montgomery?'

Aria jumped. A dark-haired woman with a microphone stood outside her car. Behind her was a guy holding a TV camera.

The woman's eyes lit up when she saw Aria's face. 'Ms Montgomery!' she cried, banging on Aria's window. 'Can I ask you a few questions?'

Aria gritted her teeth, feeling like a monkey in a zoo. She waved the woman off, started the car again, and backed out of the lot. The reporter ran alongside her. The cameraman kept his lens on Aria as she zoomed to the main road.

She had to get out of here. Now.

*

By the time Aria arrived at the Rosewood SEPTA station, the parking lot was almost full with the regular commuters' Saabs, Volvos, and BMWs. She finally found a space, shoved a bunch of change into the meter, and stood on the edge of the platform. The train tracks were under a rusty trestle bridge. Across the road was a pet store that sold homemade dog food and costumes for cats.

There wasn't a train in sight. Then again, Aria had been so frantic to leave Rosewood Day, it hadn't occurred to her to check the SEPTA schedule. Sighing, she pushed into the little station house, which consisted of a ticket window, an ATM machine, and a small coffee counter that also sold books about train travel along the historic Main Line. A few people sat on the wooden benches that lined the room, languidly staring at the flat-screen television in the corner that was tuned to *Regis & Kelly*. Aria walked over to the posted train schedules on the far wall and discovered that the next train wouldn't be leaving here for a half hour. Resigned, she plopped down on a bench. A few people gawked at her. She wondered if they recognized her from TV. Reporters had been dogging her since Sunday, after all.

'Hey,' a voice said. 'I know you.'

Aria groaned, anticipating what was coming next. *You're that murdered girl's best friend! You're that girl who was being stalked! You're that girl who saw the dead body!* When she looked one bench over, her heart stopped. A familiar blond guy was sitting on a bench across the aisle, staring at her. Aria recognized his long fingers, his bow-shaped mouth, even the little mole on his cheekbone. She felt hot, then cold.

It was Jason DiLaurentis.

'H-hi,' Aria stammered. Lately, she'd been thinking a lot about Jason – especially the crush she used to have on him. It was weird to suddenly have him here, right in front of her.

'It's Aria, right?' Jason closed the paperback book he'd been reading.

'That's right.' Aria's insides shimmered. She wasn't sure if she'd ever heard Jason say her name before. Jason used to refer to Aria and the others as simply 'the Alis'.

'You're the one who made movies.' Jason's blue eyes were steady on her.

'Yeah.' Aria felt herself blushing. They used to screen Aria's pseudo-artsy movies in Ali's den, and sometimes Jason would pause in the doorway to watch. Aria used to feel so self-conscious about him being there, but at the same time, she longed for him to comment on her movies. To say they were brilliant, maybe, or at the very least thought provoking.

'You were the only one with substance,' Jason added, giving her a kind, alluring smile. Aria's insides turned over. Substance was good ... right?

'Are you going into Philadelphia?' Aria blurted, groping for something to say. She instantly wanted to smack her forehead. *Duh*. Of course he was going into Philadelphia. This train line didn't go anywhere else.

Jason nodded. 'To Penn. I just transferred. I used to go to Yale.'

Aria refrained from saying *I know*. The day Ali told them Jason had gotten into Yale, his top-choice school, Aria had considered drawing him a *Congratulations* card. But she decided against it, afraid Ali would tease her.

'It's great,' Jason went on. 'I only have classes Mondays, Wednesdays, and Thursdays, and I get out early enough to take the three P.M. bullet train back to Yarmouth.'

'Yarmouth?' Aria repeated.

'My parents moved there for the trial.' Jason shrugged and riffled his paperback's pages through his fingers. 'I moved into the apartment above the garage. I figured they needed me to help them through this ... stuff.'

'Right.' Aria's stomach started to ache. She couldn't imagine how Jason was dealing with Ali's murder – not only had his old classmate killed her, but that he'd then vanished. She licked her lips, thinking of answers for what she guessed would be his next questions: *What was it like seeing Ian's body in the woods? Where do you think it is now? Do you think someone moved it?*

But Jason just sighed. 'I usually get on at Yarmouth, but today I had something to do in Rosewood. So here I am.'

Outside, an Amtrak bullet train roared into the station. The other people who had been waiting stood up and clattered through the door to the platform. After the train roared away, Jason walked across the aisle and sat down right next to Aria. 'So ... don't you have school?' he asked.

Aria opened her mouth, fumbling for an answer. Jason was suddenly so close to her, she could easily smell his nutty, spicy soap. It was intoxicating. 'Uh, nope. It's parent-teacher conference day.'

'Do you always wear your uniform on days off?' Jason pointed to the bottom hem of Aria's plaid Rosewood Day skirt. It was peeking out under her long wool coat.

Aria felt her cheeks blaze. 'I don't usually ditch, I swear.'

'I won't tell,' Jason teased. He leaned forward, making the bench creak. 'You know the go-kart place on Wembley Road? Once I went there for the whole day. Drove that little car around and around for hours.'

Aria chuckled. 'Was the lanky guy there? The one who wears head-to-toe NASCAR gear?' Mike used to be obsessed with that go-kart track – before he became obsessed with strippers and lacrosse.

'Jimmy?' Jason's eyes sparkled. 'Totally.'

'And he didn't ask why you weren't in school?' Aria asked, curling her hand over the bench's armrest. 'He's usually so nosy.'

'Nope.' Jason poked her shoulder. 'But *I* had sense enough to change out of my uniform so it wouldn't be so obvious. Then again, the girls' uniforms are way cuter than the guys'.'

Aria suddenly felt so bashful, she turned her head and stared fixedly at the row of potato chips and pretzels in the vending machine. Was Jason *flirting*?

Jason's eyes gleamed. He breathed in, maybe about to say something else. Aria hoped he was about to ask her on a date – or maybe even for her phone number. Then the conductor's voice blared over the loudspeaker, announcing that the eastbound train to Philadelphia would arrive in three minutes.

'I guess that's us,' Aria said, zipping up her jacket. 'Want to ride together?'

But Jason didn't answer. When Aria looked over, he was staring at the television. His skin had turned pale and his mouth was a taut, distressed line. 'I . . . uh . . . I just realized. I have to go.' He stood up sloppily, pulling his books into his chest.

'W-what? Why?' Aria cried.

Jason maneuvered around the benches, not answering. He bumped against Aria as he passed, upending her purse. 'Oops,' she mumbled, wincing as a super-plus tampon and her lucky Beanie Baby cow spilled to the sticky concrete floor. 'Sorry,' Jason muttered, pushing out the door to the parking lot.

Aria gazed after him, astonished. What the hell just happened? And why was Jason going back to his *car* . . . and not into the city?

Her cheeks burned with sudden awareness. Jason had

probably realized how Aria felt about him. And maybe, because he didn't mean to lead her on, he'd decided to drive into Philadelphia by himself instead of ride the train with her. How could she have been so stupid to think Jason was flirting? So what if he'd said she was the only one with substance, or that she looked cute in a skirt. So what that he'd given her Ali's Time Capsule flag way back in the day. None of that necessarily meant anything. In the end, Aria was nothing more than one of the nameless Alis.

Humiliated, Aria slowly turned back to the TV. To her surprise, a news broadcast had interrupted *Regis & Kelly*. The headline caught Aria's eye. *Thomas's Body a Hoax*.

The blood drained from Aria's face. She whirled around and scanned the line of cars in the parking lot. Or was *this* why Jason ran off so quickly?

On television, the Rosewood chief of police was speaking to a bevy of microphones. 'We've been searching those woods for two days straight and can't find a single trace of Mr Thomas's body,' he said. 'Maybe we need to step back and consider other … possibilities.'

Aria frowned. *What* other possibilities?

The feed cut to Ian's mother. A bunch of microphones were shoved under her chin. 'Ian e-mailed us yesterday,' she said. 'He didn't say where he was, just that he was safe … and that he didn't do it.' She paused to wipe her eyes. 'We're still verifying if it really was from him or not. I pray that it wasn't someone using his account to play a trick on us.'

Then Officer Wilden popped onto the screen. 'I wanted to believe the girls when they told me they saw Ian in the woods,' he said, looking contrite. 'But even from the start, I wasn't really sure. I had a terrible feeling this might be a ploy for our attention.'

Aria's mouth dropped open. *What?*

And finally, the camera focused on a bearded man in thick glasses and a gray sweater. *Dr Henry Warren, Psychiatrist, Rosewood Hospital*, the caption below him said. 'Being the center of attention is an addictive feeling,' the doctor explained. 'If the focus has been on someone for long enough, they begin to … *crave* it. Sometimes, people take any measure possible to keep all eyes on them, even if that means embellishing the truth. Making up false realities.'

An anchor came on again, saying they'd have more on this story at the top of the hour. As the broadcast broke for a commercial, Aria placed her palms flat on the bench and took heaping breaths. What. The. Hell?

Outside, the eastbound SEPTA roared into the station and screeched to a halt. Suddenly, Aria didn't feel like going into Philly anymore. What was the point? No matter where she went, baggage from Rosewood would always follow her.

She walked back to the parking lot, scanning for Jason's tall frame and blond hair. There wasn't a person in sight. The road in front of the station was empty, too, the traffic lights silently swinging. For just a moment, Aria felt like she was the only human left in the world. She swallowed hard, a peculiar feeling creeping down her neck to her tailbone. Jason *had* been here just now, hadn't he? And they *had* seen Ian's body in the woods … right? For a moment, she felt like she really *was* going crazy, just like the psychiatrist had insinuated.

But she quickly shook off the thought. As the train pulled out of the station, Aria walked back to her car. Not having anywhere better to go, she finally drove back to school.

7
Kate 1, Hanna 1

Hanna set her venti skim latte on the sugar and milk counter at Steam, the coffee bar adjacent to the Rosewood Day cafeteria. It was lunchtime that Tuesday, and Kate, Naomi, and Riley were still in line. One by one, Hanna heard each of them order an extra-large mint tea. Hanna had missed the memo, but apparently, mint tea was the drink du jour.

She ripped open a second Splenda packet with her teeth. If only she had a Percocet to go with her latte – or, better yet, a gun. So far, lunch had been a disaster. First, Naomi and Riley had fawned over Kate's Frye boots, saying nothing about Hanna's far-cuter Chie Mihara sling-backs. Then they'd babbled on about how much fun they'd had at Rive Gauche yesterday – one of the college-age waiters had sneaked the girls tons of pinot noir. After they'd drunk their fill, they popped into Sephora, and Kate bought Naomi and Riley gel-filled eye masks to ease their hangovers. The girls brought the masks to school today and put them on during an extra-long bathroom break during second-period study hall. The only thing that lifted Hanna's spirits was seeing that the cold mask had turned the area around Riley's brown eyes a harsh, chapped red.

'*Hmph*,' Hanna sniffed quietly. She tossed the empty Splenda packet into the little chrome trash can, vowing to buy Naomi and Riley something far better than a stupid mask. Then she noticed the flat-screen TV above the big jug of lemon water. Usually, the TV was tuned to the closed-circuit Rosewood Day channel, which showed recaps of school sporting events, choral concerts, and on-the-spot interviews, but today, someone had turned it to the news. *No Thomas Body in Woods*, said the headline.

Her stomach churned. Aria had told her about this story earlier this morning in AP English. How could the Thomases have received a note from Ian? How could there be *no trace* of Ian in those woods, no blood, no hair, nothing? Did that mean they *hadn't* seen him? Did that mean he was still … *alive*?

And why were the cops saying Hanna and the others had made it up? Wilden hadn't seemed to think they'd made it up the night of the party. In fact, if Wilden hadn't been so damn hard to find that night, they could've gotten back to the woods faster. Maybe they could've even caught Ian before he got away – or got dragged away. But *no*, the Rosewood PD couldn't look like screwups … so they had to make Hanna and the others look crazy instead. And all this time, she'd thought Wilden had her back.

Hanna quickly turned away from the TV, wanting to put the story out of her mind. Then something behind the cinnamon sifter caught her eye. It looked like … fabric. And it was the exact same color as the Rosewood Day flag.

Hanna swallowed hard, yanked the fabric free, spread it out, and gasped. It was a piece of cloth, cut into a jagged square. The very edge of the Rosewood Day crest was in the upper right-hand corner. Safety-pinned to the back was a piece of paper with the number 16 on it. Rosewood Day always numbered each piece so they'd know how to sew the flag back together.

'What's that?' said a voice. Hanna jumped, startled. Kate had slunk up behind her.

Hanna took a second to react, her mind still reeling from the Ian news. 'It's for this stupid game,' she muttered.

Kate pursed her lips. 'The game that started today? Time Warp?'

Hanna rolled her eyes. 'Time *Capsule*.'

Kate took a long sip of her tea. '"Once all twenty pieces of the flag have been found, they will be sewn back together and buried in a Time Capsule behind the soccer fields,"' she recited from the posters that had appeared all over school. Leave it to goody-goody Kate to have memorized the Time Capsule rules, as if she were going to be tested on them later. 'And then you'll get your name immortalized on a bronze plaque. That's a big deal, right?'

'Whatev,' Hanna mumbled. Talk about ironic – when she didn't give a shit about Time Capsule anymore, she found a piece without even looking at the clues posted in the school lobby. In sixth grade, the first year she'd been allowed to play, Hanna had fantasized about how she'd decorate a piece if she were lucky enough to find one. Some kids drew pointless things on their pieces, like a flower or a smiley face or – dumbest of all – the Rosewood Day crest, but Hanna understood that a well-decorated Time Capsule flag was as important as carrying the right handbag or getting highlights from the Henri Flaubert salon in the King James. When Hanna, Spencer, and the others confronted Ali in her backyard the day after the game started, Ali had described in detail what she'd drawn on her stolen piece. *A Chanel logo. The*

Louis Vuitton pattern. A manga frog. A girl playing field hockey. As soon as Hanna got home that day, she wrote down everything Ali said she'd drawn on her flag, not wanting to forget. It sounded so glamorous and exactly *right.*

Then, in eighth grade, Hanna and Mona found a Time Capsule piece together. Hanna wanted to incorporate Ali's elements into the design, but she was afraid Mona might ask her what they meant – she hated bringing up Ali to Mona, since Mona had been one of the girls Ali loved to tease. Hanna thought she was being a good friend – little did she know Mona was slowly masterminding a way to ruin Hanna's life.

Naomi and Riley bounded over, both of them immediately noticing Hanna's flag. Riley's brown eyes boggled. She reached a pale, freckly arm out to touch the piece, but Hanna snapped it back, feeling protective. It would be just like one of these bitches to steal Hanna's flag when she wasn't looking. All of a sudden, she understood what Ali meant when she told Ian she was going to guard her piece with her life. And she understood, too, why Ali had been furious the day someone had stolen it from her.

Then again, Ali had been furious, but not exactly *devastated.* In fact, Ali had been more distracted that day than anything else. Hanna distinctly remembered how Ali kept looking over at the woods and her house, as if she thought someone was listening. Then, after whining about her missing piece for a while, Ali suddenly snapped back to her bitchy, frosty self, walking away from Hanna and the others without another word, like there was something more important on her mind than talking to four losers.

When it was clear Ali wasn't coming back outside, Hanna had walked to the front yard and retrieved her bike. Ali's street had seemed so pleasant. The Cavanaughs had a pretty

66

red tree house in their side yard. Spencer's family had a big windmill spinning at the back of the property. There was a house down the street that had a humungous six-car garage and a water fountain in the front yard. Later, Hanna would learn it was where Mona lived.

And then she'd heard an engine backfiring. A sleek, vintage black car with tinted windows chugged at Ali's curb, as if waiting ... or watching. Something about it made the hair on the back of Hanna's neck stand up. *Maybe that's who stole Ali's flag*, she'd thought. Not that she ever found out for sure.

Hanna gazed at Naomi, who was adding Splenda to her mint tea. Naomi and Riley used to be Ali's best friends in sixth grade, but right after Time Capsule started, Ali ditched them both. She never explained why. Maybe Naomi and Riley had been the ones who'd stolen Ali's flag – maybe *they'd* been inside that black car Hanna had seen at the curb. And maybe that was why Ali dropped them – maybe Ali asked them for her flag back, and when they denied they'd taken it, she cut them off. But if that was what happened, why didn't Naomi or Riley turn in the flag as their own? Why did the flag stay lost?

There was a commotion at the front of Steam, and the crowd parted. Eight Rosewood Day lacrosse boys strutted by in a cocky, confident herd. Mike Montgomery was wedged between Noel Kahn and James Freed.

Riley jostled Kate's arm, making the gold bangle bracelets around Kate's wrist jingle. 'There he is.'

'You should totally go talk to him,' Naomi murmured, her blue eyes widening. At that, the three of them stood up and strolled over. Naomi ogled Noel. Riley tossed her long red hair at Mason. Now that lax boys were permitted, it was a free-for-all.

'Rosewood Day is really picky about people drawing inappropriate stuff on the Time Capsule flag,' Mike was saying to his friends. 'But if the lax team found every single piece and made one *huge* inappropriate drawing – of like, a penis – Appleton wouldn't be able to do a thing. He wouldn't even *know* it was a penis until he unveiled the flag at the assembly.'

Noel Kahn slapped him on the back. '*Nice*. I can't wait for the look on Appleton's face.'

Mike pantomimed Principal Appleton, who was getting up there in years, shakily unfolding the reconstructed flag for the school to see. 'Now, what's this?' he said in a craggy old-man voice, holding an invisible magnifying glass to his eye. 'Is this what you young whippersnappers call . . . a *schlong*?'

Kate burst out laughing. Hanna glanced at her, astonished. There was no way Kate could honestly think these cretins were funny. Mike noticed her laughing and smiled.

'That imitation of Appleton is perfect,' Kate cooed. Hanna clenched her jaw. As if Kate had even met Principal Appleton yet. She'd only been a Rosewood Day student for a week.

'Thanks,' Mike said, running his eyes up and down Kate's body, from her boots to her slender legs to her Rosewood Day blazer, which fit Kate's willowy frame perfectly. Hanna noted with annoyance that Mike didn't look at her once. 'I do a pretty good impression of Lance the shop teacher, too.'

'I'd love to hear it sometime,' Kate gushed.

Hanna gritted her teeth. That was *it*. There was no way her soon-to-be stepsister was snagging the guy who was supposed to worship *her*. She marched over to the boys, nudged Kate out of the way, and ran her fingers over the Time Capsule flag she had just found.

'I couldn't help but overhear your brilliant idea,' Hanna said loudly, 'but I'm sorry to say your *schlong* is going to be incomplete.' She waved her flag under Mike's nose.

Mike's eyes widened. He reached out for it, but Hanna yanked it away. Mike stuck out his bottom lip. 'Come on. What'll it take for you to give that piece to me?'

Hanna had to hand it to him – most sophomore guys were so nervous in Hanna's presence, they started quivering and stuttering. She pressed the flag to her chest. 'I'm not letting this baby out of my sight.'

'There's gotta be *something* I can do for you,' Mike pleaded. 'Your history homework? Hand-wash your bras? Fondle your nipples?'

Kate let out another girlish titter, trying to bring the attention back to her, but Hanna quickly grabbed Mike's arm and pulled him back toward the condiments table, away from the crowd. 'I can give you something way better than this flag,' she murmured.

'What?' Mike asked.

'Me, silly,' Hanna said flirtatiously. 'Maybe you and I could go out sometime.'

'Okay,' Mike said to Hanna emphatically. 'When?'

Hanna peeked over her shoulder. Kate's mouth had dropped open. *Ha*, Hanna thought, feeling triumphant. *That* was easy.

'How about tomorrow?' she asked Mike.

'Hmm. My dad's throwing his mistress a baby shower.' Mike stuffed his hands in his blazer pockets. Hanna flinched – Aria had told her about her dad running off with his student, but Hanna hadn't been aware that they were talking about it so candidly. 'I'd blow it off, but my dad would kill me.'

'Oh, but I *love* showers,' Hanna exclaimed, even though she sort of hated them.

'I love showers too – the kind I take with a couple of hot girls,' Mike said, winking.

Hanna fought the urge to roll her eyes. Seriously, what did Kate see in him? She peeked over Mike's shoulder again. Now, Kate, Naomi, and Riley were whispering to Noel and Mason. They were probably just trying to act secretive to throw Hanna off – but she wasn't falling for it.

'Anyway, if you really want to come, awesome,' Mike said, and Hanna turned back to him. 'Give me your number and I'll text you the deets. Oh, and you don't have to bring a gift or anything. But if you do, Meredith's really eco and shit. So, like, don't get her disposable diapers. And don't get her a breast pump – I already got that department covered.' He crossed his arms over his chest, as if terribly pleased with his idea.

'Got it,' Hanna said. Then, she stepped forward until she was just inches from Mike's mouth. She could see flecks of gray in his blue eyes. He had that sweaty boy smell, probably from a morning gym class. Surprisingly, it was kind of hot. 'I'll see you tomorrow,' she whispered, her lips touching his cheek.

'Definitely,' Mike breathed. He walked back to Noel and Mason, who were watching, and did that shoulder-punching thing all the lax boys loved.

Hanna dusted off her hands. *Done and done.* When she turned around, Kate was standing right behind her.

'Oh!' Hanna simpered. 'Hi, Kate! Sorry, I had something I had to ask Mike.'

Kate crossed her arms over her chest. 'Hanna! I *told* you I wanted to go for Mike.'

Hanna wanted to laugh at Kate's wounded tone of voice. Had Little Miss Perfect never fought for a guy before? 'Mmmm,' Hanna answered. 'Seems like he likes me.'

Kate's pale eyes darkened. A serene look came over her face. 'Well, I guess we'll have to see about that,' she said.

'I guess we will,' Hanna chirped, her voice ice.

They stared each other down. The song over Steam's speakers changed from an emo-punk ballad to a throbbing, African dance beat. It reminded Hanna of a song a tribe might play before they went off to battle.

Game on, bitch, Hanna mouthed to Kate. Then she daintily pulled her bag into her chest and waltzed around her stepsister-to-be into the Rosewood Day hallway, waggling her fingers at Mike, Noel, and the others. But as she was passing the cafeteria, she heard a sarcastic cackle reverberate off the walls. She stopped, the hair on the back of her neck rising. The laugh wasn't coming from Steam, but from the cafeteria.

All the tables in the lunchroom were full. Then, out of the corner of her eye, Hanna saw a figure behind the rotating pretzel oven slither out the back door. The person was tall and lanky and had blond, curly hair. Hanna's heart stopped. *Ian?*

But no. Ian was dead. The person who had sent his parents that text earlier today was an impostor. Shaking off the thought, Hanna pulled her school blazer around her shoulders, drained the last of her latte, and continued down the corridor, trying her best to strut like the fearless, gorgeous, unflappable girl she was.

8

If The Dolls Could Talk...

As soon as Emily finished swim practice Tuesday afternoon, she drove to Isaac's house and parked at the curb. Isaac opened the front door of his house, grabbed Emily tight, and inhaled deeply. '*Mmm*. I just love it when you smell like chlorine.'

Emily giggled. Despite the fact that she always washed her hair twice in the locker room showers after every practice, the distinct pool smell stubbornly clung to her hair.

Isaac stepped aside, and Emily walked into the house. The living room smelled like apple and peach potpourri. There was the picture on the mantel of Isaac, his mom, and Minnie Mouse at Disney World. The floral couch was covered with lacy pillows Mrs Colbert had embroidered, bearing messages like *Hugging Is Healthy* and *Prayer Changes Everything*.

Isaac pulled at one of the sleeves of Emily's coat, then the other. When he turned to open the closet door, she heard a *creak* coming from the mudroom. Emily froze, her eyes round. Isaac turned to her and touched her hand. 'Why so jumpy? The press isn't here, I promise.'

Emily licked her lips. The press had been hounding her

72

and her friends constantly, and earlier that day, she'd heard the latest: that the Thomas family had received an e-mail from Ian, and that Emily and the others had made up seeing Ian's body in the woods. *That* obviously wasn't true – but what was? Where had Ian gone? Was he really alive ... or did someone just want them to think he was?

More than that, Emily couldn't stop thinking about the Jason DiLaurentis incident on Sunday night. She had no idea what she would've done if Isaac hadn't been with her. Every time she considered the possibility of facing Jason alone, she shuddered with fear.

'Sorry,' she said to Isaac, trying to snap out of her mood. 'I'm okay.'

'Good,' Isaac said. He took her hand. 'Since we have the place to ourselves, I thought I'd show you my bedroom.'

'Are you sure?' Emily glanced at the photo of Isaac, his mom, and Minnie Mouse again. Mrs Colbert had a policy that Isaac wasn't allowed to bring any girls into his room – ever.

'Sure I'm sure,' Isaac answered. 'My mom will never know.'

Emily smiled. She *had* been curious about his bedroom. Isaac squeezed her hand and led her up the stairs. Each stair riser was decorated with a different doll. Some of them were yarn-haired rag dolls in calico dresses, and others were baby dolls with hard china heads and eyes that closed when they were laid flat. Emily averted her eyes. She'd never been one to play with dolls like other girls – they'd always kind of freaked her out.

Isaac pushed through a door at the end of the hall. 'Voilà.' There was a striped spread on the double bed in the corner, three guitars on stands, and a small desk with a new iMac. 'Very nice,' Emily said.

Then she noticed a large white object on top of the

73

dresser. 'You have a phrenology head!' She walked over to the big mold of a skull and traced her fingers over the words that were written across the head. *Guile. Forethought. Avarice.* Victorian doctors thought they could determine a person's character simply by the way his or her skull was shaped. If he had a lump in a particular spot on his head, he was a good poet. If the lump was elsewhere, he was very religious. Emily wondered what her head bumps said about her.

She grinned at Isaac. 'Where did you get this?'

Isaac walked over to her. 'Remember that aunt I told you about when we got Chinese last week? The one who's into horoscopes and stuff? She got this for me at a flea market.' He touched a spot on Emily's skull. 'Hmm, you feel very bumpy.' He glanced at the phrenology head. 'According to this, you're really good at giving affection ... or you make others *want* to give you affection. I can never remember which.'

'Very scientific,' Emily teased. She touched the top of his head, feeling for a bump. 'And you're ...' She leaned back, searching the ceramic head for an appropriate quality. *The thief. The mimic. The murderer.* Rosewood PD needed one of these heads – they could massage every cranium in town and find Ali's murderer right away. 'You're wise,' she concluded.

'*You're* beautiful,' Isaac said. He slowly steered her over to the bed and pulled her down. She felt flushed and short of breath. She hadn't anticipated lying down on Isaac's bed, but she didn't want to get up. They kissed for a while longer, easing down until they were lying flat on the pillows. Emily thrust her hand underneath his T-shirt to feel his warm, bare chest. Then she giggled, astonished at her behavior.

'What?' Isaac asked, pulling away. 'Do you want to stop?'

Emily lowered her eyes. The truth was, whenever she was

around Isaac, a calmness came over her. All of her anxieties and worries flew out the window. Being with him, she felt safe and secure … and in love.

'I don't want to stop,' she whispered, her heart fluttering. 'Do you?'

Isaac shook his head. Then, he pulled off his T-shirt. His skin was pale and soft. He unbuttoned Emily's blouse, one button at a time, until her shirt gaped open. The only sound was their breathing. Isaac touched the edge of Emily's pink scalloped bra. Ever since he had taken off her shirt two days ago in the car, she'd worn her prettier bras to school. Nicer underwear, too, not the comfy boy shorts she usually wore. Maybe she hadn't anticipated this, exactly, but maybe, just maybe, it was exactly what she'd been hoping for.

When the digital clock on Isaac's nightstand turned from 5:59 to 6:00, Emily sat up and pulled the flannel sheets around her. The streetlights up and down Isaac's block were now lit, and a woman across the street was calling her kids in from the front yard for dinner.

'I should probably go soon,' Emily said, giving Isaac another kiss. They both giggled. Isaac pulled her back down and started kissing her again. Eventually, they both stood up and got dressed, sneaking not-so-covert peeks at each other. A lot had happened … but Emily felt right about it. Isaac had gone achingly slow, kissing every inch of her body, admitting that this was his first time too. It couldn't have been more perfect.

They started down the stairs, straightening their clothes. Halfway down, Emily heard someone let out a phlegm-filled cough.

They both froze. Emily widened her eyes at Isaac. His parents weren't supposed to be back until after seven.

75

A creaky footstep sounded from the kitchen. A set of car keys jangled, then dropped into a ceramic bowl. Emily's stomach swooped. She gazed at the mute, glassy-eyed dolls on the steps. They seemed to be smirking at her.

Emily and Isaac scrambled down the stairs and flung themselves on the couch. As soon as their butts hit the cushions, Mrs Colbert walked into the room. She was dressed in a long red wool skirt and a white cable-knit sweater. Because of the way the light reflected off her glasses, Emily couldn't tell where she was looking. There was a stern, disapproving look on her face. For an agonizing second, Emily became panicked that Mrs Colbert had heard everything that had just happened.

Then, she turned and flattened her palm to her chest. 'Guys! I didn't see you there!'

Isaac leapt up, awkwardly knocking the stack of photo albums on the coffee table to the floor. 'Mom, you remember Emily, right?'

Emily stood up, too, hoping her hair wasn't a complete mess and that she didn't have a rapidly growing hickey on her neck. 'H-hi,' she stammered. 'Nice to see you again.'

'Hello, Emily.' There was a pleasant enough smile on Mrs Colbert's face, but Emily's heart continued to gallop all the same. Was she really surprised to see them, or was she just waiting until Emily left to yell at Isaac in private?

She gazed at Isaac, who looked uncomfortable. He placed his hand on top of his head, matting down his mussed hair. 'Uh, Emily, do you want to stay for dinner?' Isaac blurted. "That's okay, right, Mom?"

Mrs Colbert hesitated, drawing her lips together until they practically disappeared. 'I – I shouldn't,' Emily stammered, before Mrs Colbert could answer. 'My mom is expecting me home.'

Mrs Colbert breathed out. Emily swore she looked relieved. 'Well. Perhaps another time,' she said.

'How about tomorrow?' Isaac pressed.

Emily shot an uneasy glance at Isaac, wondering if he should just let the dinner thing drop. But Mrs Colbert brushed her hands together and said, 'Tomorrow would be fine. Wednesday is pot roast night.'

'Uh, okay,' Emily answered. 'I guess I could do that. Thanks.'

'Good.' Mrs Colbert gave her a tight smile. 'Bring your appetite!'

She glided back to the kitchen. Emily sank back onto the couch and covered her face with her hands. 'Just kill me now,' she whispered.

Isaac touched her arm. 'We're safe. She doesn't know we were upstairs.'

But as Emily glanced through the arched doorway to the kitchen, she saw Isaac's mom standing at the sink, rinsing off the breakfast dishes. Although her hands continued to manically scrub the plates, Mrs Colbert's dark eyes were fixed steadily on them. Her lips puckered, her cheeks flushed, and the cords in her neck bulged with fury.

Emily flinched, aghast. Mrs Colbert noticed Emily was watching, but her expression didn't falter. She stared unblinkingly at Emily, as if cognizant of exactly what she and Isaac had done. And maybe even blaming Emily – and only Emily – for all of it.

9
Surprise! He's Still Here …

As the sun was sinking beneath the horizon, turning all of Rosewood pitch-black, Spencer watched out her bedroom window as the remaining Rosewood PD squad cars and news vans pulled away from her street. The cops had abruptly called off the search for Ian's body, having found nothing in the woods. And a lot of people had bought into the new theory that the girls had made up seeing Ian's body, thereby allowing him to easily escape Rosewood forever.

Such bullshit. And it didn't seem possible that the cops hadn't found a single piece of evidence. There had to be something out there. A footprint. Tree bark rubbed off from someone's nails.

Her desktop computer at the other corner of the room made an angry *buzz*. Spencer looked up, eyeing the CD she and Andrew had made of her dad's hard drive yesterday. It was where she'd left it after it finished loading last night, sitting in a paper sleeve on top of her antique Tiffany blotter. She hadn't looked through the files yet, but there was no good time like the present. She walked to her desk and slid the CD into her computer.

Instantly, the computer made a farting noise, and every single icon on Spencer's desktop turned into a question mark. She tried to click on one, but it wouldn't open. Then the screen went black. She tried to reboot, but the computer wouldn't turn on.

'Shit,' she whispered, ejecting the CD. She had backups of everything on her hard drive, like her old papers, tons of pictures and videos, and her journal, which she'd kept since before Ali disappeared, but without a functional computer, she couldn't look through her dad's files for evidence.

A door slammed downstairs. Her father spoke in a muffled voice, then her mother. Spencer looked up, her stomach burbling. She hadn't really spoken to them since they'd all returned from Nana's funeral. She glanced at her computer again, then stood and walked downstairs.

The air smelled like the baked brie her parents always bought at the Fresh Fields deli counter, and the family's two labradoodles, Rufus and Beatrice, were lazing on the big round rug by the breakfast nook. Spencer's sister, Melissa, was in the kitchen, too, scuttling around, piling the design magazines and books she'd scattered around the room into a paper shopping bag. Spencer's mom was rifling through the drawer that held all the phone books and numbers for the various people who helped around the house – landscapers, driveway sealers, electricians. Mr Hastings was pacing from the kitchen to the dining room, his cell phone to his ear.

'Uh, my computer has a virus,' Spencer said.

Her dad stopped pacing. Melissa looked up. Her mother jumped and whirled around. The corners of her mouth turned down. She turned back to the drawer.

'Mom?' Spencer tried again. 'My computer. It's ... dead.'

Mrs Hastings didn't turn. 'And?'

Spencer ran her fingers along the slightly wilted floral arrangement on the island until she realized where she'd seen the flowers last – on Nana's casket. She pulled her hand away fast. 'Well, I need it to do my homework. Can I call Geek Squad?'

Her mother turned and examined Spencer for a few long beats. When Spencer gazed back helplessly, Mrs Hastings began to laugh.

'What?' Spencer asked, confused. Beatrice raised her head, then put it down again.

'Why should I pay for someone to come fix your computer when I should make *you* pay for what happened to the garage?' Mrs Hastings crowed.

Spencer blinked fast. 'The ... garage?'

Her mother snorted. 'Don't tell me you didn't see it.'

Spencer looked back and forth from one parent to the other, clueless. Then she ran to the front door and stepped out into the yard in her socks, even though the ground was frosty and soggy. A light had been turned on over the garage. When Spencer saw what was there, she clapped her hand over her mouth.

Across both garage doors, in bloodred paint, was the word *KILLER*.

It hadn't been here when she'd come home from school today. Spencer looked around, gripped with the distinct feeling that someone was watching from the woods. Did a tree branch just move? Did someone just duck behind a shrub? Was it ... A?

She faced her mother, who had marched up beside her. 'Did you call the police?'

Mrs Hastings barked out another laugh. 'Do you think the

police really want to speak to *us* right now? Do you think they're going to care that someone did this to our house?'

Spencer widened her eyes. 'Wait, you believe what the cops are saying?'

Her mom sank onto one hip. 'We both know there wasn't ever anything in those woods.'

The world started to spin. Spencer's mouth felt dry. 'Mom, I saw Ian. I really *did*.'

Her mother brought her face inches from Spencer's. 'Do you know how much it's going to cost to refinish those doors? They're one of a kind – we got them off an old barn in Maine.'

Spencer's eyes filled with tears. 'I'm sorry to be such a *liability*.' She whirled around, stomped onto the porch, and marched up the stairs without bothering to wipe her muddy socks on the doormat. Her eyes stung with hot tears as she walked up the stairs and flung open the door to her bedroom. Why did it surprise her that her mother was siding with the cops? Why should she have expected anything different?

'Spence?'

Melissa poked her head into the room. She was wearing a pale yellow cashmere twinset and dark, boot-cut jeans. Her hair was held back by a velvet ribbon, and her eyes looked tired and puffy, as if she'd been crying.

'Go away,' Spencer mumbled.

Melissa sighed. 'I just wanted to let you know that you can use my old laptop if you need it. It's in the barn. I have a new computer at the town house. I'm moving there tonight.'

Spencer turned slightly, frowning. 'The renovations are done?' Melissa's Philadelphia town house overhaul seemed to have no end – she kept tweaking the designs.

Melissa stared at the creamy Berber carpet that spread

across Spencer's bedroom floor. 'I have to get out of here.' Her voice cracked.

'Is everything ... okay?' Spencer asked.

Melissa pulled her sleeves over her hands. 'Yeah. Fine.'

Spencer shifted in her seat. She'd tried to talk to Melissa about Ian's body at Nana's funeral on Sunday, but Melissa kept waving her away. Her sister had to have some thoughts about it – when Ian was released on house arrest, Melissa had seemed sympathetic to his plight. She'd even tried to convince Spencer that Ian was innocent. Maybe, like the police, she believed that Ian's body had never been there. It would be just like Melissa to trust a bunch of possibly crooked cops over her sister, all because she didn't want to accept that her beloved might be dead.

'Really, I'm fine,' Melissa urged, as if she could read Spencer's thoughts. 'I just don't want to be here if there are going to be search parties and news vans.'

'But the cops aren't searching here anymore,' Spencer told her. 'They just called it off.'

A startled look crossed Melissa's face. Then she shrugged and turned around without answering. Spencer listened to her padding down the stairs.

The front door slammed, and Spencer could hear Mrs Hastings murmuring quietly and kindly to Melissa in the foyer. Her *real* daughter. Spencer winced, gathered up her books, shrugged into her coat and boots, and walked out the back door to Melissa's barn. As she crossed the cold, vast yard, she noticed something to the left and stopped. Someone had sprayed *LIAR* on the windmill in the same red paint as the graffiti on the garage. A glob of red dripped from the bottom edge of the *L* to the dead grass. It looked as if it were bleeding.

Spencer glanced back at the house, considering, then

pulled her books into her chest and pressed on. Her parents would see it soon enough. She certainly didn't want to be the one to break the news.

Melissa had left the barn in a hurry. There was a half-drunk bottle of wine on the counter, and a half-filled water glass her normally anal sister hadn't washed out. A lot of her clothes were still in the closet, and there was a big book called *The Principles of Mergers and Acquisitions* flung on the bed, a University of Pennsylvania bookmark wedged between the pages.

Spencer hefted her cream-colored Mulberry tote onto the brown leather couch, pulled the CD of her dad's computer from the front pocket, sat down at Melissa's desk, and slid the CD into the drive of her sister's laptop.

The disc took a while to load, and Spencer clicked on her e-mail while she waited. At the top of her in-box was a message from Olivia Caldwell. Her potential mother.

Spencer raised her hand to her mouth and opened the message. It was a link to a prepaid ticket on Amtrak's Acela line, the bullet train to New York City. *Spencer, I'm thrilled you've agreed to meet me!* said the accompanying note. *Can you come to New York tomorrow night? We have so much to talk about. Much love, Olivia.*

She peered out the window to the main house, not sure what to do. The lights in the kitchen were still on, and her mother passed from the fridge to the table, saying something to Melissa. Despite how pissed her mom had been just moments before, there was now a loving, comforting smile on her mother's face. When was the last time she had smiled like that at Spencer?

Tears welled in Spencer's eyes. She'd been trying so hard for her parents for so long . . . for what? She turned back to the computer. The Acela ticket was for 4 P.M. tomorrow. *That sounds great*, she wrote back. *See you then*. She hit send.

Almost immediately, a little *bloop* sound filled the room. Spencer closed her in-box and checked to see if the CD had finished loading, but the program was still running. Then, she noticed a flashing IM window. Instant Messenger must have automatically logged on to Melissa's account when Spencer had turned on the computer. *Hey Mel*, a new message said. *You there?*

Spencer was ready to type, *Sorry, not Melissa*, when a second message came in. *It's me. Ian.*

Her stomach flipped. *Right.* Whoever wrote this didn't have a very good sense of humor.

Another *bloop*. *You there?*

Spencer looked at the unfamiliar IM screen name. *USCMidfielderRoxx.* Ian had gone to USC, and he played midfield in soccer. But that didn't mean anything. Right?

The *bloops* kept coming. *I'm sorry I left without telling you ... but they hated me. You know that. They found out that I knew. That's why I had to run.* Spencer's hands began to shake. Someone was messing with her, just like they'd messed with Ian's parents. Ian didn't *run*. He was dead.

But why was there no trace of his remains in the woods? Why hadn't the cops found a single thing?

Spencer waved her fingers over the keys. *Prove it's really you*, she typed, not bothering to explain that it wasn't Melissa. She shut her eyes, trying to think of something personal about Ian. Something that Melissa and Spencer would know. Something that wasn't in Ali's diary, either. The press had done an exposé of everything Ali had written in her diary about Ian, like how they'd gotten together after a soccer game the fall of seventh grade, how Ian had crammed for the SATs using a Ritalin pill a friend had given him, and how he hadn't been sure if he really deserved being named the Rosewood Day varsity soccer team's MVP – Ali's brother, Jason, was far more talented. Whoever was pretending to be Ian would know all that. If only she could think of something super private.

Then the perfect thing came to her. Something she was pretty sure that even Ali didn't know. *What's your real middle name?* she typed.

There was a pause. Spencer leaned back, waiting. When Melissa was a senior in high school, she'd gotten drunk on eggnog on Christmas Day and confessed that Ian's parents wanted him to be a girl. When Mrs Thomas popped out a boy, they decided his middle name would be the girl's name they'd chosen for him. Ian never, ever used it – in old Rosewood Day yearbooks Spencer had leafed through when she was yearbook editor, he hadn't even listed a middle initial.

There was a *bloop. Elizabeth*, said the message.

Spencer blinked hard. This wasn't possible.

The light in the kitchen in the main house snapped off, enveloping the backyard in darkness. A car slid down the cul-de-sac, schussing loudly over the wet pavement. Then Spencer began to hear noises. A sigh. A snort. A giggle. She jumped up and pressed her forehead to the cold, thick windowpane. The porch was bare. There were no shadows by the pool, the hot tub, or the deck. There was no one creeping around the windmill, although the newly painted word *LIAR* seemed to glow.

Her Sidekick buzzed. Spencer jumped, her heart hammering. She glanced at the computer again. Ian had signed off Instant Messenger.

One new text message. With shaking hands, Spencer pressed Read.

Dear Spence, When I told you that he had to go, I didn't mean he had to die. Still, there's something really sketchy in this case … and it's up to you to figure out what it is. So better get searching, or the next one 'gone' is you. Au revoir! – A

10
Something's Sketchy, Indeed

The following morning, Emily cinched the hood of her pale blue anorak tight and ran across the icy blacktop to the Rosewood Day Elementary School swings, her friends' special meeting spot. For the first time all week, the long driveway was free of news vans. Since everyone now thought Emily and the others had made up seeing Ian's body in the woods, the press had no reason to interview students.

Across the courtyard, Emily's friends were gathered around Spencer, staring at a sheet of computer paper and her cell phone. Last night, Spencer had called Emily to tell her that Ian had IM'ed her and that A had sent a text. Afterward, Emily hadn't been able to sleep a wink. So A was back. And Ian ... maybe ... wasn't dead.

Something hard hit her shoulder, and Emily whirled around, her heart leaping to her throat. It was only an elementary-school boy pushing past her, running for the ball field. She placed one hand in the other, trying to stop it from trembling. Her hands had been shaking like crazy all morning.

'How could Ian have faked his death?' Emily blurted

when she reached the circle. 'We all saw him. He looked ...
blue.'

Hanna, bundled in a white wool coat and faux-fur scarf,
raised her shoulders. The only color in her face was her red-
rimmed eyes; it looked like she hadn't slept much last night,
either. Aria, wearing a thin, trendy-looking gray leather
jacket and green fingerless gloves, shook her head, saying
nothing. She wasn't wearing her usual sparkly makeup. Even
neat-as-a-pin Spencer looked disheveled – her hair was in a
greasy, lumpy ponytail.

'It fits,' Spencer croaked. 'Ian pretended to be dead, and he
called us to the woods because he knew we'd go to the police
and tell them we saw him.'

Aria sank down onto one of the swings. 'But why
wouldn't Ian just run? Why would he put on a show for us?'

'When the cops found out he was missing, they started
searching for him immediately,' Spencer explained. 'But then
when we saw his body, they turned their attention to the
woods instead. We distracted them for a few days, long
enough so Ian could really escape. We probably did exactly
what he wanted us to.' She gazed up at the clouds, a helpless
expression on her face.

Hanna sank onto her left hip. 'What do you think A has to
do with this? A lured us into the woods so we'd see Ian. A is
obviously working with him.'

'This text makes it pretty obvious that Ian and A were in
cahoots,' Spencer said, shoving her phone at them. Emily
read the first two lines again. *When I told you he had to go,
I didn't mean he had to die. Still, there's something really
sketchy in this case ... and it's up to you to figure out what
it is.* She bit her lip hard, then gazed at the dragon-shaped
slide behind them. Years ago, whenever something or someone at school scared her, she would hide inside the dragon's

head at the top until she felt better. She felt an overwhelming urge to do that now.

'It seems like A helped Ian bust out,' Spencer went on. 'They worked together – when Ian met me on my back porch last week, A threatened that if I told the cops, I'd get hurt. If I would've told them, they would've rearrested Ian … and he couldn't have escaped.'

'A was worried about *any* of us saying anything,' Emily piped up. 'All of my notes said that if I didn't tell A's secret, A wouldn't tell mine.'

Hanna looked at Emily, a curious smile on her lips. 'This A knows some secrets about you?'

Emily shrugged. For a while, A was taunting Emily about how she'd kept her sexuality from Isaac. 'Not anymore,' she said.

'What if Ian *is* A?' Aria suggested. 'It still makes a lot of sense.'

Emily shook her head. 'The texts weren't from Ian. The cops checked his phone.'

'Just because the A notes weren't coming from Ian's phone doesn't mean they weren't coming from Ian,' Hanna reminded her. 'He could have had someone else send them. Or he could have gotten a disposable cell or a phone in another name.'

Emily put her finger to her lips. She hadn't thought of that.

'And all those tricks he pulled the night we allegedly saw his body are pretty easy if you know how to use a computer,' Hanna went on. 'Ian probably figured out how to delay sending a text so that we'd get it the moment we saw what looked like his dead body. Remember how Mona sent herself an e-mail from A to throw us off? It's probably not that hard.'

89

Spencer pointed at the piece of computer paper. It was a printout of the IM exchange between her and Ian. 'Look at this,' she said, pointing to the lines that said, *They hated me. They found out that I knew. That's why I had to run.* 'Ian signed off before I could ask who 'they' were. But what if this is much bigger than Ian planning an escape? What if Ian really did find out something huge about Ali's murder? What if he thought that if he went on trial, explaining what he knew, he'd be killed? Faking his own death wouldn't just get the cops off his back, it'd get whoever wanted to hurt him off his back too.'

Aria stopped swinging. 'Do you think whoever was after Ian might come after us if we figure out too much?'

'That's what it sounds like,' Spencer said. 'But there's something else.' She pointed to a few lines of text at the bottom of the computer printout. It was the IP address of where the Instant Messages were from. 'It says Ian IM'ed us from somewhere in Rosewood.'

'*Rosewood?*' Aria shrieked. 'You mean he's still ... *here?*'

Hanna's face paled. 'Why would Ian stay here? Why wouldn't he skip town?'

'Maybe he's not done searching for the truth,' Spencer suggested.

'Or maybe he's not done with *us* ... for turning him in,' Aria said.

Emily heard a *whoop* behind her and jumped. A crow was slowly circling the playground. When she turned back to her friends, their eyes were wide, and their jaws were tense.

'Aria's right,' Hanna said, picking back up on the conversation. 'If Ian's alive, we don't know what he's up to. He still might be after us. And he still might be guilty.'

'I don't know,' Spencer protested.

Emily faced Spencer, confused. 'But *you* told the cops it

90

was him! What about that memory you had of seeing Ian with Ali on the night she died?'

Spencer shoved her hands in her coat pockets. 'I'm not sure if I really remember that ... or if it was just what I wanted to believe.'

Emily's stomach burned. What was true ... and what wasn't? She stared across the playground. A group of students were marching down the sidewalk into the sixth-grade wing. More students passed in front of the long line of classroom windows, walking to the coat closet. Emily had forgotten that sixth graders didn't have proper lockers; they had to put their stuff in cubbies in that tiny coatroom. The coatroom used to get so stinky by mid-morning, smelling like everyone's bagged lunches.

'When Ian talked to me on my back porch, he told me that we had it wrong – he didn't kill Ali,' Spencer went on. 'He wouldn't have hurt a hair on Ali's head. He and Ali always flirted, but *she* was the one who escalated it to the next level. Ian thought for a while that she was doing it to make someone angry. At first I thought she meant me – because I kind of liked him. But Ian didn't seem to buy that theory. And the night she died, he saw two blondes in the woods – one was Ali, one was someone else. At the time, I thought he meant me. But he said maybe it was someone else.'

Emily sighed, frustrated. 'We're going by *Ian's* word again.'

'Yeah, Spence.' Hanna wrinkled her nose. 'Ian killed Ali. Then he tricked us. We should go to Wilden with the IMs. Let him deal with it.'

Spencer snorted. 'Wilden? He's done a good job convincing all of Rosewood that we're crazy. Even if by some miracle he does believe us, no one else on the police force would.'

'What about Ian's parents?' Emily suggested. 'They got a note from him too. They'd believe us.'

Spencer pointed to another line on the IM exchange. 'Yeah, but what would that do? His parents would have yet more proof that Ian's alive, but they might tell the cops that his IMs came from a computer in Rosewood. And then the cops would track him down and rearrest him.'

'Which would be a *good* thing,' Emily reminded her.

Spencer gave her a helpless look. 'What if this is a test? Suppose we do tell the cops or his parents ... and something happens to one of us? Or what if something happens to Melissa? Ian thought he was IMing her, after all.' Spencer rubbed her gloved hands together. 'Melissa and I don't get along, but I don't want to put her in danger.'

Aria stepped off the swing, grabbed Spencer's phone, and looked at A's text. 'This note says now it's up to us to figure it out ... or *we'll* be next.'

'Meaning?' Emily stuck her boot into a patch of snow.

'We have to prove who Ali's real killer is,' Aria answered matter-of-factly. 'Or else.'

'Do you think the killer is the person – or people – in Ian's IMs?' Spencer asked. 'The people who hated him? The ones who found out he knew?'

'Who hated Ian?' Emily scratched her head. 'Everyone at Rosewood adored him.'

Hanna snorted. 'Guys, this is retarded. I don't really feel like playing Veronica Mars.' She unzipped her bag, pulled out an iPhone from the inside pocket, and turned it on. 'The best way to stay away from A is to do what I did: get a new phone and an unlisted number. Voilà, A can't find us.' She started jabbing at the phone's screen.

Emily exchanged a wary look with the others. 'A has gotten in touch with us in other ways, Hanna.'

Hanna pushed a strand of hair out of her eyes, still texting. 'This A hasn't.'

'It doesn't mean that this A *won't*,' Spencer said firmly.

Hanna clamped her lips together, looking annoyed. 'Well, if *Ian* is A, I guess we won't have to worry. Because Ian has no way of getting my new phone number.'

Emily gazed at Hanna, not quite sure how Hanna could be so certain ... especially if Ian really *was* still here in Rosewood.

'So do we search, or not?' Aria said after a moment.

The girls stared at each other. Emily had no idea how they could even attempt to search for Ali's real killer. They weren't cops. They didn't have forensic experience. But she understood why they couldn't turn to the cops – after the Dead Ian Scandal, the cops would just laugh at them and tell them to stop wasting their time.

She stared across the courtyard. More sixth graders paraded toward the classrooms. A few gathered around a sign hanging outside the door, talking giddily. 'I'm going to find a piece,' said a brunette girl with sparkly clips in her hair. 'Yeah, *right*,' said her friend, a petite Asian girl with a high ponytail. 'You'll never figure out those clues.'

Emily squinted at the sign's block letters, TIME CAPSULE IS HERE! HAVE YOU STARTED SEARCHING YET?

'Remember how excited everyone was for Time Capsule the first year we were able to play?' Hanna murmured, watching the girls too.

Aria pointed to the bike racks near the sixth-grade entrance. 'That was where Ali announced that she knew where one of the pieces was.'

'That was so annoying.' Spencer groaned, making a face. 'She cheated – Jason told her where it was. She didn't even have to solve the clues. That's why I wanted to steal Ali's piece – I didn't think she deserved it.'

'Except you didn't get to steal it,' Hanna singsonged. 'Because someone stole it first. And we'll never find out who.'

93

Aria coughed loudly. Bottled water spewed out of her mouth. Everyone turned to look at her. 'I'm fine,' she assured them, wheezing.

The high school bell rang, and the girls broke apart. Spencer walked off quickly, barely saying good-bye. Hanna lingered, tapping her iPhone. Emily fell in step with Aria. For a while, the only sound was their shoes crunching through the icy crust of snow on the commons. Emily wondered if Aria was thinking about the same thing she was – could Ian be telling the truth? Was someone else behind Ali's murder?

'So you'll never believe who I ran into yesterday,' Aria said. 'Jason DiLaurentis.'

Emily stopped short. Her heart started to pound. 'Where?'

Aria knotted her scarf tighter, seemingly nonchalant. 'I cut school. Jason was waiting for the train to Philly.'

A gust of wind kicked up, sneaking down the collar of Emily's shirt. 'I saw Jason the other day too,' she mustered, her voice raspy. 'I parallel-parked in back of him, and he accused me of denting his car. He was kind of ... *angry*.'

Aria gave her a sidelong glance. 'What do you mean?'

Emily fiddled with the ski lift ticket that was affixed to her jacket's zipper. She suspected that Aria used to like Jason, and she hated bad-mouthing people. Then again, Aria needed to know. 'Well, he kind of screamed for a while. And then he lunged at me, like he was going to punch me.'

'*Did* you dent his car?'

'Even if I did, it was tiny. Definitely not worth freaking out about.'

Aria shoved her hands in her pockets. 'Jason's probably really sensitive right now. I can't imagine what this must be like for him.'

'That's what I thought, too, but ...' Emily trailed off, gazing concernedly at Aria. 'Just be careful, okay? Remember

94

what Jenna said to you. Ali said she had "problems" with Jason. He could've been abusing Ali, just like Toby was abusing Jenna.'

'We don't know if that's true,' Aria barked, her eyes darkening. 'Ali wanted to find out Jenna's secret about Toby. She would've told Jenna anything to get her to talk. Jason was nothing but sweet to Ali.'

Emily looked away, staring blankly at the flagpole at the end of the school commons. She wasn't so sure about that. She remembered the shouts coming from inside Ali's house the day they'd sneaked into Ali's backyard to steal her Time Capsule flag. Someone kept imitating Ali's voice. And then there was a shattering sound and a *thud*, as if someone had been pushed. Jason stormed out of the house moments later, his face fiery red.

In fact, now that she thought about it, the very first time Emily had ever seen Ali, Jason had been teasing her. It was a few days before she started third grade, and Emily and her mom were at the grocery store, picking out juice boxes and mini bags of Doritos for school lunches. A pretty blond girl about Emily's age bounded right past them, skipping up the cereal aisle. There was something intoxicating about her, probably because she was everything plain, introverted Emily wasn't.

They saw the girl again in the frozen foods section, peering into every case, trying to decide what she wanted. Her mother trailed behind with a cart, and a boy, probably about fourteen, followed, staring at a Game Boy. 'Mom, can we get Eggos?' the girl cried, opening up a freezer door, her smile big and gap-toothed. The teenage boy rolled his eyes. '*Mom, can we get Eggos?*' he imitated, his voice sharp and mean.

And just like that, the girl wilted. Her bottom lip wobbled, and she shut the door with a disheartened *thud*. The mother grabbed the boy's arm. 'You know better.' The boy shrugged and slumped down, but Emily thought he deserved being yelled at. He ruined the girl's fun, simply because he could. A few days later, when third grade began, Emily realized that the girl in the store had been Ali. She was new to Rosewood Day, but she was so pretty and bubbly that everyone instantly wanted to sit next to her on the rug during show-and-tell. It was hard to believe anything would make her sad.

Emily kicked an icy ball of snow down the sidewalk, quietly debating whether she should tell Aria this. But before she could, Aria mumbled a terse good-bye and walked briskly toward the science wing, the tassels at the ends of her earflap hat bouncing.

Sighing, Emily slowly climbed the stairs to her locker, ducking out of the way of a bunch of younger boys from the wrestling team who were bounding down the stairs in the other direction. Yes, she'd learned that Ali had a way of manipulating people to get their secrets. And yes, she could admit that Ali had a nasty streak – Emily had been the victim of it too, especially when Ali teased Emily in front of the others about the time she kissed her in the tree house. But Jenna wasn't popular, she wasn't Ali's friend, and she didn't have anything Ali needed. Sure Ali was mean, but there was usually a grain of truth in what she said.

Emily stopped in front of her locker. As she was hanging up her coat, she heard a small snicker behind her. She whirled around, gazing into the flood of students walking down the hall to homeroom. A familiar girl swam into view. It was none other than Jenna Cavanaugh. She was standing in the doorway of the Chem II room, her golden retriever guide dog at her side. Emily's skin crawled. It was as though by just thinking about Jenna, Emily had conjured her up.

A shadow moved behind Jenna, and Emily's ex-girlfriend,

Maya St Germain, appeared in the doorway too. Emily had barely spoken to Maya since they'd broken up when Maya caught her kissing Trista, a girl she'd met when her parents sent her to live with her aunt and uncle in Iowa. By the livid look on Maya's face, it didn't seem like she'd forgiven Emily yet.

Maya whispered something in Jenna's ear before gazing across the busy hallway at Emily. Her mouth curled into a nasty sneer. Jenna's eyes were hidden behind her dark Gucci sunglasses, but her face was drawn and unsmiling.

Slamming her locker door hard, Emily scampered down the hall without even retrieving the books she needed for her morning classes. When she looked over her shoulder, Maya was waggling her fingers. *Bye*, Maya mouthed overdramatically, her eyes sparkling with mischief and amusement, as if she knew precisely how much she was making Emily squirm.

11

The Most Decked-Out Baby In Rosewood

On Wednesday afternoon, Aria stood in the foyer of the new house Byron and Meredith just purchased. She had to admit that the place was really charming. It was an old Craftsman-style bungalow on a secluded corner of the street with walnut-colored hardwood floors and quirky brass chandeliers and sconces. As Meredith had promised, there was a little attic bedroom with great light for painting.

The only glitch was that she could see the weather vane on top of Ian's house from her bedroom window. She also had a view of the barren woods where they'd found Ian's apparently fake dead body. The police vehicles and search equipment were gone, but the ground was torn up in spots, and there were lots of boot tracks in the mud. Now that she knew Ian was probably still alive – *and* still hanging out in Rosewood – she couldn't even look into the woods without feeling queasy. And when she'd stood on the front porch earlier, waiting for Meredith to unlock the door, Aria had sworn she'd caught a flash of someone disappearing behind a house at the end of the cul-de-sac. But when she stepped back to get a better look, no one was there.

Byron had sent a moving crew to Ella's house this morning to pick up some things from Aria's bedroom. Last night, Aria had finally called Ella and broken the news that she was going to move in with Byron for a while to get to know Meredith better. Ella paused, probably remembering the time Aria had painted a hateful, adulteress *A* on Meredith's blouse, and then asked if Aria was upset about something. 'Of course not!' Aria cried quickly. Ella replied that she'd really like Aria to stay; was there something she could do to make Aria happier? *Yeah, you could get rid of Xavier*, Aria wished she could suggest.

In the end, Aria backpedaled, telling Ella she'd leave some of her furniture and clothes in her old bedroom and shuttle between Ella's and Byron's houses instead. She didn't want Ella to think that Aria was abandoning *her*, specifically. Anyway, how difficult could it be to avoid Xavier? Aria would stay at Ella's on the days she was certain he wouldn't be there – like when he was out of town for an art exhibition.

The movers had left the lighter boxes in the front foyer, and Aria was in the process of bringing them upstairs. As she was bending down to pick up a box marked *Fragile*, Meredith slipped a white envelope into the back pocket of Aria's skinny jeans. 'Mail for you,' she sang, and then flitted down the hall, dust mop in hand.

Aria pulled out the envelope. Her name was printed on an anonymous green address label. She shuddered, thinking about what Emily had said to Hanna today. *A has gotten in touch with us in other ways.* She wasn't ready for a new barrage of notes.

Inside, she found an invitation and two orange tickets for a party at a new hotel called the Radley. A Post-it was attached. *Aria, I miss you already! When will you be back with us? Anyway, one of my paintings was chosen to hang in the lobby! Here are two invitations to the opening. Please join Xavier and me there! Love, Ella.*

Aria stuffed the papers back in the envelope, her heart sinking. Maybe avoiding Xavier was going to be harder than she thought.

She climbed the stairs and ducked into her small, cozy bedroom. It was the bedroom she'd always wanted, with skylights over her bed, a cushy window seat, and slightly slanted wood floors, the kind where she could place a pencil at one end of the room and it would roll slowly to the other end all on its own. Boxes from her old bedroom were stacked to the ceiling, and Aria's stuffed animal puppets were strewn out on the platform bed her parents had bought for her at a warehouse in Denmark. She'd hung up most of her clothes in an old armoire Byron had bought off Craigslist, putting her T-shirts, bras, undies, and socks in the bottom drawers. She still had to find a place for the boxes of yarn, extra blankets, too-small shoes, and board games from her old closet.

But she didn't feel like doing any of that right now. All she wanted to do was flop down on her bed and puzzle over yesterday's encounter with Jason DiLaurentis. Had he been flirting with her? Why had his mood changed so quickly? Was it because of the Ian Dead Body news report on TV?

She wondered if Jason had friends in the area anymore. In high school, he used to spend a lot of time by himself, listening to music, reading, or brooding. Ali had gone missing the last day of Jason's senior year, and Aria had barely seen him since. After the summer, he'd hightailed it to Yale, and she had no idea if he ever came home to visit after that.

So how was he handling this Ali stuff now? Did he have anyone he could talk to about it? She thought about what

Emily had said this morning at the swings – that Jason had screamed at her for denting his car. Emily had seemed worried about it, but Aria couldn't imagine what *she* might do if someone murdered Mike. She'd probably fly off the handle about dented bumpers too.

Then, a familiar Puma shoe box on the floor caught her eye. *Old Book Reports*, said the label. Aria breathed in sharply. The box was dented, the lettering on the sides faded. The last time Aria looked inside this box was the Saturday she and the others had sneaked into Ali's yard to steal her flag.

Aria had buried the memory of what happened that day for so long, but now that she was allowing herself to think about it, every sensory detail flooded back to her, crystal clear. She remembered Ali wheeling around and walking back into her house, the smell of her vanilla hand soap wafting behind her. She remembered stomping through the woods to get home, the ground still wet from the rain a few days before. She remembered how the leaves on the trees were still very green and thick, providing ample shade from the late-summer sun. The woods smelled like pine and something else ... perhaps a cigarette. Far off in the distance, a lawnmower snarled.

Then twigs cracked. Bushes rustled. Aria saw Jason's black T-shirt and blond hair and held her breath. She'd fantasized about seeing Jason that day ... and there he was. She didn't know what made her eyes go to the piece of the flag hanging out of his pocket. When Jason saw what she was looking at, he shoved the piece at her, saying nothing.

One minute it was in my bag, the next minute it was gone, Ali had told them. Why had Jason taken it from Ali? Aria wanted to think it had been for a practical and ethical reason, not just to be mean. There was no way Jason abused

101

Ali, as Jenna implied and as Emily wanted to believe. In fact, Jason had always seemed fiercely protective of Ali. He'd jumped out of nowhere to intervene when Ali and Ian were talking in the courtyard the day Time Capsule was announced. Even the day they'd tried to steal Ali's flag and Emily had shushed them to listen to a fight taking place inside Ali's house, Jason had stormed out moments later, upset about something. When Ali came out to talk to them, she still seemed worried, nervously peeking over her shoulder toward the house. If she'd had issues with Jason, wouldn't she have been relieved that he was gone?

This morning, Spencer had said she wanted to steal Ali's flag because she thought Ali had cheated her way to winning. Maybe Jason felt guilty about cheating too. Maybe he'd told Ali to keep quiet that he'd told her where he'd hidden his piece, and had gotten annoyed when he heard Ali bragging about it to everyone in the courtyard.

Aria crouched next to the shoe box, her body tingling. It had been so long since she'd looked at Ali's piece of the Time Capsule flag, she'd nearly forgotten what Ali had drawn on it. The lid bent as she pulled it off. A cloud of dust dispersed into the air.

'Aria?' Byron's voice floated from downstairs. 'Come down for Meredith's shower!'

Aria paused. The very edge of the shiny blue flag poked out from underneath a bunch of old papers. 'I'm coming,' she called, a little relieved she'd been interrupted.

Meredith, Byron, a bunch of scruffy men Aria recognized as Byron's colleagues at Hollis, and a few twentysomething girls in yoga pants or paint-spattered jeans were milling around in the living room. A French press coffeemaker, bottles of wine and sparkling water, and a large plate of cucumber-hummus sandwiches sat on the table, and there was a big pile of gifts next to the sofa. Then someone to Aria's left coughed. Mike was sitting in the corner of the sectional, a pretty brunette by his side. Aria blinked, temporarily speechless. It was Hanna's soon-to-be stepsister, Kate.

'Um, hi?' Aria said cautiously. Kate smiled smugly. Mike smiled even more smugly. He put his hand on Kate's thigh, and Kate *let him*. Aria frowned, wondering if her brain had been damaged from the dust in her new attic bedroom.

Heels clacked down the foyer, and Aria turned just in time to see Hanna enter. She wore a green silk halter-neck dress with her decorated Time Capsule flag looped around her waist as a belt. She carried a box wrapped in stork-printed paper. Aria was about to say hello, but Hanna wasn't looking in her direction. She was staring at Kate. Her mouth tightened. 'Oh.'

'Hi, Hanna!' Kate waved. 'Glad you made it!'

'You weren't invited,' Hanna blurted.

'Yes, I was.' Kate's smile didn't falter.

A muscle beneath Hanna's right eye twitched. A bloom of red traveled from her neck to her cheeks. Aria swiveled back and forth between the girls, feeling both confused and fascinated at the same time.

Meredith looked amused. 'Mike, you brought *two* dates?'

'Hey, it's a party,' Mike said, shrugging. 'The more the merrier, right?'

'That's what I say!' Kate crowed. When superthin Kate smiled a certain way, she reminded Aria of the screeching gibbon on her *National Geographic* Animals of the World poster that still hung on her old bedroom door. Hanna was definitely the prettier of the two.

Hanna rolled her shoulders back, strutted over to Meredith, and stuck out her hand. 'Hanna Marin. I'm an old

103

friend of the family.' She proffered her gift to Meredith, and Meredith put it in the pile with the other things. Hanna glowered at Kate, then settled on the other side of Mike, squishing in so that their butts shared a couch cushion.

Kate ogled Hanna's Time Capsule flag belt. 'What's that thing?' She pointed at a black blob Hanna had drawn.

Hanna shot her a haughty look. 'It's a manga frog. Duh.'

Aria sat down on the rocker, overwhelmingly weirded out. She caught Hanna's eye, pointed to her cell phone, and started typing Hanna a text – Hanna had reluctantly given Aria and the others the number to her iPhone that morning. *What R U doing here?*

Hanna's iPhone beeped. She read the text, glanced at Aria, and typed. Seconds later, Aria's phone buzzed. *Y didn't U tell us U were moving 4 drs down from Ian?*

Aria opened up a reply text. Hanna couldn't dodge the question that easily. *I just found out myself*, she wrote back. *So do U like Mike?*

Maybe, Hanna wrote. *He's the one guy you can't steal from me.*

Aria gritted her teeth. Hanna was referring to the time last fall when Aria had dated her ex, Sean Ackard. To this day, Hanna seemed certain that Aria had stolen Sean from her.

Meredith began unwrapping her large pile of gifts, displaying everything on the coffee table. So far, she'd received a bunch of baby toys, a receiving blanket, and a breast pump from Mike. When she got to a gift wrapped in striped paper, Kate sat up straighter. 'Oh, that one's mine!' She rubbed her hands together gleefully. Hanna's scowl deepened.

Meredith sat back down on the couch and unwrapped the box. 'Oh my God,' she breathed, lifting a cream-colored onesie from a layer of pink tissue paper.

'It's organic Mongolian cashmere,' Kate recited. 'Completely fair trade.'

'Thank you so much.' Meredith pressed the onesie to her face. Byron felt it between his fingers, nodding sagely as if he were a cashmere connoisseur. Frayed cotton T-shirts and flannel pajama pants were usually more his thing.

Hanna abruptly stood up, letting out a small squeak. 'Did you snoop in my room?'

'Excuse me?' Kate asked, widening her eyes.

'You *knew*,' Hanna shrieked. 'I searched for hours for the perfect thing.'

'I don't know what you're talking about.' Kate shrugged.

At that moment, Meredith was unwrapping the stork-wrapped gift that Hanna had brought. Inside was another box from Sunshine. 'Oh,' Meredith said pleasantly, lifting an identical cashmere onesie out of identical pink tissue paper. 'It's beautiful. Again.'

'One can never have too many of those,' Tate, one of Byron's Hollis colleagues, guffawed, a glob of hummus falling into his scraggly beard.

Kate tittered good-naturedly too. 'Great minds think alike, I guess,' she said, which made Hanna's face contort with rage. Mike's head swiveled from one girl to the other; he was obviously lapping up the catfight drama.

Suddenly, Aria noticed a dark shape moving outside the front window. Goose bumps rose on her arms. Someone was standing in the yard, watching the party.

She looked around the room, but no one else seemed to notice. Clearing her throat, she rose from the couch and crept down the hall. Her heart pounded as she turned the door-knob and stepped outside. The neighborhood was deathly quiet, and the air smelled like a woodstove. The sky was getting dark, and the lamp at the end of Aria's new driveway cast

105

a pale gold circle on the grass. When she saw the figure again by the mailbox, she jumped back. Thankfully, it wasn't Ian. It was ...

'Jenna?' Aria cried softly.

Jenna Cavanaugh was wearing a heavy quilted black coat, black mittens, and a gray hat with earflaps. Her golden retriever's tongue dangled from his mouth. She cocked her head toward the sound of Aria's voice. Her lips parted.

'It's Aria,' Aria explained. 'I moved here with my dad yesterday.'

Jenna nodded faintly. 'I know.' She didn't move. There was a guilty look on her face.

'Are you ... okay?' Aria asked after a moment, her heart pounding. 'Do you need something?'

Jenna pushed her big Gucci sunglasses up the bridge of her nose. It was strange, seeing someone wearing sunglasses at dusk. She looked as if she was about to say something, but then she turned, waving her hand. 'No.'

'Wait!' Aria called, but Jenna kept walking. Her dog's tags jingled. Her shoes made no sound. After a moment, all Aria could see of her was her glowing white cane, slowly drifting from side to side to the end of the street.

12
Off With Her Head!

Wednesday evening, Emily placed four cream-colored dinner plates around the square farmhouse table in the Colberts' dining room. When she got to the silverware, she paused, puzzled. Did knives go next to forks, or spoons? Her own family's dinners were casual free-for-alls. Emily and her sister Carolyn often ate later than their parents because of swim practice.

Isaac strolled in from the kitchen, his eyes looking extra blue in his shrunken V-neck sweater and dark denim jeans. He took Emily's hand and pressed something smooth and round into it. She stared into her palm. It was a teal blue ceramic ring. 'What's this for?'

Isaac's eyes were bright. 'No reason. Because I love you.'

Emily pressed her lips together tightly, overcome. No one she'd dated had given her a gift before. 'I love you too,' she said, and slid the ring onto her pointer finger, where it fit best. She couldn't stop thinking about what had happened between them yesterday. It felt surreal ... but wonderful, too – a great distraction from thinking about A's return. All day at school, she kept sneaking into the girls' bathroom, inspecting herself in the mirror, looking for changes. It was always the same Emily staring back at her, with the same sprinkling of freckles, the same wide brown eyes, the same slightly upturned nose. She kept waiting to see a special glow or a knowing smile, something to indicate a transformation. She wished she could grab Isaac's shoulders, kiss him hard, and whisper that she wanted to do it again. *Soon.*

A loud crash in the kitchen shattered Emily's thoughts into a million pieces. Not that she'd dare tell Isaac *now*, of course. Not with his parents around.

Isaac took the silverware from Emily and started placing it next to the plates – spoons next to knives on the right, forks alone on the left. 'You look nervous,' he said. 'Don't worry. I told my parents not to bring up Ali's trial.'

'Thanks.' Emily tried to smile. Prying questions about Ali's trial were the least of her problems tonight – she was more worried about what exactly Mrs Colbert had heard about yesterday. When she'd arrived at the door, Mrs Colbert had greeted her stiffly, as if she wasn't pleased to see her. And after Emily came out of the powder room just now, she swore Mrs Colbert was watching her judgingly, as if she thought Emily had forgotten to wash her hands.

Emily scurried into the kitchen to help Isaac's mom carry the pot roast and casserole dishes of broccoli, garlic mashed potatoes, and rolls to the table. Mr Colbert blustered into the dining room, loosening his tie. After the family said grace, Mrs Colbert passed the pot roast in Emily's direction, looking at her squarely for the first time of the evening.

'Here you go, dear.' The corners of Mrs Colbert's mouth curled up. 'You like meat, don't you?'

Emily blinked. Was it her, or did that statement seem … *loaded*? She checked Isaac for his reaction, but he was innocently selecting a roll from a wicker basket. 'Uh, thanks,'

Emily said, pulling the platter toward her. She *did* like meat. The kind you, um, eat.

'So, Emily.' Mr Colbert dug a large spoon into the bowl of potatoes. 'I asked some of my catering employees about you. Apparently, you have a reputation.'

Mrs Colbert snorted quietly. Emily's fork clattered to her plate. The only sound in the room was the vent fan over the stove. 'I-I do?'

'Everyone says you're a great swimmer,' Mr Colbert finished. 'Nationally ranked in butterfly? That's amazing – it's a tough stroke, right?'

'Oh.' Emily took a long, shaky drink from her glass of water. 'Yeah.' What had she expected, that Mr Colbert was going to ask her what it was like to make out with girls? 'It is a tough stroke, but for some reason I'm naturally fast at it.'

And then Mrs Colbert murmured something else under her breath. Emily could have sworn it was, 'You're naturally fast, all right.'

Emily lowered her glass. Mrs Colbert chewed calmly, watching Emily. It felt like her eyes were beaming into Emily's skull. 'What was that, Mom?' Isaac asked, squinting.

Mrs Colbert's expression morphed into a sweet smile. 'I said Emily's naturally *modest*. I'm sure she's worked very hard to become such a good swimmer.'

'Totally.' Isaac smiled. Emily stared at her pile of mashed potatoes, feeling a little like she was going insane. Was *that* what Mrs Colbert had said?

For dessert, Mrs Colbert brought out an apple pie and a pot of coffee. Mr Colbert looked at his wife. 'By the way, we're set for the opening this Saturday. I thought we weren't going to have enough people to work it, since the party is so big, but we've got enough.'

'That's great,' Mrs Colbert said.

'That party's going to be sweet,' Isaac murmured.

Emily grabbed a plate of pie. 'Party?'

'My dad's catering the opening of a new hotel outside town,' Isaac explained. He took her hand under the table. 'It used to be a school or something, right?'

'A mental institution,' Mrs Colbert interjected, wrinkling her nose.

'Not exactly,' Mr Colbert corrected her. 'It was a facility for troubled kids called the Radley. The hotel's going to be called that too. The owners are kicking themselves for scheduling the opening party for this weekend – renovations aren't all done. But the rooms they haven't gotten to yet are all on the upper levels – the guests won't even see them. But you know hotel people – everything's gotta be perfect.'

'The hotel is really gorgeous,' Isaac said to Emily. 'It's like an old castle. There's even a labyrinth maze in the garden. I'd love it if you would come with me.'

'Sure,' Emily said, beaming. She popped a bite of pie in her mouth.

'So it's a dinner,' Isaac explained. 'But there will also be drinks and dancing.'

'But they'll only serve you *virgin* drinks, Emily,' Mrs Colbert clarified.

Emily's skin prickled. *Virgin?* She glanced at Isaac, unable to control the muscles around her mouth. *She knows*, she thought. *She definitely knows*.

Isaac smiled appeasingly. 'Don't worry. We won't drink.'

'Good,' Mrs Colbert said. 'I worry about you guys going to these adult functions. A lot of the bartenders don't even ask for IDs.' She sighed dramatically. 'I thought you'd be more excited about the church trip to Boston next week than the Radley opening, Isaac. You were never interested in going to fancy adult parties until a few weeks ago.' She glanced pointedly at Emily, as if to say that Emily's partying ways had corrupted him.

'I've always liked parties,' Isaac defended quickly.

'Oh, let them have some fun, Margaret,' Mr Colbert said gently. 'They'll be good.'

The phone rang, and Mrs Colbert jumped up to get it. Isaac excused himself to go to the bathroom, and Mr Colbert disappeared to his office. Emily sliced her pie into tinier and tinier pieces, her hands slick and her cheeks hot. What was wrong with her? Was she being unreasonably sensitive? This had to be all in her head. Mrs Colbert didn't have it in for Emily and wasn't trying to mess with her mind. She wasn't A.

She gathered the plates and carried them to the sink, hoping she'd seem helpful. After a few minutes of scrubbing, she felt in her pocket for her cell phone. This would be an opportune time for A to write a snarky message about Mommy Dearest's behavior. In fact, maybe Mrs Colbert *hadn't* known about Emily and Isaac yesterday ... but A had tipped her off just in time for tonight's dinner. Just like the old A, New A always seemed to know everything, after all.

But the little screen on Emily's Nokia was blank. Suddenly, Emily realized she actually wanted a text from A. If A was behind this, then at least Isaac's mom would be a victim of A's manipulative wrath instead of simply being a passive-aggressive ogre.

As Mrs Colbert let out a peal of laughter in the other room, Emily looked around the kitchen. Isaac's mom collected cow stuff in the same way Emily's mom collected chickens. They had the exact same refrigerator magnets of a thatched-roof French cottage, a tall-steepled church, and a *boulangerie*. Mrs Colbert was a regular mom with a regular kitchen, just like Mrs Fields. Maybe Emily was overreacting.

Emily gathered the washed forks, spoons, and knives and

dried them on a dish towel, wondering where the silverware drawer was. She tried the one nearest the sink. A double-A battery rolled to the front. There were scissors, scattered paper clips, a cow-print oven mitt, and a bunch of takeout menus held together by a purple rubber band. Emily started to close it, but a picture shoved to the back of the drawer caught her eye.

She slid it forward. Isaac was standing in the family's front foyer, wearing the slightly oversize suit that belonged to his father. He had his arm around Emily, who was wearing a pink satin dress she'd swiped from Carolyn's closet. This had been taken the week before when they were on their way to the Rosewood Day benefit. Mrs Colbert had flitted around them, her cheeks pink, her eyes shining. 'You two look so cute!' she'd crowed. She'd adjusted Emily's corsage, reknotted Isaac's tie, and then offered both of them fresh-baked chocolate chip cookies.

The photo told that happy story ... except for one thing. Emily no longer had a head. It had been cut out of the picture entirely, the scissors cleanly removing every last strand of her hair.

Emily shut the drawer fast. She ran her fingers over her neck, then up her jaw, then around her ears, cheeks, and forehead. Her head was still attached. As she stared out the kitchen window, trying to figure out what to do, her cell phone chimed.

Emily's heart sank. So A *was* involved. She reached for the phone, her fingers trembling. *One new picture message.*

An image appeared on the screen. It was an old photo of someone's backyard. *Ali's* backyard – Emily recognized the tree house in the big oak off to the side. And there was Ali, her face young and smiling and bright. She was wearing a field hockey uniform from Rosewood Youth League, mean-

112

ing the photo was from fifth or sixth grade – after that, Ali played JV for Rosewood Day. There were two other girls in the picture too. One had blond hair and was mostly concealed by a tree – it had to be Naomi Zeigler, one of Ali's best friends at the time. The other girl was in profile. She had dark hair, pale skin, and naturally red lips.

Jenna Cavanaugh.

Emily held the phone outstretched, puzzled. Where was the blackmail about her? Where was the gleeful, *Gotcha! Mommy thinks you're a big dirty slut!* message? Why wasn't A behaving like ... *A*?

Then she noticed the accompanying text at the bottom of the photo. Emily read it four times, trying to understand.

One of these things doesn't belong. Figure it out quickly ... or else. – A

13
That Mother–Daughter Bond

That same Wednesday evening, Spencer boarded the Amtrak Acela bullet train at the 30th Street Station, settled into a plushy seat by the window, adjusted the belt of her gray wool wrap dress, and brushed a piece of dried grass off the pointy toe of her Loeffler Randall boots. She'd spent over an hour choosing her outfit, and hoped the dress said *young fashionista, serious young woman*, and *I'm an awesome bio-daughter, really!* It was a hard balance to strike.

The conductor, a gray-haired, kindly looking man in a jaunty blue Amtrak uniform, examined her ticket. 'Going to New York?'

'Uh-huh.' Spencer gulped.

'Business or pleasure?'

Spencer licked her lips. 'I'm visiting my mom,' she blurted.

The conductor smiled. An older woman across the aisle clucked approvingly. Spencer hoped none of her mother's friends or her father's business associates were coincidentally on this train. It wasn't like she wanted her parents to know what she was doing.

She'd tried to confront her family about being adopted

one last time before she left. Her dad was working from home, and Spencer had stood in the doorway of his office, watching as he read the *New York Times* on his computer. When she cleared her throat, Mr Hastings turned. His face softened. 'Spencer?' he said, concern in his voice. It was as if he'd temporarily forgotten he was supposed to hate her.

Tons of words had welled in Spencer's head. She wanted to ask her dad if any of this could be real. She wanted to ask him why he'd never told her. She wanted to ask him if this was why they treated her like shit a good deal of the time – because she wasn't really theirs. But then she lost her nerve.

Now her cell phone beeped. Spencer pulled it out of the front pocket of her tote. It was from Andrew. *Want to come over?*

An Amtrak train going in the other direction thundered past. Spencer opened a reply text. *Having dinner with my family, sorry*, she typed back. It wasn't a *complete* lie. She wanted to tell Andrew about Olivia, but she was afraid; if she told him, he'd be waiting in anticipation tonight, dying to know how her meeting had gone. But what if it went badly? What if Spencer and Olivia hated each other? She already felt vulnerable enough.

The train clickety-clacked on. A man in front of Spencer laid down a section of newspaper, and Spencer spied yet another story about Rosewood. *Was Initial Investigation of DiLaurentis Disappearance Flawed?* squawked a headline. *Is the DiLaurentis Family Hiding Something?* said another.

Spencer pulled her Eugenia Kim hand-knitted newsboy cap over her eyes and slumped lower in her seat. These crazy news stories were relentless. Still, what if the cops who'd initially investigated Ali's disappearance over three years ago *did* miss something huge? She thought of Ian's IMs. *They found out I knew. Do you see why I had to run? They hated me. You know that.*

It was puzzling. First, Ian assumed he was IMing Melissa, not Spencer. So did Melissa know who hated Ian … and why? Had Ian shared his suspicions about Ali's murder with her? But if Melissa knew an alternate story about what happened to Ali the night she died, why hadn't she come forward with it?

Unless … someone was scaring Melissa into silence. Spencer had called her sister repeatedly over the past forty-eight hours, eager to ask Melissa if there was anything more that she knew. But Melissa hadn't returned any of her calls.

The door that connected two train cars clattered open, and a woman in a navy business suit teetered down the aisle, carrying a cardboard container of burnt-smelling coffees and bottled waters. Spencer leaned her head against the window, watching the bare trees and weathered telephone poles slide by. And what did Ian mean when he wrote *they hated me*? Did it have anything to do with the picture message Emily had forwarded to Spencer about a half hour ago, the old photo of Ali, a partially concealed Naomi Zeigler, and Jenna Cavanaugh in Ali's yard? A's accompanying text implied that the photo was a clue … but to what? Okay, it was weird that Ali was hanging out with dorky Jenna Cavanaugh, but Jenna herself had told Aria that she and Ali were covert friends. And what did that have to do with Ian?

Only one incident of anyone hating Ian stuck out in Spencer's mind. When Spencer and the others sneaked into Ali's backyard to steal her Time Capsule piece, Jason DiLaurentis had stormed out of the house and frozen in the middle of the yard, glaring at Melissa and Ian, who were sitting at the edge of the hot tub. They'd just started dating – Spencer remembered how Melissa had agonized over choosing

116

the perfect first-day-of-school bag and shoes a few days before, eager to impress her new boyfriend. After Ali ditched them and Spencer returned home, she heard the new couple whispering in the living room. 'He'll get over it,' Melissa was saying. 'It's not him I'm worried about,' Ian answered. Then he mumbled something Spencer didn't catch.

Were they talking about Jason ... or someone else? From what Spencer understood, Jason and Melissa weren't really friends. They had some classes together – sometimes when Melissa was sick, Spencer had to go next door and collect her class assignments from Jason – but Jason was never part of the big clique that rented stretch Hummer limos for school formals or spent spring breaks in Cannes, Cabo San Lucas, or Martha's Vineyard. Jason ran around with some of the other soccer boys – they were famous for making up the 'Not It' game that Ali, Spencer, and the others played – but Ali's brother also seemed to need a lot of personal space. Half the time, Jason didn't even hang out with his family. The Hastings and the DiLaurentis families were both members of the Rosewood Country Club, and both faithfully attended the weekly Sunday jazz brunches ... except for Jason, who faithfully didn't. Spencer recalled Ali mentioning that their parents let Jason go to their lake house in the Pocono Mountains alone on the weekends; was that where he was all those Sundays? Whatever the answer, the DiLaurentises didn't even seem to mind he was gone, going on about their brunch happily, savoring their eggs Benedict, drinking mimosas, and doting on Ali. It was almost as if they only had one child, not two.

Spencer shut her eyes, listening as the train blew its whistle. She was so tired of thinking about this. Maybe the farther away she got from Rosewood, the less everything would matter.

After a while, the train slowed. 'Penn Station,' the conductor called. Spencer grabbed her purse and stood, her knees quivering. *This was really happening.* She followed the line of passengers down the narrow aisle, onto the platform, and up the escalator to the main hall.

The station smelled like soft pretzels, beer, and perfume. An anonymous announcer blared over the PA system that the train to Boston had pulled into gate 14 East. A crush of people ran for 14 East at the same time, nearly knocking Spencer over. She looked around fretfully. How could she find Olivia in this crowd? How would Olivia know it was her? What on earth were they going to say to each other?

Somewhere in the throng of people, Spencer heard a familiar, high-pitched giggle. And then she considered the worst of the possibilities: What if Olivia didn't exist? What if this was some cruel joke orchestrated by A?

'Spencer?' cried a voice.

Spencer whirled around. A young blond woman in a gray J. Crew cashmere sweater and brown riding boots was walking toward her. She carried a petite snakeskin clutch and a large accordion folder stuffed with papers.

When Spencer raised her hand, the woman grinned. Spencer's heart stopped. The woman had the same broad smile Spencer saw whenever she looked in a mirror.

'I'm Olivia,' the woman announced, taking Spencer's hands. Even her fingers were similar to Spencer's, small and slender. And Olivia had her same green eyes and a familiar clear, mid-range voice. 'I knew it was you as soon as you stepped off the train. I just *knew* it.'

Spencer's eyes filled with giddy tears. Just like that, her fears began to melt away. Something about this seemed so ... *right.*

'Come on.' Olivia pulled Spencer toward one of the exits,

skirting a bunch of NYPD officers and a drug-sniffing dog. 'I have lots of things planned for us.'

Spencer beamed. It suddenly felt like her life was beginning.

It was an unusually warm January night, and the streets teemed with people. They took a cab to the West Village, where Olivia had just moved, and stopped into Diane von Furstenberg, one of Olivia's – and Spencer's – favorite stores. As they sifted through the racks, Spencer learned that Olivia was an art director at a new magazine dedicated to New York City nightlife. She was born and raised in New York City, and had gone to school at NYU.

'I'm going to apply to NYU,' Spencer chirped. Admittedly, it was her safety school – or it had been, back when she was first in the class.

'I loved it there,' Olivia gushed. Then, she let out a small *ooh* of delight and pulled out a sage green sweaterdress. Spencer laughed – she'd just selected the same thing. Olivia blushed. 'I always pick things that are this color green,' she admitted.

'Because it matches our eyes,' Spencer concluded.

'Exactly.' Olivia gazed at Spencer gratefully. Her expression seemed to say, *I'm so glad I found you.*

After shopping, they strolled slowly up Fifth Avenue. Olivia told Spencer that she'd recently married a wealthy man named Morgan Frick in a private ceremony in the Hamptons. 'We're leaving for a honeymoon to Paris tonight, in fact,' she said. 'I have to catch a helicopter to his plane later. It's at a private airport in Connecticut.'

'*Tonight?*' Spencer stopped, surprised. 'Where's your luggage?'

'Morgan's driver is bringing it to the airport,' Olivia explained.

Spencer nodded, impressed. Morgan must be loaded if he had a driver and a private plane.

'That's why it was so important that we meet today,' Olivia went on. 'I'm going away for two weeks, and I couldn't stand the idea of putting it off until I got back.'

Spencer nodded. She wasn't sure if she would've been able to bear the suspense for two extra weeks either.

The accordion file under Olivia's arm started to slip, and she stuck out her hip to catch it from spilling to the sidewalk. 'Do you want me to take that for you?' Spencer asked. The folder would fit easily into Spencer's oversize tote.

'Would you?' Olivia pushed it toward her gratefully. 'Thanks. It's driving me nuts. Morgan wanted me to bring the information about our new apartment so he could look it over.'

They turned down a side street, passing a row of beautiful brownstones. The parlor levels were lit up in golden light, and Spencer locked eyes with a big calico cat lazing in one of the front bay windows. She and Olivia fell silent, the only sound their clicking heels on the sidewalk. Gaps in conversation always made Spencer uneasy – she always worried that the awkwardness was some fault of hers – so she started to babble about her accomplishments. She'd scored a total of twelve goals this hockey season. She'd gotten the lead role in every school play since seventh grade. 'And I have A's in almost all my classes,' she boasted, and then realized her mistake. She winced and braced herself, certain of what was coming.

Olivia grinned. 'That's fantastic, Spencer! I'm so impressed.'

Spencer cautiously opened one eye. She'd expected Olivia to react the same way her mom would. '*Almost* all your classes?' she could practically hear Mrs Hastings sneer. 'Which class do you *not* have an A in? And why are they *just*

A's? Why aren't they A-*pluses*?' And then Spencer would feel like shit for the rest of the day.

But Olivia wasn't doing that. Who knew, if Olivia had kept Spencer, maybe she would've turned out differently. Maybe she wouldn't be so OCD about her grades or feel so inferior around other people, always desperate to prove that she was good enough, worthy enough, lovable enough. She would've never met Ali. Ali's murder would simply be another story in the newspaper.

'Why did you give me up?' Spencer blurted out.

Olivia stopped at the crosswalk, staring contemplatively at the tall buildings across the street. 'Well . . . I was eighteen when I had you. Far too young to have a baby – I'd just started college. I agonized about my decision. When I found out that a wealthy family in suburban Philadelphia was adopting you, I felt like that was the right choice. But I've always wondered about you.'

The light changed. Spencer skirted around a woman walking a pug dressed in a white cable-knit sweater as they crossed. 'Do my parents know who you are?'

Olivia shook her head. 'I screened them on paper, but we didn't meet. I wanted everything to be anonymous, and so did they. I cried after I delivered you, though, knowing I had to give you up.' She smiled sadly, then touched Spencer's arm. 'I know I can't make up for sixteen years in one visit, Spencer. But I've thought about you all your life.' She rolled her eyes. 'Sorry. That's cheesy, right?'

Spencer's eyes welled with tears. 'No,' she said quickly. 'Not at all.' How long had she been waiting for someone to say these things to her?

At the corner of Sixth Avenue and 12th Street, Olivia abruptly stopped. 'There's my new apartment.' She pointed to the top floor of a luxury apartment building. Beneath it was a quaint market and a home accessories store. A limo pulled up to the entrance, and a woman in a mink stole got out and whisked through the revolving doors.

'Can we go up?' Spencer squealed. The place seemed so glamorous, even from the outside.

Olivia checked the Rolex that dangled from her wrist. 'I'm not sure we have enough time before our reservations. Next visit, though. I promise.'

Spencer shrugged off her disappointment, not wanting Olivia to think she was bratty. Olivia hurried Spencer to a small, cozy restaurant a few blocks away. The room smelled of saffron, garlic, and mussels, and was packed with people. Spencer and Olivia sat down at a table, the candlelight flickering on their faces. Olivia immediately ordered a bottle of wine, instructing the waiter to pour some in Spencer's glass too. 'A toast,' she said, raising her glass to Spencer's. 'To many more visits like this.'

Spencer beamed and looked around. A young guy who looked a lot like Noel Kahn – except probably less puerile – was sitting at the bar. A girl in nut brown boots tucked into her jeans sat next to him, laughing. Next to them was a handsome older couple, the woman in a silvery poncho, the man in a narrow, pin-striped suit. A French pop song was playing over the speakers. Everything in New York seemed a billion times more fashionable than Rosewood. 'I wish I could live here,' she sighed.

Olivia tilted her head, her eyes lighting up. 'I know. I wish you could too. But it must be so nice out in Pennsylvania. All that space and clean air.' She touched Spencer's hand.

'Rosewood is nice.' Spencer swirled her wine and weighed her words carefully. 'But my family ... isn't.'

Olivia opened her mouth, a concerned look on her face. 'They just don't care about me,' Spencer clarified. 'I'd give anything not to live there anymore. They wouldn't even miss me.'

There was a peppery feeling in her nose that she always got when she was about to cry. She looked stubbornly into her lap, trying to harness her emotions.

Olivia stroked Spencer's arm. 'I'd give anything for you to live here,' she said. 'But I have a confession to make. Morgan has a hard time trusting people – some close friends have used him for his money in the past, and now he's very careful about people he doesn't know. I haven't told him about you yet – he knew I gave up a baby when I was young, but he didn't know I was searching for you. I wanted to make sure this was real first.'

Spencer nodded. She certainly understood why Olivia hadn't told Morgan they were meeting – it wasn't like she'd told people either.

'I'm going to tell him about you in Paris,' Olivia added. 'And once he meets you, I know he'll adore you.'

Spencer bit off a crust of bread, considering her options. 'If I moved here, I wouldn't even have to live with you guys,' she sounded out. 'I could get my own place.'

Olivia got a hopeful look on her face. 'Could you handle living on your own?'

Spencer shrugged. 'Sure.' Her parents were barely around these days; she was practically living on her own as it was.

'I *would* love to have you here,' Olivia admitted, her eyes bright. 'Just think – you could get a one-bedroom in the Village near us. I'm sure our Realtor, Michael, could find you something really special.'

'I could start college next year, a year early,' Spencer added, her excitement beginning to build. 'I was thinking about doing that anyway.' When she'd secretly dated Wren, Melissa's boyfriend, she'd considered applying to Penn early

123

to get out of the house and be with him. In fact, she'd already spoken to the Rosewood Day administration about graduating as a junior. With all the AP classes she'd taken, she was more than qualified.

Olivia breathed in, about to say something else, but then stopped, took a long sip of wine, and held out her palms, as if to say, *Hold up*. 'I shouldn't be getting so excited,' she said. 'I'm supposed to be the responsible one here. You should stay with your family, Spencer. Let's stick to visits for now at least, okay?' She patted Spencer's hand, probably noting Spencer's disappointed look. 'Don't worry. I've only just found you, and I don't want to lose you again.'

After polishing off the bottle of wine and two orders of pasta puttanesca, they strolled to the helipad on the Hudson River, acting more like best friends than mother and daughter. When Spencer saw Olivia's helicopter waiting, she clutched her arm. 'I'm going to miss you.'

Olivia's bottom lip quivered. 'I'll be back soon. And we'll make plans to do this again. Maybe a Madison Avenue shopping trip next time? You'll die over the Louboutin store.'

'It's a deal.' Spencer wrapped her arms around Olivia. She smelled like Narciso Rodriguez, one of Spencer's favorite perfumes. Olivia blew a kiss and boarded the helicopter. The propeller began to whirl, and Spencer pivoted and looked back at the city. Cabs zoomed up the West Side Highway. People jogged down the West Side path, even though it was past 10 P.M. Lights twinkled in the apartment windows. A party boat on the Hudson drifted by, guests dressed in elegant suits and gowns clearly visible on the deck.

She was *dying* to live here. Now she had a reason to.

The helicopter lifted off the ground. Olivia slid big headphones over her ears, leaned out the window, and waved enthusiastically at Spencer. 'Bon voyage!' Spencer cried.

When she hefted her bag higher on her shoulder, something poked her arm. Olivia's accordion folder.

She pulled it out and waved it over her head. 'You forgot this!' But Olivia was saying something to the pilot, her eyes on the skyline. Spencer waved until the helicopter was a tiny dot on the horizon, finally lowering her arms and turning away. At least she had an excuse to see Olivia again.

14

And On A Westbound Train The Next Day . . .

The following afternoon, Aria stood on the westbound SEPTA platform in Yarmouth, a town a few miles from Rosewood. The sun was still high in the sky, but the air was chilly, and Aria's fingers had gone numb. She craned her neck and looked down the tracks. The train was a few stops away, glimmering in the distance. Her heart sped up.

After she'd seen not one but *two* hot girls fawn over Mike yesterday, she'd decided that life was too short to brood. She distinctly remembered Jason telling her that he got out of Thursday classes early enough to catch the 3 P.M. bullet train back to Yarmouth. Which meant she knew just where to find him now.

She turned and looked at the houses across the tracks. Many had junk on their porches and peeling paint around the windows, and none had been converted into antique shops or upscale spas like the old houses around the Rosewood station. Nor was there a fancy Wawa or Starbucks nearby, just a dingy head shop that offered palm readings and 'other psychic services' – whatever that meant – and a bar called the Yee-Haw Saloon, with a big placard out front that said CHUG ALL YOU CAN FOR $5! Even the spindly trees didn't seem as picturesque. Aria understood why the DiLaurentises wouldn't have wanted to move back to Rosewood for the duration of the trial, but why had they chosen Yarmouth?

She heard a snort behind her. As she turned, a shadow slipped behind the station on the other side of the tracks. Aria stood on her tiptoes, blinking hard, but she couldn't make out who it was. She thought about seeing Jenna Cavanaugh in her front yard yesterday. It had seemed as if Jenna was about to tell Aria something ... but then decided against it. On top of that, Emily had forwarded Aria a text from A, a photo of Ali and Jenna together that Aria had never seen. *See?* said Emily's text. *It looks like Ali and Jenna were friends.* But wasn't it possible that Ali was *pretending* to be Jenna's friend, in order to get Jenna to trust her? It was just like Ali to bring someone into her inner circle only to steal all her secrets.

The train roared into the station and screeched to a halt. The conductor banged the door open, and people slowly climbed down the metal stairs. When Aria saw Jason's blond hair and gray jacket, her mouth went dry. She ran to him and touched his elbow. 'Jason?'

Jason turned around with a jerk, seemingly on guard. When he saw it was Aria, he relaxed. 'Oh,' he said. 'Hey.' His eyes flickered back and forth. 'What are you doing here?'

Aria cleared her throat, resisting the urge to turn around, run back to her car, and drive away. 'Maybe I'm making a fool out of myself, but I liked talking to you the other day. And ... I wanted to know if we could hang out some time. But if not, that's cool too.'

Jason grinned, looking impressed. He stepped out of the

way of a crowd of businessmen. 'You're not making a fool out of yourself,' he said, meeting Aria's eyes.

'I'm not?' Aria's heart flipped over.

Jason checked his oversize watch. 'Do you want to get a drink right now? I've got some time.'

'S-sure,' Aria stammered, her voice cracking.

'I know the perfect place in Hollis,' Jason said. 'You can follow me there, okay?'

Aria nodded, grateful he hadn't suggested the Yee-Haw Saloon down the street. Jason let her go first up the narrow stairs that led to the station. As they walked to their cars, something flickered in Aria's peripheral vision. The figure she'd seen earlier was standing at the station window, looking out. Whoever it was wore big sunglasses and a puffy coat with the hood pulled tight, obscuring his or her facial features. Even so, Aria had the distinct sense that the person was staring right at her.

Aria followed Jason's black BMW into Hollis. She made a point to check his back bumper for any big dents, remembering what Emily had said about her and Jason's altercation the other day. But as far as she could tell, the bumper was flawless and dent-free.

After they both found parking spaces on the street, Jason led her down a narrow alley and up the stairs of an old Victorian house with the word BATES hanging on a sign over the front porch. There was a creaky black rocking chair off to the right, as spindly as a skeleton.

'*This* is a bar?' Aria looked around. The Hollis bars *she* knew, like Snooker's and the Victory Brewery, were dark, foul-smelling places that had no decoration besides a few neon Guinness and Budweiser signs. Bates, on the other hand, had stained-glass windows, a brass knocker on the front door, and a bunch of long-dead hanging plants swinging from the porch ceiling. It reminded Aria of the creaky mansion her Reykjavík piano teacher, Brynja, lived in.

The door swung open, leading to an enormous parquet-floored parlor. Red velvet couches lined the sides of the room, and dramatic curtains billowed over the windows. 'Supposedly the place is haunted,' Jason whispered to her. 'That's why they call it Bates, like the Bates Motel from *Psycho*.' He walked up to the bar and sat on a stool.

Aria looked away. Back before Ali's body had been found, she'd thought A was Ali – or maybe her ghost. The blond flashes she'd seen had probably been Mona, who'd stalked each of them for their dirtiest secrets. But now that Mona was dead, Aria still sometimes swore she saw someone with blond hair just like Ali's duck behind trees and appear at windows, watching her from beyond the grave.

A short-haired bartender dressed in black took their orders. Aria asked for pinot noir – she thought it seemed sophisticated – and Jason ordered a gimlet. When he noticed Aria's confused expression, he said, 'It's vodka and lime juice. A girlfriend at Yale got me into it.'

'Oh.' Aria ducked her head at the word *girlfriend*.

'She's not my girlfriend anymore,' Jason added, which made Aria blush more.

They got their drinks, and Jason slid his gimlet over to her. 'Try it.' She took a dainty sip. 'It's good,' she said. It tasted like Sprite, except way more fun.

Jason folded his hands, a curious smile on his lips. 'You seem awfully comfortable drinking in a bar.' He dropped his voice to a whisper. 'You almost have me fooled that you're twenty-one.'

Aria slid the gimlet back to him. 'I spent the last three years in Iceland. They're not as strict about drinking, and my parents were pretty lenient. Plus, I never had to drive home, either – my house was a couple of blocks away from the main drag. The worst thing that happened was I once tripped over the cobblestones after having too much Brennivín schnapps and skinned my knee.'

'Europe seemed to really change you.' Jason leaned back and appraised her. 'I remember you as this awkward kid. Now, you're ...' He trailed off.

Aria's heart pounded. She was ... *what?* 'I fit in better in Iceland,' she admitted when it was clear he wasn't going to finish his sentence.

'How so?'

'Well ...' Aria stared at the oil portraits around the room of old aristocratic women. Underneath each of their portraits were their birth and death dates. 'Guys, for one. In Iceland, they didn't care if I was popular. They cared about what music I listened to or what books I liked to read. In Rosewood, guys only like one kind of girl.'

Jason propped his elbows on the bar. 'A girl like my sister, you mean.'

Aria shrugged, looking away. That *was* what she meant, but she hadn't wanted to say Ali's name out loud.

An expression Aria couldn't parse floated over Jason's face. She wondered if Jason knew the effect Ali had had on guys – even older ones. Had Jason known about Ali's secret relationship with Ian at the time, or had that come as a surprise after he was arrested? How did Jason feel about it?

Jason sipped his gimlet, his serious look gone. 'So did you fall in love a lot in Iceland?'

Aria shook her head. 'I had some boyfriends, but I've only been in love once.' She clumsily took another swig of wine. She'd hardly eaten anything today, and the wine was taking

130

hold fast. 'It was with my AP English teacher. Maybe you heard about it.'

A crease formed between Jason's eyes. Maybe he hadn't.

'It's over now,' she said. 'Honestly, it was a disaster. He was asked to leave his teaching position ... because of me. He left town a couple of months ago and said he'd keep in touch, but I haven't heard from him.'

Jason nodded sympathetically. Aria was surprised how comfortable it felt to tell him this. Something about him made her feel safe, like he wasn't going to judge her.

'Have you ever been in love?' she asked.

'Only once.' Jason tipped his head back and swallowed the rest of his drink. The ice rattled against the empty glass. 'She broke my heart.'

'Who was it?'

Jason shrugged. 'No one important. Not now, at least.'

The bartender brought Jason another gimlet. Then Jason poked Aria's arm. 'You know, I thought you were going to say the person you were in love with was *me*.'

Aria's mouth fell open. Jason ... *knew*? 'I guess it was really obvious.'

Jason smiled. 'Nah. I'm just really perceptive.'

Aria signaled the bartender to refill her wine, too, her cheeks blazing. She'd always taken extra precaution to hide her crush from Jason, certain she'd die if he ever found out. Now she kind of wanted to crawl under the bar.

'I remember this one time when you were waiting outside the journalism barn at Rosewood Day,' Jason explained gently. 'I noticed you right away. You were looking around ... and when you saw me, your eyes lit up.'

Aria gripped the bulky wooden lip of the bar. For a second, she'd almost thought Jason was going to bring up the time he gave her Ali's Time Capsule flag. But he was

131

referencing the day she'd waited outside his journalism class, wanting to show him her dad's signed copy of *Slaughterhouse-Five*. That had happened the Friday before they all sneaked into Ali's backyard.

Then again, maybe Jason didn't want to bring up stealing Ali's flag. Maybe he felt guilty about it.

'Sure, I remember that day,' Aria mustered. 'I really wanted to talk to you. Except the school secretary got to you first. She said you had a phone call from a girl.'

Jason squinted, as if trying to see the memory. 'Really?'

Aria nodded. The secretary had taken Jason's arm and guided him toward the office. And now that Aria thought about it, the secretary had also said, *She says she's your sister*. But hadn't Aria seen Ali earlier that day, heading into the gym locker room? Maybe it was Jason's secret girlfriend calling, knowing that the only way the Rosewood Day staff would page him was if she said she was a family member. 'I figured it was a beautiful and mature girl you actually *wanted* to speak to, not a crazy sixth grader,' Aria added, blushing.

Jason nodded slowly, recognition flickering over his face. He muttered something under his breath, something that sounded a lot like, *Not exactly*.

'Pardon?' Aria asked.

'Nothing.' Jason downed the rest of his second gimlet. Then he eyed her coyly. 'Well. I'm glad you're making your crush a little more obvious now.'

A ripple cascaded down Aria's back. 'Maybe it's more than a crush,' she whispered.

'I hope so,' Jason said. They smiled shyly at each other. Aria's heart thudded in her ears.

The front door whooshed open, and a bunch of Hollis students paraded in. Someone in the corner lit a cigarette, blowing filmy smoke into the air. Jason checked his watch and reached into his pocket. 'I'm really late.' He pulled out his wallet and fished out a twenty, enough to cover both their drinks. Then he looked at Aria. 'So,' he started.

'So,' Aria echoed. And then she leaned forward, grabbed his hand, and kissed him the way she'd wanted him to kiss her years ago outside the journalism barn. His lips tasted like lime juice and vodka. Jason pulled her close, kneading his hands in her hair. After a moment, they broke apart, grinning. Aria thought she might faint.

'So I'll see you later,' Jason said.

'Definitely,' Aria breathed. Jason strode across the room, opened the door, and was gone.

'Oh my God,' Aria whispered, turning back to the bar. A huge part of her wanted to climb up on the bar stool and scream to the whole room what just happened. She had to tell *someone*. But Ella was busy with Xavier. Mike wouldn't care. There was Emily, but Emily might be a buzzkill, determined to believe that Ali was truly good at heart and Jason wasn't.

Her phone began to bleat. Aria jumped and stared at it. *One new text message*, the little window said. The sender was *Caller Unknown*.

Aria's excitement instantly dimmed. She looked around the packed bar. People sat on couches, deep in conversation. A college-age guy with dreadlocks whispered to the bartender, every so often gazing in Aria's direction. A draft wafted from the back of the room, making the candle flames bow to the right. It was as if an unseen back door had just opened and shut.

One new text message. Aria ran her hands through her hair. Slowly, she pressed read.

Enjoy your gimlets? Well, sorry, darling, but the fantasy's over. Big Brother is hiding something from you. And trust me ... you don't want to know what it is. – A

15
En Garde, Kate

An hour later that same night, Hanna idled outside the Montgomerys' freaky modernist house, waiting for Mike to emerge. Earlier this afternoon, she'd called her dad at work and asked if she could please go to the library tonight to study for a French test ... *without* Kate. She needed to be alone to sufficiently memorize the long list of irregular verbs, she explained.

'Fine,' her father agreed gruffly. Thankfully, he was loosening up on his go-everywhere-Kate-goes rule – yesterday, he'd let Hanna shop for Meredith's baby shower present alone too. It appeared that he'd also allowed Kate to do some private baby gift shopping ... at the very same store. Immediately after Hanna had received her get-out-of-Kate-jail-free pass from her dad, she'd texted Mike and told him she wanted him to take her on a date ... *one-on-one*. What her dad didn't know wouldn't hurt him.

She stared out the window at the small cubic lights over the Montgomerys' front porch. It had been ages since she'd been to Aria's house, and she'd forgotten how strange it was. The front of the house had just one window, positioned off-kilter above the stairwell. The back of the house, on the other hand, was nothing *but* windows, stretching from the first floor to the third. Once, when Hanna and the others were in Aria's den watching a family of deer traipse through her backyard, Ali gazed at the huge windows and clucked her tongue. 'Don't you guys worry about people spying on you?' She gave Aria a nudge. 'But then, I guess your parents don't have any secrets they don't want anyone to know about, huh?' Aria had blushed and left the room. Hanna hadn't known why Aria had gotten so upset, but now she did – Ali had discovered that Aria's dad was having an affair, and she was torturing Aria with the information, the same way she used to torture Hanna about bingeing and purging.

Such a bitch.

Mike appeared on the front porch. He wore dark jeans, a long wool coat with the collar turned up, and carried an enormous bouquet of roses. Hanna felt tingles in her stomach. Not that she was excited for this date or anything. It was simply nice to get flowers on such a gray winter day.

'Those are gorgeous,' she said as Mike opened the door. 'You shouldn't have.'

'Okay.' Mike pulled the flowers back to his chest, the cellophane crinkling. 'I'll give them to my *other* girlfriend.'

Hanna caught his arm. 'Don't you dare.' That definitely wasn't funny, not after the stunt he'd pulled with Hanna and Kate at the baby shower yesterday. She drummed her fingers on the steering wheel of her Prius. 'So. Where are we going?'

'The King James,' Mike quipped.

Hanna glanced at him warily. 'No Rive Gauche.' With her luck, Lucas would be their waiter. *Très* awkward.

'I know,' Mike said. 'We're going shopping.'

Hanna wrinkled her nose. 'Ha.'

'I'm serious.' Mike held up his hands. 'I want you to shop

all night. I know that's what girls love to do, and I'm all about making you happy.'

His earnest expression didn't waver. Hanna thrust the car into gear. 'We'd better get there, then, before you change your mind.'

They took the back roads to the mall, Hanna slowing every time she saw a DEER CROSSING sign – they were relentless this time of year. Mike slipped a CD into the Prius's stereo. A throbbing bass filled the car, then a singer's screechy voice. Mike immediately started singing. Hanna recognized the song, and sang along quietly, too. Mike stared at her. 'You know who this is?'

'It's Led Zeppelin,' Hanna said matter-of-factly. Sean Ackard, Hanna's ex-ex-boyfriend, had tried to get into the band last summer – it seemed to be a Rosewood Day soccer and lax boy thing – but he'd decided they were too dark and moody for his pure, virginal ears. Mike's brow was furrowed with disbelief. 'What, did you think I listened to Miley Cyrus?' she snapped. 'The Jonas Brothers?' Actually, *Kate* listened to the Jonas Brothers. That and Broadway show tunes.

By the time they were pulling into the King James Mall, both were belting out the lyrics to 'Dazed and Confused'. Mike knew every verse by heart and even did a dramatic air guitar solo, which made Hanna buckle over in laughter.

The mall parking lot was packed. A Home Depot was off to their left, the Bloomingdale's doors in the middle, and the haute section – with stores like Louis Vuitton and Jimmy Choo – was on the right. As they stepped out into the crisp night air, Hanna heard someone grunt. A man stood next to a white car in the Home Depot lot, struggling to lift a heavy barrel of what looked like propane into the trunk of his car. When he moved out of the way, she noticed the writing on the car doors. *Rosewood Police Department.* The guy had an angular chin and a pointy nose. A shock of dark hair stuck out from the bottom of his black wool hat.

Wilden?

Hanna watched as he lifted the second tub of propane, struggling to fit it in the trunk next to the other one. Did his house not have a normal heater? She considered waving, but then turned away. Wilden had told the press that they'd made up seeing Ian's body in the woods. He'd turned all of Rosewood against them. *Asshole.*

'Come on,' she said to Mike, giving Wilden one last look. He had shut the trunk and was now holding his cell phone to his ear, his posture rigid, his shoulders square. It reminded Hanna of a time a few months ago, back when Wilden and her mom had been dating. He'd spent the night, and early in the morning, Hanna had heard whispers in the hall. When she peeked out, she saw Wilden standing in front of the hall window, looking out into the yard, his body rigid and his voice hoarse and harsh. Who the hell was he talking to? Was he sleepwalking? Hanna had slunk back to bed before Wilden noticed her.

Really, what did Hanna's mom ever see in that guy, anyway? Wilden was cute, but not *that* cute. When Hanna caught him getting out of the shower all those months ago, he didn't even look that fabulous half-naked. Not that she was into him or anything, but Hanna had a feeling lacrosse-obsessed Mike would look way hotter.

Otter, Hanna's favorite boutique, was tucked next to Cartier and Louis Vuitton. She strode in, inhaling the Ceylon-scented Diptyque candles. Fergie was on the stereo, and racks of Catherine Malandrino, Nanette Lepore, and Moschino spread out before her. She sighed, blissful. The leather jackets were glossy and lush. The silk dresses and diaphanous, oversize scarves looked spun from gold. Sasha, one of the salesgirls, noticed Hanna and waved. Hanna was one of Otter's best customers.

Hanna immediately selected a few dresses, enjoying the noise the wooden hangers made when they clonked together. 'Would you like me to put those in your dressing room?' said a fake high-pitched voice. Hanna turned. Mike was standing next to her. 'I've already started a room for you with some of *my* favorite selections,' he added.

Hanna stepped back. '*You* picked things out for me?' This she had to see. She marched to the only dressing room that had its velvet curtain tied to the side. A few things hung on the knob next to the mirror. First was a pair of high-waisted, tight black leather pants. Then there was a slinky silver tunic with a deep V in the front and big, gaping side vents. Behind that were three string bikinis with Wonderbra tops and thong bottoms.

Hanna turned to Mike and rolled her eyes. 'Nice try, but hell has to freeze over before you get me into any of that stuff.' She eyed the leather pants again. Interestingly, Mike thought she was a size zero.

Mike's expression wilted. 'You won't even try on the bikinis?'

'Not for you,' Hanna teased. 'You'll have to use your imagination.' Whipping the curtain closed, she couldn't help but smile. Mike deserved a few points for being so creative.

She put her plum-colored suede satchel on the little leather footstool and smoothed out her piece of the Time Capsule flag, which she'd wrapped around the strap. After some consideration, Hanna had decided to decorate the piece in homage to Ali, incorporating Ali's original designs from sixth grade. The Chanel logo was next to the manga frog. A field hockey girl swatted a ball into the Louis Vuitton initials. Hanna was quite pleased with the end result.

Turning, she peeled off her sweater, unhooked her bra, and unzipped her pants and kicked them off. Just as she was reaching for the first dress, the dressing room curtain parted. Mike poked his head in.

Hanna let out a yelp and covered up her boobs. 'What the hell?' she squealed.

'Oops!' Mike brayed. 'Shit. Sorry, Hanna. I thought this was the bathroom. This place is like a maze!' His eyes landed on Hanna's cleavage. Then they moved down to her skimpy lace underwear.

'Get out!' Hanna roared, giving Mike a kick with her bare foot. A few minutes later, she emerged from the dressing room, one of the dresses draped over her arm. Mike was perched on the chaise by the three-way mirrors. He looked like a naughty puppy who'd just chewed up his owner's Ugg slippers. 'Are you mad?' he asked.

'Yes,' Hanna said frostily. Truthfully, though, she wasn't that bothered – it was kind of flattering that Mike was *that* eager to see Hanna's body. But she did want to get revenge.

She paid for her dress, and Mike asked if she wanted to get some dinner. '*Not* Rive Gauche,' Hanna reminded him.

'I know, I know,' Mike said. 'But there's a place that's even better.'

He led her to Year of the Rabbit, the Chinese place near Prada. Hanna wrinkled her nose. She could practically feel her butt expanding from simply being around the oil, fat, and sauce all Chinese restaurants seemed to use in their entrees.

Mike registered her look of disgust. 'Don't worry,' he assured her. 'I got you covered.'

A bone-thin Asian woman with chopsticks in her bun led them to an intimate booth and poured them both cups of hot green tea. There was a gong in the corner and a large jade Buddha leering down at them from a high shelf. An elderly Chinese waiter appeared and handed them their menus. To Hanna's astonishment, Mike mumbled a few words in Mandarin. He pointed at Hanna, and the waiter nodded and turned away. Mike sat back, smugly flicking the center of the gong with his thumb and forefinger.

Hanna gawked. 'What the hell did you say?'

'I told him you were an underwear model and needed to keep your hot body in top shape, and we'd like to see the special healthy low-fat menu,' Mike explained nonchalantly. 'They hate giving that menu to people. You have to know how to ask for it.'

'You know how to say *underwear model* in Chinese?' Hanna blurted.

Mike draped his arms over the back of the leather booth. 'I picked up a thing or two during that boring-ass time I spent in Europe. The term *underwear model* is the first thing I learn in every language.'

Hanna shook her head, fascinated. 'Wow.'

'So you don't mind that the waiter thinks you're an underwear model?' Mike asked.

Hanna shrugged. 'Not really.' Underwear models were pretty, after all. And rail thin.

Mike brightened. 'Sweet. I brought my last girlfriend here, but she didn't find the whole special diet menu trick so funny. She thought I was objectifying her or some shit.'

Hanna took a slow sip of tea, unaware that Mike had *had* previous girlfriends. 'Was this ... a recent girlfriend?'

The waiter handed them their menus – the regular one for him, the diet one for Hanna. After he left, Mike nodded. 'We just broke up. She kept bitching about how I was too concerned with being popular.'

'Lucas said that too,' Hanna squealed, before she could stop herself. 'He didn't like that I told everyone Kate had herpes.' She flinched, annoyed she'd said Kate's name out loud – Mike would probably step in and defend her. But he just shrugged.

'I had to do it,' Hanna went on. 'I thought she was going to . . .' She trailed off.

'Thought she was going to what?' Mike asked.

Hanna shook her head. 'I just thought she was going to say something nasty about me.' Hanna had thought Kate was going to tell everyone that she used to make herself throw up, something she'd unfortunately admitted to Kate in a moment of weakness. And she was pretty sure Kate *would* have said it, if Hanna hadn't said the herpes thing first.

Mike smiled empathetically. 'Sometimes you have to play dirty.'

'Cheers to that.' Hanna raised her water glass and clinked it with Mike's, thankful he hadn't pressed to know what the nasty thing was that Kate was going to spill.

They finished eating their dinners and sucked on the orange wedges that came with the check. Mike suggestively complimented Hanna on her sucking abilities and advised her to save some sucking power for later. Then he excused himself to the bathroom. Hanna watched him snake around the tables, realizing her chance to get him back. Slowly, she stood, laid her napkin on her plate, and crept down the hall. She waited until the men's room door swung closed, counted to ten, and burst inside. 'Oops!' she called out. Her voice echoed throughout the shiny, empty room.

There was a line of urinals, but Mike wasn't at any of them. Nor did she see his Tod's loafers underneath the stall doors. She heard a small noise coming from the walled-off sink area and walked over. Mike was standing at the sink, a

141

comb, a can of deodorant, and a tube of toothpaste on the counter next to him. He held a toothbrush in his hand. When he saw Hanna in the mirror, the color drained from his face.

Hanna bleated out a laugh. 'Are you *primping*?'

'What are you doing here?' he croaked.

'Sorry, I thought this was a dressing room,' Hanna recited. It didn't quite have the effect she was going for.

Mike blinked and quickly shoved his toiletries back into his Jack Spade messenger bag. Hanna felt a little bad – he didn't have to *stop*. She backed out of the sink area. 'I'll be outside,' she muttered. She pushed her way out the door and returned to her seat, smiling to herself. Mike had been brushing his teeth. Did that mean he wanted to kiss her?

On the drive back to Mike's house, they listened to 'Whole Lotta Love', again belting out the lyrics. She pulled up to Mike's curb and turned off the ignition. 'Want to walk me to my door?'

'Sure,' Hanna answered, realizing her heart was pounding. She followed Mike up the stone steps to the Montgomerys' porch. There was a Zen rock garden to the left of the door, but it had frozen over by now, a thin crust of ice on the sand.

Mike faced her. Hanna liked that he was quite a bit taller – Lucas had been about her height, and Sean, her ex-ex, had been a tad shorter. 'So this was almost as fun as when I go out with my hookers,' Mike announced.

Hanna rolled her eyes. 'Maybe you can give the hookers a night off this Saturday too. Come with me to the Radley opening.'

Mike put his thumb to his chin, pretending to give it some thought. 'I think that could be arranged.'

Hanna giggled. Mike touched the inside of her arm lightly. His breath smelled minty. Almost unconsciously, she leaned in a little more.

The door flung open. Bright light streamed out from the Montgomerys' foyer, and Hanna shot back. A tall brunette stood inside. It wasn't Mike's mom, and it certainly wasn't Aria. Hanna's heart plummeted.

'*Kate?*' she shrieked.

'Hi, Mike!' Kate whooped at the same time.

Hanna pointed at her. 'What are *you* doing here?'

Kate blinked innocently. 'I got here early, so Mike's mom let me in.' She looked at Mike. 'She's *super* nice. And her artwork is amazing. She told me that she has a piece that's going to be in the lobby of the Radley – and that there's a big opening this Saturday. We should totally go together, don't you think?'

'What do you mean, you *got here early*?' Hanna interrupted.

Kate put her hand to her chest. 'Didn't Mike tell you? We have a date.'

Hanna faced Mike. 'No, Mike *didn't* tell me.'

Mike licked his lips, looking guilty.

'Well, that's strange!' Kate bleated. 'We set it up yesterday.'

Mike gazed at Kate. 'But you told me not to say anyth—'

'Besides,' Kate interrupted, using her innocent sweetie-pie voice again. 'Aren't you supposed to be at the library, Han? When I didn't see you in the auditorium during *Hamlet* practice, I called Tom. He said you needed to study for a big French test.'

She pushed around Hanna and took Mike's arm. 'You ready? I'm taking you to this awesome place for dessert.'

Mike nodded, then glanced back at Hanna, whose jaw was practically on the stoop. He apologetically raised his shoulders, as though to say, *We're not exclusive, are we?*

Dumbstruck, Hanna watched them walk back down the steps to the driveway, where the Audi that belonged to Isabel, Kate's mother, was parked. Hanna had been so distracted about how to end her date with Mike, she hadn't even noticed it. Was this why Mike had been primping at the restaurant? To freshen up for date number two? After their fabulous date, why was Mike still keeping his options open? How could he not *want* to be exclusive?

The Audi growled to life, rolled down the driveway, and disappeared. In the ensuing silence, Hanna heard a sniff behind her. She whipped around, her body tense. Another sniff. It sounded like someone was stifling a laugh.

'Hello?' Hanna called quietly into the Montgomerys' dark yard. No one answered, but Hanna still had the distinct feeling that someone was there. *A?* An eerie chill came over her, burrowing deep to her bones, and she scampered off the porch as fast as she could.

16
Spencer Hastings,
Future Wawa Counterperson

That same night, Spencer perched on the arm of the sofa in the media room, watching the news. A reporter was talking yet again about how the police had vacated the woods behind her house and were now searching the United States for Ian. Today, someone on the police force had received a hot tip about where he might be, but they weren't disclosing any more details at this time.

Spencer groaned. Then, the news broke to yet another new commercial for the Elk Ridge Ski Resort – they'd opened six more runs and were introducing Girls Ski for Free Thursdays.

The doorbell rang, and Spencer bounded up, eager to focus her attention on more positive things. Andrew stood on the stoop, shivering. 'I have so much to tell you,' Spencer squealed.

'Really?' Andrew walked in, carrying his AP econ textbook under his arm. Spencer sniffed apathetically. AP econ hardly mattered anymore.

Spencer led him by the hand into the media room, shut the

door, and turned off the TV. 'So you know how I e-mailed my biological mom on Monday? She e-mailed me back. And yesterday, I went to see her in New York.'

Andrew blinked quickly. 'New York?'

Spencer nodded. 'She sent me an Amtrak ticket and told me to meet her at Penn Station. And it was *wonderful*.' She squeezed Andrew's hands. 'Olivia's young, she's smart, and she's ... *normal*. We instantly clicked. Isn't that awesome?' She pulled out her phone and showed him a text Olivia had written late last night, presumably when she reached the airport. *Dear Spencer, I miss you already! See you soon! XX, O.* Spencer had written Olivia back, saying she had her accordion folder, and Olivia had responded that she should just hold on to it – she and Morgan would look it over once they returned.

Andrew picked at a piece of dry skin on his thumb. 'When I asked you what you were doing yesterday, you said you were having dinner with your family. So ... you lied?'

Spencer lowered her shoulders. Why was Andrew quibbling about semantics? 'I didn't want to talk about it before I met her. I was afraid it would jinx things. I was going to tell you in school, but we had a busy day.' She leaned back. 'I'm seriously considering moving to New York to be with Olivia. We've been separated for so long, and I don't want to spend another minute apart. She and her husband moved into this great neighborhood in the Village, and there are so many great schools in the city, and ...' She noticed Andrew's dour expression and stopped. 'Are you okay?'

Andrew stared at the floor. 'Sure,' he mumbled. 'That's great news. I'm happy for you.'

Spencer ran her hands over the back of her neck, suddenly feeling insecure. She'd expected Andrew to be thrilled that she'd found her birth mother – he was the one who'd pushed her to register for the bio mom-matching site in the first place. 'You don't sound that happy,' she said slowly.

'No, I am.' Andrew jumped up, bumping his knee hard on the coffee table. 'Um, I forgot. I ... I left my calc book back at school. I should probably go get it. We have all those problem sets for homework.' He grabbed his books and headed for the door.

Spencer grabbed his arm. He stopped, but he wouldn't look at her. 'What's going on?' she urged, her heart beating fast.

Andrew clutched his books tightly to his chest. 'Well ... I mean ... maybe you're moving a little fast with all this New York stuff. Shouldn't you discuss it with your parents?'

Spencer frowned. 'They'd probably be happy I was gone.'

'You don't know that,' Andrew argued, glancing at her cagily, then quickly cutting his eyes away. 'Your parents are mad at you, but I'm sure they don't *hate* you. You're still their kid. They might not let you go to New York at all.'

Spencer opened her mouth, then quickly shut it again. Her parents wouldn't stand in the way of this opportunity ... would they?

'And you just met your mom,' Andrew mumbled, looking more and more pained. 'I mean, you barely know her. Don't you think you're moving a little too fast?'

'Yeah, but it felt right,' Spencer urged, wishing that he could understand. 'And if I'm closer to her, I can *get* to know her.'

Andrew shrugged, then turned away again. 'I don't want to see you get hurt.'

'What do you mean?' Spencer pressed, frustrated. 'Olivia would never hurt me.'

Andrew mashed his lips together. In the kitchen, one of the family's labradoodles started drinking from his water bowl.

The phone rang, but Spencer made no motion to get it, waiting for Andrew to explain himself. She looked at Andrew's pile of books in his arms. On top of their AP econ text was a small, square invitation. *Please join us for the opening of the Radley hotel*, the invitation said in elegant script.

'What's that?' Spencer pointed at it.

Andrew glanced at the invitation, then pushed it under his notebook. 'Just this thing I got in the mail. I must have picked it up by mistake.'

Spencer stared at him. Andrew's cheeks were blotchy, as though he was trying hard not to cry. Suddenly . . . she got it. She imagined Andrew receiving the Radley invitation and rushing over here, eager to ask her to be his date. *This will make up for Foxy*, he might have planned to say, referring to the disastrous benefit they'd attended together this fall. Maybe all this nonsense about Spencer taking things slow and not wanting her to get hurt was really because Andrew didn't want her to leave.

She touched his arm gently. 'I'll come back and visit you. And you can visit me too.'

A look of extreme embarrassment fluttered over Andrew's face. He shook her off. 'I-I have to go.' He stumbled out the door and down the hall. 'I'll see you in school tomorrow.'

'Andrew!' Spencer protested, but he had already put on his jacket and was out the door. The wind slammed it shut so hard, the little wooden labradoodle statue that sat on the console table toppled over.

Spencer walked to the window next to the front door and watched Andrew run down the path to his Mini Cooper. She touched the doorknob, about to go after him, but a part of her didn't want to. Andrew peeled away fast, the tires squealing. And then he was gone.

A huge lump formed in her throat. What had just

happened? Had they broken up? Now that Spencer might leave, did Andrew want nothing else to do with her? Why wasn't he happier for her? Why was he only thinking about himself and what *he* wanted?

Moments later, the back door slammed, and Spencer jumped. There were footsteps, then Mr Hastings's voice. Spencer hadn't spoken to her parents since before her trip to New York, but she knew she had to. Only, what if Andrew was right? What if they prevented her from moving there?

She snatched her funnel-neck tweed jacket off the back of the living room chair and grabbed her car keys, suddenly afraid. There was no way she could talk to them about this right now. She needed to leave the house for a while, have a cappuccino, and clear her head. As she walked down the front steps toward the driveway, she stopped short, looking right, then left. Something was wrong.

Her car was gone.

The spot where she normally parked the little Mercedes coupe was empty. But Spencer had parked it here a few hours ago after school. Had she forgotten to turn on the alarm? Had someone stolen it? *A?*

She sprinted back to the kitchen. Mrs Hastings was standing by the stove, putting some veggies in a big soup pot. Mr Hastings was pouring himself a glass of Malbec. 'My car is gone,' Spencer bleated. 'I think someone stole it.'

Mr Hastings kept calmly pouring. Mrs Hastings pulled out a plastic cutting board, not even flinching. 'No one stole it,' she said.

Spencer stopped. She gripped the edge of the kitchen island. 'How do you know no one stole it?'

Her mother's mouth was pursed, as if she was sucking on something sour. Her black T-shirt pulled tightly against her trim shoulders and chest. She held a paring knife tightly in her fist, wielding it like a weapon. 'Because. Your father turned it into the dealer this afternoon.'

Spencer's knees felt weak. She turned to her dad. '*What? Why?*'

'It was a gas guzzler,' Mrs Hastings spoke for him. 'We have to start thinking about the economy and the environment.' She shot Spencer a self-righteous smile and turned back to her cutting board.

'But …' Spencer's body felt electrified. 'You guys just inherited millions of dollars! And … that car is *not* a gas guzzler! It's way more efficient than Melissa's SUV!' She turned to her dad. He was still ignoring her, savoring his wine. Didn't he care at all?

Enraged, Spencer grabbed his wrist. 'Do *you* have anything to say?'

'Spencer,' Mr Hastings said in an even voice, wrenching his hand away. The spicy smell of red wine filled Spencer's nose. 'You're being dramatic. We've been talking about turning in your car for a long time, remember? You don't *need* a car of your own.'

'But how am I supposed to get around?' Spencer wailed.

Mrs Hastings kept chopping the carrots into smaller and smaller bits. The knife made a gnawing sound against the cutting board. 'If you want to buy a new car, do what plenty of other kids your age do.' She brushed the carrots into the pot. 'Get a job.'

'A *job*?' Spencer sputtered. Her parents had never made her work before. She thought about the people at Rosewood Day who had jobs. They worked at the Gap at the King James. At Auntie Anne's pretzels. At Wawa, making sandwiches.

'Or borrow our car,' Mrs Hastings said. 'Or I hear there's a wonderful new invention that takes you places the same as a car does.' She laid the knife on the cutting board. 'It's called the bus.'

Spencer gaped at both of them, her ears ringing. Then, to her surprise, a peaceful feeling settled over her. She had her answer. Her parents truly *didn't* love her. If they did, they wouldn't be trying to take away everything from her.

'Fine,' she said tersely, whirling around. 'It's not like I'll be here much longer, anyway.' As she strode out of the kitchen, she heard her father's glass clink against the granite counter-top. 'Spencer,' Mr Hastings called. But it was too little, too late.

Spencer ran upstairs to her bedroom. Usually, after her parents dissed her, tears would stream down her face, and she'd fling herself on the bed, wondering what she'd done wrong. But not this time. She marched over to her desk and picked up the expandable file Olivia had been lugging around yesterday. Taking a deep breath, she peered inside. Just as Olivia said, it was filled with papers about the apart-ment Olivia and her husband had purchased, things like dimensions of rooms, floor and cabinet materials, and the amenities in the building – a pet groomer, an indoor Olympic-length swimming pool, and an Elizabeth Arden salon. Clipped to the front of the file was a business card. *Michael Hutchins, Real Estate.*

Michael, our Realtor, could find you something really spe-cial, Olivia had said at dinner.

Spencer looked around the room, assessing its contents. All the furniture, from her four-poster bed to her antique writing desk to the mahogany armoire and Chippendale vanity table, was hers. She'd inherited it from her great-aunt Millicent – apparently *she* didn't have the same animosity toward adopted children. Of course she'd have to take her clothes, shoes, bags, and collection of books, too. It would probably fit in a U-Haul. She could even drive the thing herself if she had to.

Her phone buzzed, and Spencer flinched. She eagerly reached for it, hoping Andrew was calling to make up, but when she saw it was a text from *Caller Unknown*, her heart plummeted to the floor.

Dear Little Miss Spencer-Whatever-Your-Name-Is,
Shouldn't you know by now what happens if you don't listen to me? I'll use small words this time, so even you'll understand. Either give Long-Lost Mommy a rest and keep searching for what really happened . . . or pay my price. How does disappearing forever sound? – A

17
Just Like Old Times …

Later that night, after swimming practice ended, Emily slid into her favorite booth at Applebee's, the one with the old-fashioned tandem bicycle suspended from the ceiling and the colorful license plates on the walls. Her sister Carolyn, Gemma Curran, and Lanie Iler – two other Rosewood Day swimmers – piled in beside her. The dining room smelled like salty french fries and burgers, and an old Beatles song was playing loudly on the stereo. When Emily opened the menu, she was pleased to see that mozzarella sticks and hot wings were still featured appetizers. The southwest chicken salad still came with spicy ranch dressing. If Emily closed her eyes, she could almost pretend it was last year at this time, when she used to come to Applebee's every Thursday night – back when nothing bad had happened yet.

'Coach Lauren had to be smoking crack when she wrote that set of five hundreds,' Gemma whined, flipping through the laminated menu.

'Seriously,' Carolyn echoed, shrugging out of her Rosewood Day Swim Team jacket. 'I can barely lift my arms!'

Emily laughed with the others, then saw a flash of blond

hair out of the corner of her eyes. She stiffened and glanced toward the bar, which was packed with people watching an Eagles game on the flat-screen TVs. There was a blond guy at the very end of the bar, talking animatedly to his date. Emily's heart slowed down. For a second, she'd thought he was Jason DiLaurentis.

Emily couldn't get Jason off her mind. She hated that Aria had brushed off her warnings about him in the courtyard on Tuesday, making excuses for his anger. And she really didn't know what to make of the strange photo A had sent her yesterday, the one of Ali, Naomi, and Jenna all together, presumably friends. If Jenna was Ali's friend, Ali might've opened up to her truthfully, right? She might've told Jenna a deep, dark secret about her brother, having no idea that Jenna was going to reveal something similar.

A few months ago, before the cops arrested Ian for Ali's murder, Emily had seen an interview with Jason DiLaurentis on TV. Well, it was *sort of* an interview – a reporter had tracked him down at Yale, asking him what he thought of the investigation into his sister's murder, and he'd waved them away, saying he didn't want to talk about it. He stayed away from his family as much as possible, he said – they were too messed up. But what if *Jason* was the one who was messed up? The summer between sixth and seventh grade, Emily had been over at Ali's house when the DiLaurentises were packing up to go to their mountain house in the Poconos. While the whole family industriously carried suitcases to the car, Jason slumped on the recliner in the den, flipping through the TV channels. When Emily asked Ali why Jason wasn't helping, Ali just shrugged. 'He's in one of his Elliott Smith moods.' She rolled her eyes. 'They should put him in the mental ward, where he belongs.'

A shiver traveled down Emily's back. 'Jason needs to be in a mental ward?'

Ali rolled her eyes again. 'It was a *joke*,' she groaned. 'You're so literal!'

But as she turned to carry another suitcase to the car, Ali's mouth flickered slightly. It seemed like something was going on deep beneath Ali's cool exterior, something she wouldn't admit.

Emily had forwarded A's picture to each of her old friends. Both Spencer and Hanna had responded, saying they had no idea what it could mean, but Aria hadn't acknowledged it at all. What if they *should* be worrying about Jason? There was a lot about him they didn't know.

A blond waitress in a green Applebee's button-down and an Eagles baseball cap took their orders. Then the swimmers started talking about the party at the Radley. 'Topher managed to snag an invite, and he wants me to go,' Carolyn was saying. 'But what do you wear to something like that?'

Emily sipped her vanilla Coke. Topher was Carolyn's boyfriend, but usually the two of them preferred *Heroes* marathons to fancy parties. 'What about the pink dress I wore to the Rosewood Day benefit?' she suggested. Then she drummed her fingers on the table. 'You don't have to worry about me borrowing from your closet yet again. I already *got* a dress.'

Carolyn's eyes lit up. 'You're going?'

'Someone asked me,' Emily blurted out. Lanie and Gemma leaned forward, intrigued.

Carolyn squeezed Emily's arm. 'Let me guess,' she whispered. 'Renee Jeffries from Tate? You guys were so cute when you were talking before the two hundred fly last month. And someone told me she's ... you know.' Carolyn trailed off.

Emily fiddled with the red straw in her vanilla Coke.

She hadn't told her family or swimming friends about Isaac yet.

She took a deep breath and looked at the others. 'Actually ... it's a guy.'

Carolyn blinked hard. Lanie and Gemma smiled, puzzled. On TV, the Eagles scored a touchdown. The whole room cheered, but none of them turned.

'I met him at church,' Emily went on. 'He goes to Holy Trinity Academy. His name's Isaac. We're sort of ... dating.'

Carolyn placed her palms flat on the table. 'Isaac *Colbert*? The hot guy in that band, Carpe Diem?'

Emily nodded, pleased color rising to her cheeks.

'I know him,' Gemma said, swooning. 'We worked on the same Habitat for Humanity project last year. He's gorgeous.'

'Is it *serious*?' Carolyn's eyes popped wider and wider.

Emily nodded again, gazing at her sister. 'I plan to tell Mom and Dad. Don't break the news to them first. I just needed to make sure it was ... for real.'

Carolyn picked up a piece of garlic bread that had just arrived. 'Go you.' Gemma gave Emily a high five, and Lanie patted her on the back.

Emily breathed out, relieved. She'd worried about how that would go. And she'd especially fretted that Carolyn would make a face and ask her why she'd put the family through the lesbian stuff if she was going to eventually date guys again.

But now that her thoughts had turned to Isaac, she couldn't help but think about what had happened at dinner last night. All those awful, jabbing digs. All those bitter looks. And that photo in the drawer, the one of Emily beheaded. *Would* Emily and Isaac be able to go to the Radley party together, if Mrs Colbert knew what they'd done?

She'd left Isaac's house soon after seeing the photo in the drawer, not telling Isaac a word about it. But she had to say something. They were a couple. They were in love. Surely he would understand. She could say, *Are you sure your mom likes me? Does your mom like to haze your new girlfriends? Did you know your mom is a psychopath and beheaded me in a photo?*

Their dinners came, and the swimmers scarfed them down. As the waitress cleared their plates, Emily's phone rang. *Spencer Hastings*, said the name in the Caller ID window. A flutter of nerves streaked through Emily's stomach. She glanced apologetically at her friends, slid out of the booth, and walked down the hall toward the bathrooms. It was way too loud in the bar area to even attempt a phone conversation.

'What's up?' Emily said when she pushed through the bathroom door.

'I got another note,' Spencer said.

Emily placed a shaky hand on the marble sink and stared in the mirror. Her eyes were round, and her face had gone very pale. 'W-what did it say?'

'Basically that we have to keep searching or pay A's price.'

'Searching ... for the killer?' Emily whispered.

'I guess. I don't know what else it could mean.'

'Do you think it has to do with that photo I got? The one of Ali and Jenna?'

'I don't know.' Spencer sounded hopeless. 'That doesn't make much sense either.'

A toilet flushed, and a pair of loafers shuffled behind one of the stall doors. Emily tensed. She hadn't realized anyone else was in the bathroom. 'I have to go,' she hissed into the phone.

'Okay,' Spencer said. 'Be careful.'

Emily clapped her phone shut and stuffed it back into her pocket. When the stall door opened and the woman emerged, Emily's blood went cold.

'Oh.' Mrs Colbert stopped short. She was dressed in a silk blouse and black pants, as if she'd come from work. The corners of her mouth turned sharply down.

'Hi,' Emily chirped, her voice an octave higher than it normally was. Her hands shook. 'H-how are you?'

Mrs Colbert whisked past her to the sink and turned on the hot tap. She plunged her hands underneath the stream of water, rubbing so vigorously it was a wonder her skin didn't peel off in curls. She was blocking the paper towel dispenser, but Emily didn't dare ask her to move.

'Are you and Mr Colbert having dinner here?' Emily asked, mustering a smile. 'I love their burgers.'

Mrs Colbert whirled around and glared at her. 'Cut the sweet act. It's insulting.'

Emily sucked in her stomach. Another cheer erupted from the bar. 'I'm ... sorry?'

Mrs Colbert turned off the tap and tore off a piece of paper towel violently, wadding it up in her hands. 'I didn't want to say this in front of my son, which is why I tolerated you at dinner the other night. But you've disrespected me and my home. As far as I'm concerned, you're trash. Don't you dare set foot in my house again.'

Emily paled. All other sounds fell away. Dizzily, she backed out of the room butt-first and sprinted back to her table. She snatched her coat off her chair and darted for the door. 'Emily?' Carolyn called, standing halfway up. But Emily didn't answer. She had to get out of here. She had to get away from Isaac's mom before she could say anything else.

Bitter wind swept across her cheeks as she walked into the parking lot. Carolyn was right behind her, tugging at her sleeve. 'What's wrong?' her sister asked. 'What happened?'

Emily didn't answer. She wasn't sure she *could* answer.

You've disrespected me and my home. Mrs Colbert had said it all.

She stared at the bright Applebee's sign, cursing her terrible luck. Why did Mrs Colbert have to eat at Applebee's tonight of all nights? And it was 8 P.M., not exactly the normal dinnertime hour. It was bitter cold out, too, a good night to stay indoors.

Then, from deep inside her purse, Emily's phone chimed. Suddenly, it hit her. Maybe it wasn't luck or coincidence that Mrs Colbert was at Applebee's tonight. Maybe someone had told her to come.

'Just ... give me a sec,' she said to her sister. She walked over to the curb near the takeout door and lowered herself down. Her cell phone's greenish window glowed in the darkness. *One new photo message*, the screen said.

A picture appeared on the Nokia's screen. But it had nothing to do with Emily, Isaac, or Isaac's mom. Instead, it was of a big room with stained-glass windows, glossy wooden pews, and thick red carpeting. Emily frowned. It was Holy Trinity, her family's church. There was Father Tyson's confessional, the little wooden alcove near the lobby. Someone was emerging from the confession booth, his head bowed. Emily brought the phone close to her face. The guy in the photo was tall, with short, dark hair. A Rosewood Police Department badge glowed on his jacket, and a pair of handcuffs dangled from his belt.

Wilden?

Then she noticed the text at the bottom of the photo. Even though she wasn't quite sure what it meant, an uneasy shiver rippled from the top of her head down to the soles of her feet.

I guess we all have stuff to feel guilty about, huh? – A

159

18
Something's Rotten In Rosewood...

Friday morning, as the sky was turning from dark blue to pale purple, Hanna zipped up her green Puma running jacket and did a couple of calf stretches against the big maple tree in her front yard. Then she set off running down her driveway, listening to music on her iPhone. She'd been an idiot not to get an iPhone sooner – armed with a new unlisted phone number, she hadn't received a single text from New A.

New A was certainly texting Emily up a storm, though – Hanna had received a forward from Emily early this morning, a photo of Darren Wilden skulking around a church. *What do you think this means?* Emily wrote, as if Hanna really would know. Lots of people went to church. She didn't buy that A was sending Emily texts as all-important clues. More than likely, A was just messing with poor Emily's already addled mind.

But Hanna *had* received quite a few texts from Mike Montgomery. Like the one that came in right now: *U awake?*

Yes, Hanna typed back quickly. *On a run.*

Sexy, Mike wrote back. *What R U wearing?*

Hanna smirked. *Spandex. Super tight.*

Mike: *Run by my house!*

You wish, Hanna answered, giggling.

Mike had even texted her last night, presumably after he'd returned from his date with Kate. Hanna considered scolding him about double booking, but then she worried she might sound whiny and insecure. Did Mike think Kate was prettier? Thinner? Did he take her shopping and try and bust into her dressing room, too? What did Kate do? Laugh ... or freak?

What time do U want me to pick U up for the Radley party 2morro? Hanna texted.

She was at the bottom of her street before Mike responded. *Do U mind if we add a third?* Hanna came to an abrupt stop at the corner. It was obvious who the third person Mike wanted to add was – *Kate*.

She kicked the metal post of the stop sign hard. It made a loud clanging sound, startling a few birds from a nearby tree. Her dad might have relaxed the all-Kate-all-the-time punishment, but he was still trying to coerce Hanna and Kate into being BFFs. Like yesterday, when Kate had returned from her date with Mike, she'd joined Hanna and Mr Marin in the kitchen, where Hanna was proudly showing her father her decorated Time Capsule flag. Mr Marin studied it, then Kate, and then gently asked Hanna if Kate could have some of the credit for finding the flag too. Maybe Hanna could let her draw a little decoration in one of the corners?

Hanna's mouth had dropped open. 'It's my flag,' she cried, astonished her dad could even suggest such a thing. 'I found it.' Her father looked at her disappointedly, then walked away. Kate didn't say a word the whole time, probably figuring that a silent, humble daughter was better than a screechy, bratty one. But Hanna knew Kate was thrilled that Hanna and her father's relationship was dying a slow, painful death.

There was a *swish* behind her, and Hanna whirled around, suddenly struck with the distinct feeling that someone was on her tail. Only the narrow road was empty. She let out a long sigh and decided not to answer Mike at all, sliding her iPhone into her pocket and cranking up the music. She ran down the hill from her neighborhood, cut across a narrow footbridge between two yards, and found herself at a familiar intersection. There was an old gray farmhouse on the corner, set back from the street. Two cinnamon-colored horses and one spotted Shetland pony stood calmly next to the wood fence. This was the turn to Ali's.

The first time Hanna stood at the crossroads was the day she'd tried to steal Ali's piece of the Time Capsule flag. Hanna remembered gazing into the pony's big, soft eyes, wishing she could ask its opinion about what she was about to do. Who did she think she was, assuming she could march in and snatch Ali's flag? What if Naomi and Riley were there and they all laughed in Hanna's face? *Maybe I should face the fact that I'll never be popular*, she'd almost said out loud to the pony. But then a car had passed, and she'd squared her shoulders and biked on.

Now she jogged into Ali's neighborhood, breathing hard. Mona's house was one of the first houses on the street, its grand circular driveway and gabled six-car garage painfully familiar. Hanna looked away. Next came Jenna's house, the red colonial with the big tree off to the side, the one that had once held Toby's tree house. Then Spencer's estate, which sat aloofly behind a large wrought-iron gate. Hints of the *KILLER* graffiti were visible through the repainted barn garage doors. Ali's old house was last, looming at the end of the cul-de-sac.

Hanna ran up to the Ali shrine, which was still assembled at the curb. A few of the candles had been replaced, and one was lit, dancing in the wind. There were a few hand-lettered signs on poster board that said things like, WE'LL FIND HIM, ALI, and IAN WILL PAY FOR THIS!

She crouched down and looked at the photograph that had been part of the shrine ever since it was first assembled, back when Ali's body had been recovered. The photo was warped and faded from months of rain and snow. It was a picture of sixth-grade Ali, wearing a blue Von Dutch T-shirt and Seven jeans, standing in Spencer's grand foyer. The photo had been taken the night Melissa and Ian were going to the Rosewood Day Winter Ball – Ali had been vehement about spying on them, giggling hysterically when Melissa tripped on the stairs during her grand entrance. Who knew, maybe Ali had something going on with Ian even back *then*.

Hanna frowned, looking closer at the photo. Behind Ali, the Hastingses' front door was slightly open, offering a partial view of Spencer's front yard. Standing in Spencer's driveway next to Ian and Melissa's Hummer limo was a lone figure in a down jacket and jeans. Hanna couldn't really make out who it was, his face a blur. Still, there was something intrusive and voyeuristic about the person's posture, as if whoever it was wanted to spy on Ian and Melissa too.

A door slammed. Hanna jumped, looking up. For a moment, she couldn't locate where the noise had come from. Then she saw Darren Wilden standing at the bottom of the Cavanaughs' driveway. When he saw Hanna, he did a double take.

'Hanna,' Wilden said. 'What are you ... doing?'

Hanna's heart started to beat faster, like she'd just been caught shoplifting. 'Running. What are *you* doing?'

Wilden looked shaken. He turned halfway, gesturing across the street to the woods behind Spencer's house. 'I was, um, just, you know. Checking things out back there.'

163

Hanna crossed her arms. The cops had abandoned the search in the woods a few days ago. And Wilden had come from Jenna's house, which was across the street from the woods, not in the right direction at all. 'Did you find something?'

Wilden rubbed his gloved hands together. 'You shouldn't be here,' he blurted.

Hanna stared at him.

'It's cold out,' Wilden fumbled.

Hanna extended her left leg. 'That's what running tights are for. And mittens and hats.'

'Still.' Wilden slapped his right fist into his left palm. 'I'd rather you were running somewhere safer. Like the Marwyn trail.'

Hanna squirmed. Was Wilden truly concerned for her ... or did he just want her to leave? He glanced over his shoulder again toward Spencer's woods. Hanna craned her neck too. Was there something there? Something he didn't want her to see? But hadn't he told the press that he'd never believed anything was back there? Didn't he think Hanna and the others made it up?

A's text about Wilden at confession flashed through her mind. *We all have stuff to feel guilty about, huh?*

'Do you need a ride somewhere?' Wilden asked loudly, making Hanna jump. 'I'm finished here.'

Truthfully, Hanna's toes *were* going numb. 'Okay,' she stammered, trying to stay calm. She gave the Ali shrine a final look, then followed Wilden to a car covered in a dirty layer of caked-on snow and ice. 'That's your car?' Hanna asked. There was something familiar about it.

Wilden nodded. 'My cruiser's in the shop, so I had to resort to this old beater.' He opened the passenger door. The inside of the car smelled like old McDonald's hamburger wrappers. He quickly tossed a bunch of file folders, shoe boxes, CDs, empty packs of cigarettes, unopened mail, and an extra pair of gloves to the backseat. 'Sorry for the mess.'

An oval-shaped sticker in the front-seat foot well caught Hanna's eye. There was a drawing of a fish on it, with a few initials and the words *Day Pass*. The sticker hadn't been pulled off the shiny backing, and the ink seemed bright and new.

'Did you recently go ice fishing?' Hanna teased, pointing at it. Back when her dad was Hanna's friend instead of the soulless drone who only wanted to make Princess Kate happy, they used to go fishing at Keuka Lake in upstate New York. They always had to buy a similar-looking fishing pass at the local bait shop in order to use the lake without getting fined.

Wilden glanced at the sticker, an odd expression flickering over his face. He tweezed it between his fingers and tossed it quickly to the back. 'I haven't cleaned out this car in years.' His words tumbled out in a rush. 'That thing's old.'

The motor started up, and Wilden shifted into reverse so forcefully Hanna was knocked back. He swung around the cul-de-sac, nearly running over the Ali shrine, then whipped past Spencer's house, Jenna's, and Mona's. Hanna grasped the little handle above the window. 'This isn't a race,' she joked shakily, growing more and more weirded out.

Wilden looked at her out of the corner of his eye, saying nothing. Hanna noticed he didn't have his Rosewood PD jacket on, but instead wore a simple, oversize gray hoodie and black jeans. An oversize hoodie, in fact, that looked a lot like the one the Grim Reaperish person who'd stood over her in the woods Saturday night had worn. But that was just a coincidence ... right?

Hanna ran her hand over the back of her neck and cleared her throat. 'So, um, how's the Ian investigation?'

Wilden looked at her, his foot still pressed firmly on the gas pedal. They took the turn at the top of the hill fast, and the car's tires made a screeching noise. 'We have a pretty good lead that Ian's in California.'

Hanna opened her mouth, then closed it fast. The IP address from Ian's IMs had said that he was still in Rosewood. 'Uh, how did you find out that?' she asked.

'A tip,' Wilden growled.

'From who?'

He shot her a frozen glare. 'You know I can't tell you that.'

A gray Nissan Pathfinder was in front of them, slowly ascending the hill. Wilden revved the engine and veered into the lane of oncoming traffic, speeding to get around. The Pathfinder honked. Two hazy lights appeared in the distance, heading the opposite direction. 'What are you doing?' Hanna screamed, growing nervous. Wilden didn't move back into the right lane. 'Stop!' Hanna screamed. All at once, she was catapulted back to the night she'd stood in the Rosewood Day parking lot, Mona's SUV heading straight for her. By the time she'd realized the SUV wasn't going to swerve, she couldn't move, petrified and helpless. It had felt as if there was nothing she could have done to stop what had happened.

Hanna shut her eyes, anxiety overpowering her. There was a loud, blaring horn, and Wilden's car swerved. When Hanna opened her eyes again, they were back in their own lane.

'What is *wrong* with you?' Hanna demanded, her whole body trembling.

Wilden glanced at her out of the corner of his eye. He looked ... *amused*. 'Calm down.'

Calm down? Hanna ran her hand down the length of her face, about to throw up. The incident flashed through her mind again and again, on rapid fast-forward. Ever since her accident, she'd tried very, very hard not to think about that

166

night, and here Wilden was, laughing at her for being scared. Maybe she shouldn't have been so quick to discount A's texts about Wilden after all.

Hanna was about to tell him to pull over and let her out when she realized Wilden was zooming up her winding driveway. When they reached the top, she quickly unbuckled her seat belt and got out of the car, never so grateful to see her house.

She slammed the door anyway, but Wilden didn't seem to notice. He just sped in reverse down the driveway, not even bothering to make the three-point turn. Some of the snow had fallen off the nose of the car. Hanna could see that it had a pointed end and mean-looking headlights.

A sense of déjà vu suddenly nagged at her. Something about what had just happened had happened before – and not just the night of her accident. She had the same feeling as when she couldn't remember a vocabulary word in French class, the term on the tip of her tongue. Usually, the word came to her later at the weirdest time, like when she was surfing on iTunes or walking Dot. Soon enough, this would come back to her too.

But she wasn't exactly looking forward to finding it.

19
Spencer Wheels And Deals

After school on Friday, Spencer's closest field hockey friend, Kirsten Cullen, pulled up to Spencer's curb and yanked up the parking brake.

'Thanks so much for the ride,' Spencer said. Just because her parents had taken away her wheels didn't mean she was about to climb aboard the smelly Rosewood Day school bus.

'No worries,' Kirsten said. 'You need a ride on Monday, too?'

'If it's not too much trouble,' Spencer mumbled.

She'd tried calling Aria for a ride, since Aria now lived one neighborhood over, but Aria had said she had 'something to do' this afternoon, mysteriously not saying what it was. And it wasn't like she could ask Andrew. All day, she'd thought he was going to apologize – if he had, she would have apologized to him too, and promised they would stay together if she moved. Andrew pointedly didn't say a word to her in any of their shared classes. That, Spencer figured, was that.

Kirsten gave Spencer a wave and pulled away from the curb one-handed. Turning, Spencer walked up the driveway.

The neighborhood was still and silent, and the sky was a drab, purplish-gray. The *KILLER* graffiti on the garage doors had been painted over, but the new color didn't quite match, and the word still showed through faintly. Spencer averted her eyes, not wanting to look at it. Who had put it there? A? But ... why? To scare her, or to warn her?

The house was empty, smelling like Murphy's Oil Soap and Windex, meaning the Hastingses' cleaning lady, Candace, had just left. Spencer ran upstairs, grabbed Olivia's expandable folder from the desk in her room, and exited the house through the back door. Even though her parents weren't here, she didn't want to be in their house when she did this. She needed complete privacy.

She unlocked the barn's front door and flipped on the kitchen and living room lights. Everything was as she'd left it since the last time she'd been in here, down to the half-filled water glass by the computer. She plopped down on the couch and pulled out her Sidekick. A's message was the last text she'd received. *How does disappearing forever sound?*

At first, the note had scared her, but after a while, she'd seen it another way. Disappearing forever sounded fine – disappearing from Rosewood, that was. And Spencer knew just how she could.

She dumped Olivia's file folder on the coffee table, its contents practically spilling out onto the throw rug. The Realtor's card was right on top. With shaking hands, Spencer dialed his number. The phone rang once, then twice. 'Michael Hutchins,' a man's voice squawked.

Spencer sat up and cleared her throat. 'Hi. My name is Spencer Hastings,' she said, trying to sound older and professional. 'My mom is your client. Olivia Caldwell?'

'Of course, of course.' Michael sounded overjoyed. 'I

didn't realize she had a daughter. Have you seen their new place yet? It's going to be photographed for the *New York Times* Home section next month.'

Spencer wound a piece of hair around her finger. 'Not yet. But . . . I will. Soon.'

'So what can I do for you?'

She crossed and uncrossed her legs. Her heart thudded through her ears. 'Well . . . I'd like an apartment. In New York. Preferably somewhere near Olivia. Is that doable?'

She heard Michael flipping some papers. 'I believe so. Hang on. Let me pull up the database of what's available.'

Spencer bit down hard on her thumbnail. This felt surreal. She stared out the window at the rock-lined pool and hot tub, the tiered back deck, the two dogs frolicking near the fence. Then, she turned and gazed at the windmill. *LIAR*. It was still there, not yet painted over. Maybe her parents had left it for Spencer as a reminder, the equivalent of the big red *A* in *The Scarlet Letter*. Ali's old house next door no longer had the *Do Not Cross* tape over the half-dug hole – the new owners had finally had the sense to take it down – but the hole hadn't been filled yet. Behind the barn were the woods, thick and black and brimming with secrets.

Olivia had told her to take things slow, but moving out of Rosewood was the smartest – and safest – thing she could do.

'You there?' Michael's voice called. Spencer jumped. 'There's a new listing at two twenty-three Perry Street. It hasn't even gone on the market yet – the landlord is cleaning and painting – but it'll probably go up on our Web site on Monday. It's a one-bedroom on the parlor level of a brownstone. I'm looking at the pictures right now, and the place looks gorgeous. High ceilings, wood floors, crown molding, an eat-in kitchen, a back deck, a claw-foot tub. You'd be near the subway *and* a block from Marc Jacobs. You sound like you might be a Marc Jacobs girl.'

'You're right about that.' Spencer smiled.

'You near a computer?' Michael said. 'I can e-mail you some pictures of the place right now.'

'Sure,' Spencer said, giving him her e-mail address. She sprang up and walked to Melissa's laptop, which was sitting closed on the desk. In seconds, a new e-mail appeared in her in-box. The attached photos were of a quaint brownstone with slate stairs. The apartment had wide oak floors, two bay windows, exposed brick, marble countertops, and even a little washer and dryer.

'It looks awesome,' Spencer breathed, nearly swooning. 'I'm in Philadelphia at the moment, but could I come to the city on Monday afternoon and check it out?'

She heard a horn honk outside Michael's window. 'That could work, sure,' he said, the hesitation in his voice practically palpable. 'But I've gotta warn you. Apartments like this don't come up very often, and New York City real estate is insane. This is one of the best blocks in the Village, and people are going to jump on it. It's likely that on Monday morning someone's going to show up at our office as soon as the place lists with a check, sight unseen. By the time you get here, the place might be gone. But I don't want to pressure you. There are other places I could show you in that neighborhood, too ...'

Spencer tensed her shoulders, adrenaline coursing through her veins. She suddenly felt as if she were running for the ball in field hockey or fighting for a teacher's approval in class. This was *her* rightful apartment, not someone else's. She imagined her furniture in the bedroom. She pictured herself wearing her Chanel poncho on Saturday mornings while

171

strolling to Starbucks. She could get a dog and hire one of those dog walkers that walked fifteen dogs at once. Earlier today, she'd looked into private schools in New York City if she didn't opt to graduate early.

When she glanced down at the blank piece of paper next to the laptop, she realized that she'd doodled 223 Perry Street over and over, in cursive and block letters and calligraphy. No other apartment would do.

'Please don't list it,' Spencer blurted out. 'I want it. I don't even have to look at it. What if I give you money now? Would that work?'

Michael paused. 'We could do that.' He sounded surprised. 'Believe me, you won't be disappointed. It's a wonderful find.' He clattered on his keyboard. 'Okay. We'll need some cash up front, enough for the first month's rent, security, and a broker fee. So we should get your mom on the phone. She's going to be your guarantor for the lease and authorize the transfer of the deposit, right?'

Spencer wiggled her fingers over the laptop keyboard. Olivia had made it clear that her husband, Morgan, was suspicious of people he didn't know. If she asked Olivia and Morgan for money, she risked losing his trust. She glanced at the screen. There was the folder in the right-hand corner of the desktop. *Spencer, College.*

She slowly opened the folder and then the PDF. All the information she needed was there. The account was in her name. Olivia had said that once Morgan met her, he'd love her. He'd probably reimburse this account ten times over.

'We don't need my mother to be involved,' Spencer said. 'I have an account in my name I'd like to use.'

'Okay,' Michael said, not missing a beat. He probably dealt with rich city kids with their own accounts all the time. Spencer read Michael the numbers on the screen, her voice quivering. Michael repeated them back to her, and then told her all he had to do was call the landlord and they'd be set. They made arrangements to meet in front of the building at 4 P.M. on Monday so Spencer could sign the lease and collect the keys. After that, the apartment would be hers.

'Great,' Spencer said. Then, she hung up her phone and stared blankly at the wall.

She had done it. She had *really done it*. In mere days, she wouldn't live here anymore. She'd be a New Yorker, away from Rosewood for good. Olivia would come home from Paris, and Spencer would be adjusted to city life. She imagined meeting Olivia and Morgan for casual dinners in their apartment and fancier dinners at the Gotham Bar and Grill and Le Bernardin. She pictured the group of new friends she'd make, people who loved going to art exhibitions and benefits and didn't give a shit that she had once been pursued by a bunch of jealous losers who called themselves A. When she thought of the boys she'd meet, she felt a twinge of sadness – none of them would be Andrew. But then she thought of how he'd treated her today and shook her head. She couldn't dwell on him right now. Her life was about to change.

Her head felt soft and hollow, as if she were drunk. Her limbs shook with glee. And it almost seemed like she was hallucinating – when she looked out the back window, she thought she saw sparkling beams of light bouncing off the trees, like a fireworks display just for her.

Wait a minute.

Spencer stood. The beams were from a flashlight, crisscrossing over the tree trunks. A figure crouched and started rummaging in the dirt. Whoever it was tried one spot, stopped, and then crab-walked a few paces to the left and tried another.

173

Her stomach dropped. It couldn't be a cop – they'd abandoned these woods days ago. She hefted up the window, curious as to whether the person was making any noise. To her horror, the window made a loud scraping sound against the jamb. Spencer winced, curling away.

The figure stopped, turning toward the barn. The flashlight beamed erratically, first right, then left, and then, for a moment, on the figure's face. Spencer saw the whites of two blue eyes. The edges of a black hooded sweatshirt. A few pale strands of familiar blond hair.

Spencer wrinkled her nose in disbelief. Was that … *Melissa*?

The figure flinched in the darkness, as if Spencer had spoken out loud. Before Spencer could determine if it really was her sister, the flashlight in the woods snapped off. A few twigs cracked. It appeared that whoever was out there was walking away. The footsteps grew fainter and fainter until Spencer couldn't distinguish them from the swishing trees.

When Spencer was certain the person was gone, she ran outside and crouched in the dirt. Sure enough, the soil was soft and loose. She felt around for a moment, touching only stones and sticks, but the ground still felt warm, as if someone else's hands had just been there. As she looked up, she heard a thin sound, far off in the trees. Goose bumps rose on her arms. It almost sounded like … a *giggle*.

But as Spencer cocked her head, the noise vanished, and she couldn't help but wonder if it had just been the wind.

20
Aria's Free Fall

That same afternoon, Aria met Jason outside Rocks and Ropes, an indoor rock-climbing facility a few miles outside Rosewood. 'After you,' Jason said, holding the front door.

'Thanks.' Aria swooned. She hitched up the slightly too-big spandex yoga tights she'd stolen from Meredith's closet, hoping that Jason wouldn't notice how baggy they were in the butt. Jason, on the other hand, looked comfortable and sexy in a long-sleeved gray T-shirt and Nike warm-up pants, as though he climbed rock walls all the time. Maybe he did.

Once inside, the light was fluorescent and harsh. Aggressive guitar rock blared through the speakers, and the high-ceilinged, rubbery-smelling room had thousands of colorful, plastic-looking outcroppings on the walls. Jason had asked Aria to Rocks and Ropes in a text message this morning, admitting he wasn't the type of guy to take girls to dinner and a movie. Really, Aria would have stood in line at the DMV with Jason if that was what he considered a date.

After signing in, they walked over to the big wall and looked around. Aria ogled a few girls as they scuttled up the side of the wall, harnesses tied tightly around their waists.

How could they stand being up that high? Just craning her neck gave Aria vertigo. She shuddered.

'Are you scared?' Jason asked.

Aria giggled nervously. 'I'm not that athletic.'

Jason smiled and took her hand. 'It's fun, I promise.'

Aria flushed with pleasure, thrilled Jason was touching her. She still had to pinch herself to make sure this was really happening.

One of the instructors, a dark-haired guy with a scruffy beard, came over with their gear, which included harnesses, helmets, and special climbing gloves. He asked which of them wanted to be hitched up first. Jason pointed to Aria. '*Madame.*'

'Such a gentleman,' she teased.

'My mom brought me up well,' Jason answered.

The instructor started to hook a harness around Aria's torso. When he walked off to find a different clamp, Aria turned to Jason. 'So how *is* your family?' she asked as casually as she could. 'Are they ... okay?'

Jason stared at a few climbers on the other side of the room for a long time. 'They're wrecked,' he said after a while. He raised his blue eyes to her and smiled sadly. 'We all are. But what can we do?'

Aria nodded, having no clue what to say. A's note from yesterday popped into her mind. *Big Brother is hiding something from you. And trust me ... you don't want to know what it is*. Aria hadn't forwarded the note to any of her friends, for fear they would jump to conclusions about Jason. A had to be messing with them – that was Old *and* New A's M.O., after all.

Aria assumed A was implying that Jason's secret had to do with his and Ali's 'sibling problems', as Jenna put it, but she wasn't buying it. There was no way Jason and Ali had had anything but a loving sibling relationship. Aria had tried to mine her memories for times when Jason had been mean to Ali, but she couldn't come up with a single incident. Instead, Jason seemed fiercely protective of his sister. Once, not long after they'd become friends, Aria and the others had been over at Ali's house for a sleepover. They were planning to give each other makeovers, and everyone had brought over their makeup bags to share – except for Emily, because she wasn't allowed to wear makeup yet. As they were oohing over Hanna's Dior eye shadow, Mrs DiLaurentis walked into the room. There was a frazzled look on her face.

'Ali, did you feed the cat a whole can of wet food?' Ali's mom asked. Ali looked at her blankly. Mrs DiLaurentis lowered her arms to her sides with a slap. 'Honey, you're supposed to mix dry food in, remember? And put a few drops of hairball medicine on top?' Ali bit her lip. Mrs DiLaurentis let out a groan and turned. 'You forgot that too? She's going to have hairballs all over the new basement carpet!'

Ali tossed Hanna's blush brush on the table. 'Would you *chill*? I'm in sixth grade now, and we have a lot of homework! Sorry if I'm a little too distracted to remember how I'm supposed to feed the cat!'

Mrs DiLaurentis had shaken her head, exasperated. 'Ali, you've been feeding the cat this way since third grade.' Then she stormed away.

An instant later, Jason appeared from the kitchen, a bag of pretzels in his hand. 'Mom's in a mood, huh?' he said gently. 'I can feed the cat for you for a while, if that helps.'

He touched Ali's shoulder, but Ali shook him off. 'Stop it. I'm fine.'

Jason recoiled, a wounded look on his face. Aria had wanted to leap up and throw her arms around him. Ali had

177

behaved the same way the day Time Capsule was announced, too – Jason had approached Ali and Ian in front of the bike racks, telling Ian to leave Ali alone, and Ali had shooed him away, mocking him for caring so much. Maybe Jason had sensed that Ian's feelings for Ali weren't exactly innocent and wanted to protect her. Maybe Ali *knew* Jason had sensed it and wanted him off her back. If Ali and Jason had sibling problems, maybe *Ali* was the one creating them, not the other way around.

Or what if *Jenna* was lying? Maybe Jenna had made up Ali and Jason having sibling problems. Perhaps that was why Jenna was standing at the edge of Aria's yard two days ago, a guilty look on her face. Maybe she wanted to tell Aria that what she'd told her in the art room a few months ago hadn't been quite the truth.

But why would Jenna lie? Could Jenna have something against Jason, some reason to turn the girls against him? Could *Jenna* be A?

'You're all set,' the instructor said to Aria, snapping her to the present. He was back, pointing to the large rope that was attached to both the ceiling *and* the middle of her waist. 'Do you need a lesson?'

'I'll teach her,' Jason said. The instructor nodded and went to get the clamps for Jason's tethers. Then Jason crept closer to Aria and poked her side. 'Don't look now,' he said in a low voice. 'But I think the old school nurse is here. I used to have nightmares about her.'

Aria glanced over her shoulder. Sure enough, a stumpy, bulldog-faced woman was standing in the lounge next to a neon-lit Mountain Dew machine. 'That's Mrs Boot!' Aria whispered.

Jason's eyes widened. 'She still works there?'

Aria nodded. 'Whenever I see her in the halls, my scalp

immediately itches. I'll never forget lining up in her office in elementary school for lice tests.'

'I *hated* that.' Jason shuddered. They turned back to Mrs Boot. She was scowling at the rock wall harshly, as if it were a Rosewood Day student feigning a fever. Then a little boy ran out of the locker room, straight into Mrs Boot's arms. The crusty old woman smiled slightly, and the two of them walked out of Rocks and Ropes together.

'I had to spend a lot of time in the nurse's office,' Jason murmured. 'Whenever I'd go in there, Mrs Boot would glower at me with her good eye. I once heard a rumor that her gaze was a laser beam that could melt your brain.'

Aria giggled. 'I heard that rumor too.' Then she frowned. 'Why were you at the nurse's office a lot?' She didn't recall Jason being particularly sickly – he was a star soccer player in the fall and played baseball in the spring.

'I wasn't sick,' Jason corrected. He flicked the little zipper on the pocket of his warm-up pants. 'I, um, went to the school psychologist. Dr Atkinson. Well, he asked that I call him Dave.'

'Oh,' Aria chirped, struggling to smile. Psychologists were fine, weren't they? In fact, Aria herself had asked her parents to send *her* to one when they first moved to Reykjavík – Ali had vanished just a few months before. Ella had suggested Aria do hatha yoga instead.

'It was my parents' idea.' Jason shrugged his shoulders. 'I had a hard time adjusting to the move to Rosewood in eighth grade.' He rolled his eyes. 'I was really shy, and my parents thought it would do me some good to talk to someone with an objective point of view. Dave wasn't so bad. Plus, talking to him got me out of class.'

'I know lots of people who went to Dave,' Aria said fast, although truthfully, she didn't know anyone. Maybe *this* was the big secret Jason was hiding. It was hardly anything to get panicked about.

The instructor returned, hitched Jason up, and walked away. Jason faced Aria and asked what type of climb she wanted to start on – easy, medium, or hard. Aria snorted. 'That's a pretty stupid question, don't you think?' She giggled.

'Just checking,' Jason said, grinning. He led her to the easy section of the wall and showed her how to place her left foot on one rock and pull herself with her right hand to the rock above it, climbing up a few feet to demonstrate. When Jason climbed, it looked easy. Aria stepped onto the first rock, her muscles twitching. She reached for the rock above it and pulled herself up. Amazingly, she didn't fall. Jason had his eyes on her the whole time. 'You're doing great!' he cried, grinning.

'That's what you say to all the girls,' Aria groaned. But she continued up a few more rocks. *Don't look down*, she repeated to herself. She used to get dizzy just standing on the edge of the low diving board at the local swimming pool.

'So you told me the other day that you just moved in with your dad and his girlfriend,' Jason called, keeping pace with her. 'What's that about?'

Aria reached for another rock. 'My parents separated when I moved back from Iceland,' she started, wondering how to word this. 'My dad had an affair with his old student. Now they're getting married. *And* she's pregnant.'

Jason glanced at her. 'Whoa.'

'It's weird. She's not much older than you.'

Jason made a face. 'When did they start seeing each other?'

'When I was in seventh grade,' Aria admitted. She scanned the rocks above her, looking for the best handhold. It was

180

nice that they were talking – it took her mind off how hard climbing was. 'I caught them kissing in my dad's car.' And then, maybe because she'd remembered the time Ali had snapped at Jason so heartlessly about the cat, she added, 'Your, um, sister ... she was with me. And she wouldn't let me hear the end of it.'

She peeked at Jason, wondering if she'd overstepped her bounds. He had a neutral expression on his face, one she couldn't gauge. 'I'm sorry,' she called. 'I shouldn't have said that.'

'No ... I get it. My sister was like that. She knew everyone's precise button to push.'

Aria hung on to the wall, suddenly too tired to move. 'You had a button, too?'

'Uh-huh. It was girls.'

'Girls?'

Jason nodded. 'Sometimes she used to tease me about girls. I could be ... awkward, I guess. She used to needle me about it.'

'She knew all of our weaknesses, all right,' Aria said. She looked up again, radiating with guilt. 'I still feel bad talking about her to you.'

Suddenly, Jason pushed off the wall, swinging freely from the tether. 'Come down to the ground for a minute,' he called. 'Slide down with your harness.'

Aria slid down as he instructed, landing clumsily on the mat. Jason studied her very seriously, and Aria wondered if she'd made a mistake bringing up Ali. But then he said, 'Maybe it's good we're talking about her. I mean, right now, Alison's this big elephant in the room that no one will discuss with me. When I'm at home, my parents don't bring her up. When I'm out with friends, they don't say a word. I know people are talking about her, but whenever they get around

181

me, they shut up. I know my sister had faults. I know some people didn't like her. Some people more than …' He mumbled something else and then trailed off, pressing his lips together tightly.

'What was that?' Aria asked, leaning forward.

Jason fluttered his hand, waving away what he'd just said. 'I'd like you to talk about Ali with me.'

Aria smiled, comforted. Talking about Ali with Jason would give her a whole new perspective on who Ali really was. She wondered if she should tell Jason about how Ali had spread rumors about him to Jenna Cavanaugh – or how Jenna had spread rumors about Jason to Aria. Or how Ian had reached out on IM, saying someone had forced him to flee. Or how New A had helped Ian escape.

Something else took hold of her. *This* was why A was trying to seed the idea that Jason was hiding something – A wanted to make Aria paranoid and scare her away. If Aria began dating Jason, it was pretty likely that she'd tell him not just that A was sending them notes, but that A was in on Ian's evil plan. The cops might not believe that A was real … but Jason probably would. This was his sister's murder they were talking about.

Aria curled her toes, furious that someone was yet again trying to manipulate her. Ian probably *had* done it, and now was crafting some elaborate game. She looked at Jason, ready to tell him everything.

'You climbing here?' a junior high-age boy interrupted, making Aria jump. He gestured to the spot on the wall that Aria was leaning against. Aria shook her head and moved out of the way. Then three girls strolled past, gazing suspiciously at Jason and Aria, as if they recognized them from the news. Even the music seemed quieter, as if everyone sensed an important conversation was happening.

182

Aria shut her mouth. This didn't seem like the right place to talk about the Ali and Ian stuff. Maybe she could tell Jason about it in the car going home, when they were alone.

Then she remembered the invitation that was wedged into the front pocket of her yak-fur bag, which she'd left with her and Jason's coats at the side of the wall. Still tethered, she tottered over to her bag and pulled it out. 'Do you have plans tomorrow?' she asked Jason.

'I don't think so. Why?'

'My mom has one of her paintings in the lobby of this new hotel.' She handed him the invitation. 'There's a fancy party tomorrow for the opening. My mom's going to be there with her new boyfriend, and I don't really like him. You would be a lovely distraction.' She tilted her head coquettishly.

Jason smiled back. 'I haven't been to a fancy party in quite a while.' He pulled the invitation closer and read it. Then his face clouded. His Adam's apple bobbed up and down.

'Is something wrong?' Aria asked.

'Is this some kind of joke?' Jason's voice was hoarse.

Aria blinked. 'W-what do you mean?'

'Because it's not funny,' Jason said, his eyes wide. He didn't look angry, exactly, more like ... scared.

'What's the matter?' Aria cried. 'I don't understand.'

Jason stared at her for a beat longer. His expression changed, becoming cagey and maybe even a bit disgusted, as if Aria was covered head to toe in leeches. Then, to her horror, he unhooked the ropes from his harness, pulled it off, strode over to their stuff, and put on his coat. 'I-I have to go.'

'What?' Aria tried to grab his arm, but she was still awkwardly tethered and couldn't figure out how to get the harness off. Jason wouldn't even look at her. Shoving his hands in his pockets, he breezed by the front desk, nearly bumping into a group of teenagers just coming in.

A few moments later, Aria finally managed to wriggle out of her harness. She struggled to put her coat on and then ran outside. There was a group of guys getting out of a Range Rover. A mother was holding a little girl's hand, helping her inside. Aria looked right, then left. 'Jason!' she called out. It was cold enough to see her breath. An SUV made a squealing left turn into the Wawa across the street. Jason was gone.

Aria stood under the lamp at the front of the facility and stared hard at the Radley invitation. It gave the address and time. A man named George Fritz had been the architect on the hotel's redesign. There was a list of featured artists, Ella's name among them. What on this invitation had gotten Jason so spooked? What did he mean, *Is this some kind of joke?* Did he not want to meet her mom? Was he embarrassed to be seen with her?

'Jason!' she called again, more weakly this time. Just then, she heard a peal of laughter. Aria looked around, startled and frightened. She didn't see anyone, but the laughter continued, like someone was laughing at her and her alone.

21
Nothing But The Truth

That same Friday night, Emily idled at the curb of Isaac's house, watching nervously as he slipped out the front door and jogged to her car. 'Hey!' he cried, then looked up at the sky. 'It looks like it might snow. Are you sure you want to go for a drive?'

Emily nodded quickly. Isaac had texted her after school, asking if she'd come over this evening. At first, Emily had thought it was a joke. But when he texted her again, asking why she hadn't answered him, she wondered if Mrs Colbert hadn't told him that she'd confronted Emily at Applebee's last night – or that she knew they'd slept together. Maybe Isaac was still under the impression that everything was fine.

But there was no way Emily could set foot in the Colberts' house, even if his parents were going to be at the Radley opening party run-through all evening. Emily wasn't the type of girl who disobeyed adults' orders, even if they seemed harsh and mean and unreasonable. Only, what was she supposed to do, never visit Isaac at his house again? Come up with crazy excuses every time he wanted her to stop in?

Last night, when Emily and Carolyn were settling into

their beds in their shared bedroom, Carolyn asked her again why she'd run out of Applebee's crying. Emily broke down and told her what Mrs Colbert had said. Carolyn sat up in bed, gaping in horror. 'Why would she say you disrespected her home?' she asked. 'Is it because of the Maya stuff?'

Emily shook her head. 'I doubt it.' She felt ashamed. If her parents caught Emily and Isaac doing it in Emily's bedroom, they'd probably serve him with a restraining order. 'Maybe I deserved it,' she mumbled.

They both fell silent, listening to the cornstalks in the field outside their house twisting in the wind. 'I don't know what I'd do if Topher's mom hated me,' Carolyn said into the darkness. 'I'm not sure we could be together.'

'I know,' Emily answered, a big lump in her throat.

'But you have to talk to Isaac about it,' Carolyn told her. 'You have to be honest.'

'Emily?'

She blinked. Isaac had buckled his seat belt and was ready to go. Her whole body throbbed. Isaac's hair was pushed off his face, and he had a dark green scarf wrapped many times around his neck. When he smiled, his white teeth gleamed. He leaned forward to kiss her, but she stiffened, half-expecting a siren to go off and Mrs Colbert to pop out from behind a bush, ready to yank him away.

She turned her head, pretending to fumble with her car keys. Isaac pulled back. Even in the dark car, Emily could see the little parenthesis that formed at the corner of Isaac's right eye whenever he was worried. 'You okay?' he asked.

Emily faced forward. 'Yep.' She shifted the Volvo into drive and pulled away from the curb.

'You excited for the Radley party tomorrow?' Isaac asked. 'I rented a tux this time. Better than my dad's old suit, right?' He chuckled.

Emily pulled in her bottom lip, astonished. He still assumed they could go to the Radley party? 'Sure,' she said.

'My dad's totally stressed about the catering, and he keeps ribbing me about how I'm not helping *yet again* because I've got a date.' Isaac grinned and poked her in the ribs.

Emily squeezed the steering wheel, her eyes welling. She couldn't take this anymore. 'So ... your parents haven't said anything about us not going together?' she blurted out.

Isaac looked at her curiously. 'Well, I've barely seen them the past few days, they've been so busy. But why would they have a problem with us going together? They were there when I asked you.'

A car passed going the other direction, its xenon headlights blinding. She said nothing.

'Are you sure you're okay?' Isaac asked again.

Emily swallowed hard. She tasted peanut butter in her mouth, the sensation she always got when she was about to have a fight-or-flight reaction. There was a Wawa off to the right, and before she knew what she was doing, she was jerkily pulling into the parking lot and driving around to the back near a green Dumpster. After she shoved the car into park, she rested her head on the steering wheel and let out a pent-up sob.

'Emily?' Isaac said, concerned. 'What is it?'

Tears blurred her vision. As much as she didn't want to say this, she knew she had to. She turned the blue ring he'd given her the other day around her finger. 'It's ... your mom.'

Isaac traced figure eights on her back. 'What about my mom?'

Emily ran her palms along the legs of her jeans, heaving a sigh. *Just be honest*, Carolyn had said. She could be honest with Isaac, couldn't she?

'She knows we ... you know. Slept together,' Emily

187

moaned. 'And she said all these weird things to me at dinner. Like, she kept insinuating that I was ... fast. Or loose. And then when I was doing the dishes later that night, I found a photo of you and me from the Rosewood Day benefit last week. Your mom had cut my head out of the picture. *Only* my head.' She swallowed hard, not brave enough to look up. 'Still, I thought maybe I was overreacting. I didn't want to say anything. But then, last night, I was at Applebee's with Carolyn. And ... your mom was *there*. She came up to me and said I could never come over to your house ever again.' Her voice broke on the word *again*.

The car was silent. Emily squeezed her eyes shut. She felt awful and relieved at the same time. It was a weight off her shoulders to say it out loud.

Finally, she looked at Isaac. His nose wrinkled, as if he had smelled something rancid from the Dumpster. A new worry filled her. What if this ruined Isaac's relationship with his mom for good?

He blew air out his cheeks. 'Emily, come on.'

Emily blinked. 'Sorry?'

Isaac shifted in his seat, facing her. His expression looked hurt and disappointed. 'My mom wouldn't cut your head out of a picture. That sounds like something a kid would do. And she would never confront you at Applebee's and say those things. Maybe you misunderstood.'

Emily's blood began to pulse. 'I didn't misunderstand.'

Isaac shook his head. 'My mom *loves* you. She told me so. She's happy we're together. She never said anything about banning you from the house. Don't you think she'd *tell* me that?'

Emily barked out a laugh. 'Maybe she didn't want to tell you because she wanted *me* to. She wanted me to be the bad guy. Which is exactly what's happening.'

Isaac was quiet for a long time, staring at his hands. The tips of his fingers were callused from years of playing guitar. 'My girlfriend last year did this exact same thing,' he said slowly. 'She said my family was telling her to stay away from me.'

'Maybe your mom was doing the same thing to her!' Emily cried.

Isaac shook his head. 'She told me later that she made it all up. She did it to get attention.' He gazed at her evenly, as if waiting for her to get his drift.

Emily's skin went from steaming hot to ice cold. 'What, like seeing Ian's dead body in the woods was a way to get attention?' she squeaked.

Isaac raised his hands, helpless. 'I'm not saying that. It's just ... I wanted to go out with someone who wasn't into drama. I thought you did too. Whoever I go out with has to like my family, not battle against them.'

'That's not what I'm doing!' Emily pleaded.

Isaac shoved open the passenger door and stepped out. Icy air swirled in, harsh against her bare skin. 'What are you doing?' Emily demanded.

He leaned over the open door, his mouth small and solemn. 'I should go home.'

'No!' Emily cried. She lurched out her own door and followed him across the parking lot. 'Come on!'

Isaac was walking toward the little wooded path that led from the Wawa lot to the street. He glanced over his shoulder. 'This is my mom you're talking about. Think about what you're saying. Think really hard.'

'I *have* thought about it!' Emily shouted. But Isaac kept going, not answering. She came to a stop in front of the store, going limp. Above her, the neon Wawa sign buzzed fiercely. There was a line of kids at the counter buying coffees and

189

sodas and candy. She waited for Isaac to turn back, but he didn't. Finally, she walked back to her car and got in. The inside of the Volvo smelled like the Colberts' detergent. The passenger seat was still warm from Isaac's butt. For at least ten minutes, she stared numbly at the Dumpster, not knowing what to make of what had happened.

A little chime went off inside her backpack. Emily swiveled around, reaching for her phone. Maybe it was Isaac, writing to apologize. And maybe she should apologize too. He and his mom were close, and she certainly didn't *want* to hate his family. Maybe she should've found another way to break the news instead of blindsiding him with it.

Emily opened the new text, swallowing a sniffle. It wasn't from Isaac.

Too distracted to decipher my clues? Go to your first love's old house and maybe it'll all make sense. – A

Emily glowered at the screen. She'd had it with these vague clues. What did A want?

She slowly pulled out of the Wawa parking lot, braking to let a Jeep full of high school boys cut in front of her. *Go to your first love's old house*. A obviously meant Ali. She'd take the bait; Ali's old neighborhood was only a few blocks away. What else did she have to do right now? It wasn't like she could bang on Isaac's door, begging for him to come back.

She turned onto a quiet road with acres of rolling farmland, tears still stinging her eyes. The stop sign to Ali's street came up fast. There was a WATCH CHILDREN sign at the entrance to the neighborhood. Years ago on a warm, sticky summer night, Ali and Emily had decorated the sign with smiley-face stickers they'd bought at a party store. They were all gone now.

Ali's old house loomed at the end of the street, the Ali shrine a dark, shadowy lump at the curb. Maya's family lived in the house now. A few of the lights were on, including the one in Ali's old bedroom – Maya's *new* bedroom. As Emily stared up at it, Maya appeared, almost as though she'd known Emily was going to be there. Emily gasped, shrank away from the window, gripped the steering wheel, and peeled around the cul-de-sac. Once she was in front of Spencer's driveway, she pulled over, too overcome to go on.

Then she saw a flicker of something to her right. Someone in a white T-shirt was standing in the front window of the Cavanaughs' house.

Emily turned off the headlights. Whoever was in the window was tall and somewhat broad, probably a guy. His face was obscured by a large, square-shaped floor lamp. Suddenly, Jenna appeared next to him. Emily sucked in her breath. Jenna's dark hair cascaded down her shoulders. She wore a black T-shirt and plaid pajama pants. Her dog sat next to her, scratching his neck with his hind leg.

Jenna turned and spoke to the guy. She spoke for a long time, and then he said something back. Jenna nodded, listening. The guy waved his arms, as if Jenna could see his gestures. His face was still hidden. Jenna's posture got defensive. The guy spoke again, and Jenna lowered her head, as if ashamed. She brushed a few strands of hair away from her big Gucci sunglasses. She said something else, her face contorted with an expression Emily couldn't rightly determine. Sorrow? Worry? Fear? Then Jenna walked away, her dog following.

The guy rubbed his hands through his hair, obviously flustered. Then the living room lamp snapped off. Emily leaned forward, squinting hard, but she couldn't see anything. She looked around at Jenna's yard. There were still wood blocks fastened to the tree trunk, makeshift steps to get into Toby's old tree house. Mr Cavanaugh had taken the tree house down shortly after the firework blinded Jenna. It was amazing that after all this time, the Cavanaughs still blamed Toby for blinding his sister. In truth, it had been Ali who had done it. And it had been Jenna who had wanted to set up the prank to get rid of Toby for good.

The Cavanaughs' front door opened, and Emily ducked again. The guy from the living room stomped down the front steps to the dark front path. When the motion-sensor light above the garage doors snapped on, he froze, startled. Emily saw him head-on, flooded with light. He wore running sneakers and a heavy down parka. Both hands were curled into tight, angry fists. When Emily's eyes got to his face, her stomach dropped to the bottom of her boots. He was glaring right at her. She instantly realized who it was. 'Oh my God,' she whispered. That shaggy blond hair, those bow-shaped lips, those stark blue eyes, still locked with hers.

It was Jason DiLaurentis.

Emily shifted into drive and gunned down the street. Only at the corner did she turn her lights on again. And then she heard her cell phone beep. She rifled through her purse, grabbed it, and looked at the screen. *One new text message*.

What do you think HE'S so angry about? – A

192

22
Nothing Like An Ultimatum To Kick Off The Weekend

There it was. The big Victorian house at the corner of the cul-de-sac, the one with the rose trellises along the fence and the wraparound teak deck in the back. Yellow *Do Not Cross* police tape was supposed to be around the half-dug hole in the backyard ... only there was no tape anywhere. As a matter of fact, there wasn't a *hole* anywhere. The yard was a wide, flat expanse of freshly mown grass, untouched by backhoes or bulldozers.

Hanna looked down. She was on her old mountain bike, the one she hadn't touched since she got a driver's license. And her hands looked swollen. Her jeans strained across her butt. Her thighs bulged. A strand of poop-brown hair fell over her eyes. She ran her tongue over her teeth and felt rough, metal braces. When she gazed into Ali's backyard, she saw Spencer crouched behind the raspberry bushes that bordered Ali's house and hers. Spencer's hair was shorter and a little lighter, the way it looked in sixth grade. There was

193

skinny, baby-faced Emily behind the tomato vines, her eyes darting nervously back and forth. Aria, with big pink streaks in her hair and wearing a freaky German tunic, ducked next to a big oak.

Hanna shuddered. She knew why they were here – they wanted to steal Ali's flag. This was the Saturday after Time Capsule had begun.

The four girls marched to one another, annoyed. Then they heard a *thud*, and the back door opened. Hanna and the others crouched behind the trees while Jason stormed across the yard. The patio door slammed again. Ali stood on the porch, her hands on her hips, her blond hair spilling down her shoulders, her lips pink and shiny. 'You can come out,' she called.

Sighing, Ali marched across the yard, her wedge heels sinking into the wet grass. When she approached Hanna and the others, she reached into her pocket and pulled out a shiny piece of blue cloth. It looked exactly like the piece of the Time Capsule flag Hanna had found at Steam a few days ago.

But hadn't Ali lost her flag? Hanna looked at the others, confused, but her old friends didn't seem to notice that anything was amiss.

'So this is how I've decorated it,' Ali explained, pointing at the different drawings on the flag. 'Here's the Chanel logo. And this is the manga frog, and here's the field hockey girl. And don't you love this Louis Vuitton pattern?'

'The flag looks like a purse,' Spencer oohed.

Hanna regarded them uneasily. Something felt scrambled. This wasn't happening like it was supposed to. And then, Ali snapped her fingers, and Hanna's old friends froze. Aria's hand hung motionless, almost touching Ali's flag. A few strands of Emily's hair were suspended in air, caught by a

194

breeze. Spencer had an odd expression on her face, something between a fake smile and a grimace.

Hanna wiggled her fingers. She was the only one not frozen. She stared at Ali, her heart pounding hard.

Ali smiled sweetly. 'You're looking much better, Hanna. Completely recovered, huh?'

Hanna gazed down at her too-tight jeans and ran her hands through her limp hair. *Recovered* wasn't the word she'd have chosen. Her *recovery* from loser to diva wouldn't happen for another few years.

Ali shook her head, noting Hanna's confusion. 'From the accident, silly. Don't you remember me from the hospital?'

'H-hospital?'

Ali brought her face close to Hanna's. 'They say people should always talk to coma patients. They can hear. Did you hear me?'

Hanna felt dizzy. Suddenly, she was back in her hospital room at Rosewood Memorial, where the EMTs had taken her after her car accident. There was a round, bright fluorescent light above her head. She could hear the *hiss* of the various machines that monitored her vital signs and fed her intravenously. In the hazy space between coma and consciousness, Hanna thought she saw someone looming over her bed. Someone who looked startlingly like Ali. '*It's okay*,' the girl lilted, her voice exactly the same as Ali's. '*I'm okay*.'

Hanna glowered at Ali. 'That was a dream.'

Ali raised a flirtatious eyebrow as if to say, *was it?* Hanna glanced at her old friends. They were still immobile. She wished they'd unfreeze – she felt way too alone with Ali, as if they were the only two people left in the whole world.

Ali waved her Time Capsule flag in Hanna's face. 'See this? You need to find it, Hanna.'

Hanna shook her head. 'Ali, your piece is lost forever. Remember?'

'Uh-uh,' Ali protested. 'It's still here. And if you find it, I'll tell you all about it.'

Hanna widened her eyes. 'All about ... *what*?'

Ali put a finger to her lips. 'The two of them.' She cackled eerily.

'Two of them ... what?'

'They know everything.'

Hanna blinked. 'Huh? Who?'

Ali rolled her eyes. 'Hanna, you are so slow.' She stared right at her. '*Sometimes, I don't notice I'm singing.* Remember that?'

'What do you mean?' Hanna asked, desperate. 'Singing ... what?'

'Come on, Hanna.' Ali looked bored. She tipped her head to the sky, thinking for a moment. 'Okay, how about ... go fish?'

'Go ... fish?' Hanna repeated. 'The card game?'

Ali grunted, frustrated. 'No. Go *fish*.' She waved her arms, trying to make Hanna get it. 'Go fish!'

'What are you talking about?' Hanna cried desperately.

'GO FISH!' Ali screamed. 'Go fish! Go fish!' She repeated it over and over, like it was the only thing she could say. When she grazed Hanna's cheek with her fingers, Hanna's skin felt sticky and wet. Hanna touched her face, alarmed. When she pulled her hands away, they were covered in blood.

Hanna shot up, her eyes popping open. She was in her bedroom. Pale morning light streamed through the windows. It was Saturday morning – but a Saturday morning in eleventh grade, not sixth. Dot was standing on Hanna's pillow, licking Hanna's face. She touched her cheek. There wasn't blood there, just doggie drool.

196

You need to find it, Hanna. If you find it, I'll tell you all about it.

Hanna groaned, rubbed her eyes, and reached for her Time Capsule flag, which was smoothed out on her nightstand. It was a stupid dream, end of story.

She heard voices in the hallway, first her father's joking tone, then Kate's shrill laugh. Hanna grabbed a handful of sheets and squeezed. That was *it*. Kate might have stolen Hanna's father, but she wasn't stealing Mike too.

Abruptly, the urgent images from her dream faded away. Hanna bolted out of bed and pulled on her snug-fitting cashmere sweaterdress. In English class yesterday, she'd overheard Noel Kahn tell Mason Byers that the lacrosse team was meeting for a weekend workout at Philly Sports Club. She had a feeling wherever Noel went, Mike would go too. She hadn't yet gotten back to Mike about bringing Kate to the Radley party because she hadn't known what to say. Now she did.

There was one girl Mike should be exclusive with – Hanna. It was time to kick Kate out of the picture for good.

Philly Sports was in the section of the King James Mall that contained the *non*-luxe stores, ghetto places like Old Navy and Charlotte Russe and – *shudder* – JCPenney. Hanna hadn't set foot in here for years – acrylic-blend fabrics, mass-market T-shirts, and designer collections by has-been celebutantes gave her hives.

She parked the Prius and forcefully hit the lock button three times, taking stock of the rusted Honda next to her. As she walked through the parking lot, her iPhone blinked, indicating she had a text. She reached for it, her stomach churning. Surely A couldn't have found her, right?

197

The text was just from Emily. *U around? I got another note. We need to talk.*

Hanna slid the phone back in her pocket, biting her lip hard. She knew she should call Emily back – *and* tell her about how strangely Wilden had behaved when he drove Hanna home from running yesterday – but she was busy right now. Still, the dream she'd had this morning drifted back to her. What was her brain trying to tell her? Did Ali know where her flag had gone? Could it be true that there was something on Ali's flag that hinted at what had happened to her? And then Ali said, *Sometimes, I don't notice I'm singing*, expecting Hanna to know what she meant. Was that something Ali used to say, or was it something someone used to say to Ali? Hanna couldn't remember either way. She'd even culled through the minor characters in Ali's life, like the exchange student from Holland who'd given Ali a pair of wooden shoes as a token of his affection, the greasy-haired Jet Ski operator in the Poconos who always told Ali he'd 'warmed up the seat just for her', or Mr Salt, the school's only male librarian, who always told Ali he would bring in his first-edition *Harry Potter*s especially for her if she ever wanted to read them – *gag*. Hanna couldn't remember anyone saying anything creepy about singing. The phrase was somehow familiar, but it was probably just a stupid line from one of Kate's show tunes, or some dorky slogan on a Rosewood Day Masterworks Choir bumper sticker.

The techno music inside the gym assaulted Hanna's ears before she opened the front door. A girl in a perky pink bra top and black yoga pants beamed from behind the gym's front desk. 'Welcome to Philly Sports!' she chirped. 'Can you sign in, please?' She held up a contraption that looked like a price scanner to check Hanna's membership.

'I'm a guest,' Hanna answered.

'Oh!' The girl had wide, unblinking eyes, a round face, and a dopey expression. She reminded Hanna of the Tickle Me Elmo doll that belonged to her six-year-old twin neighbors. 'Can you fill out the guest form, then?' the receptionist tweeted. 'And it costs ten dollars to work out for the day.'

'No, thanks!' Hanna sang, breezing right past. As if she'd ever, *ever* pay to use this dump. The front-desk girl let out a small, indignant squeak, but Hanna didn't turn. Her high heels clicked as she passed the shop that sold spandex shorts, neoprene iPod holders, and sports bras, and the large shelves where the towels were kept. Hanna sniffed haughtily. This shithole didn't even have a smoothie bar? People probably peed in the locker room showers, too.

Bass from the piped-in music throbbed in Hanna's ears. Across the room, a stick-thin girl with veiny arms whirled frantically on an elliptical machine. A guy with wet, curly hair mopped sweat off a treadmill. Hanna heard the clanging of barbells in the distance. Sure enough, the entire Rosewood Day lacrosse team was in the corner by the free weights. Noel was doing arm curls in front of a mirror, admiring himself. James Freed was making faces while balancing on a BOSU ball. And Mike Montgomery was lying down on the bench press, wrapping his hands around the bar, getting ready to lift.

Jackpot.

Hanna waited until Mike had brought the bar to his chest, then walked right up and shooed away Mason Byers, Mike's spotter. 'I can take over from here.' Then she leaned over Mike and smiled.

Mike's eyes bugged out. 'Hanna!'

'Hello,' Hanna said coolly.

Mike started to lift the bar back up to return it to the

stand, but Hanna stopped him. 'Not so fast,' she said. 'I have something to discuss with you first.'

A few beads of sweat dotted Mike's forehead, and his arms shook. 'What?'

Hanna tossed her hair over her shoulder. 'So. If you want to go out with me, you can't go out with anyone else. Including Kate.'

Mike let out a grunt. His biceps started to wobble. He looked at her pleadingly. 'Please. I'm going to drop this on my chest.' His face began to turn red.

Hanna made a *tsk* sound. 'I thought you were stronger than that.'

'*Please*,' Mike begged.

'Promise me first,' Hanna urged. She leaned over a little farther, offering him more of a view down her dress.

Mike's eyes slid to the right. The tendons in his neck popped out. 'Kate asked me to go to the Radley party before I knew you wanted to be exclusive and whatever. I can't *uninvite* her.'

'Yes, you can,' Hanna growled. 'It's easy.'

'I have an idea,' Mike gasped. 'Let me put this down, and I'll tell you.'

Hanna stepped aside and let him return the bar. He let out a huge sigh, sat up, and stretched. Hanna was surprised to see how defined his arms were. She'd been right the other day when she'd guessed that Mike would look way better post-shower than Officer Wilden.

She laid down a towel on an empty leg-press bench next to him and sat down. 'Okay. Spill it.'

Mike grabbed a towel that was sitting on the floor next to the bench press and mopped off his face. 'I can be bought, if you're interested. If you do something for me, I'll uninvite Kate.'

'What do you want?'

'Your flag.'

'No way.' She shook her head.

'Okay, then take me to prom,' Mike said.

Hanna's mouth hung open, temporarily stunned. 'The prom's four months away.'

'Hey, a guy needs to lock down his date early.' Mike shrugged. 'It'll give me time to find the *perfect* pair of shoes.' He fluttered his eyelashes girlishly.

Hanna ran her hands over the back of her neck, trying to tune out the other lax players, who were catcalling her from the weight circuit. If Mike wanted Hanna to take him to her prom, that meant that he liked Hanna best, right? And that meant she had won. A smile spread across her lips. *Take that, bitch*. She couldn't wait to see Kate's face when she told her.

'Okay,' she said. 'I'll take you to my prom.'

'Nice,' Mike said. He glanced at his wet T-shirt. 'I'd feel you up right now to celebrate, but I don't want to get you all sweaty.'

'*Gracias*,' Hanna simpered, rolling her eyes. She sauntered out of the weight room, making exaggerated movements with her hips. 'I'll pick you up tonight at eight,' she called over her shoulder. 'Alone.'

Tickle Me Elmo girl was waiting for Hanna by the snack bar. A bald man with tattooed biceps and a handlebar mustache loomed behind her. 'Miss, if you want to use this gym, you're going to have to pay a guest fee,' the girl said haltingly. Her cheeks matched the bright red sweatband on her forehead. 'And if you don't want to do that, then—'

'I'm done here,' Hanna cut her off, skirting around both of them. The girl and her bouncer whirled around, watching her go. Neither moved. Neither stepped forward to apprehend her. And that, of course, was because she was Hanna Marin. And she was unstoppably, unbelievably fabulous.

23

Yearbook Memories To Last A Lifetime

That afternoon, a UPS truck pulled up to the curb of Aria's father's new house. The deliveryman, wearing blue long underwear under his short-sleeved brown UPS shirt and shorts, handed Aria a box. Aria thanked him and looked at the mailing label. *Organic Baby Booties.* The return address was from Santa Fe, New Mexico. Who knew such little baby booties could leave such an adult-size carbon footprint?

Her phone beeped, and she reached into the pocket of her bulky-knit sweater coat to grab it. She'd received a text from Ella. *Are you coming to the Radley party tonight?* Another text quickly followed. *I hope you can … I've missed you!* And then another. *It would mean so much!*

Aria sighed. Ella had been texting Aria like this all morning, begging her for an answer. If Aria said she didn't want to go to the Radley party, Ella would inevitably ask why, and then what would Aria do? Tell her that she didn't want to be within six feet of her creepy boyfriend? Concoct a lie, which might make her mom think she didn't want to support her art career? It was bad enough that Aria hadn't been to Ella's house even once this week. There was no way out of it –

she'd have to suck it up and deal with Xavier as best she could. If only Jason were coming with her.

Her phone beeped again. Aria clicked on the new message, expecting it to be another missive from Ella. Instead, it was an e-mail. The sender's name was Jason DiLaurentis.

Aria's heart leapt. She opened the note fast. *Listen. I've been thinking*, Jason wrote. *I overreacted at Rocks and Ropes yesterday. I want to explain. Want to meet me at my house in an hour?*

Beneath it was his address in Yarmouth. *Don't go in the regular entrance*, Jason explained. *I'm up the steps in the apartment above the garage.*

Sounds good, Aria wrote back. She hugged herself, giddy and relieved. So there *was* an explanation for this. Maybe Jason didn't hate her.

Her phone rang once more. Aria glanced at the screen. It was Emily. After a reluctant pause, Aria answered.

'I need to talk to you,' Emily said in an urgent voice. 'It's about Jason.'

Aria groaned. 'You're jumping to conclusions. Ali lied to Jenna about him.'

'Don't be so sure.'

Emily was about to say something else, but Aria cut her off. 'I wish I'd never told you what Jenna said. It's caused nothing but trouble.'

'But ...' Emily protested. 'It was the truth.'

Aria smacked her hand to her forehead. 'Emily, you have Ali on *such* a pedestal. She was a lying, conniving, manipulative bitch – to me, to Jason, and to you too. Deal with it.'

Then Aria hit end, dropped her phone into her bag, and walked back inside for the keys to the Subaru. It was maddening how clouded Emily's judgment was. If she even considered the notion that Ali had lied to Jenna about her brother just to get Jenna to spill her secrets, Ali would no longer be the perfect girl of Emily's dreams. It was easier for Emily to believe that Jason was the bad one, even though there was nothing supporting that whatsoever.

It was funny how love could make people believe anything.

The DiLaurentises' new house was on a quiet, pretty street, far away from the grungy Yarmouth train station. The first thing Aria noticed were the leaf-shaped wind chimes hanging from the front porch – they'd been on the front porch at Ali's old house, too. When Aria used to stand on Ali's welcome mat, waiting for Ali to come downstairs, she'd always make the chimes clang together, trying to compose a song.

The driveway was empty, and the main house looked dark, the curtains pulled shut and the lights turned off. The structure that housed the three-car garage and Jason's second-floor apartment was separated by a low stone wall, and on the other side of that was a high wrought-iron fence. Surprisingly, there weren't any Ali shrines in the yard or at the street – but then, maybe the DiLaurentises had asked the media to keep quiet about them living here. And maybe, amazingly, the media had respected their wishes.

Aria started up the driveway toward the garage, an excited burn in her stomach. Then she heard a *clink* and a loud *woof*. A Rottweiler ran out from the narrow space between the garage and the wrought-iron fence, dragging a long metal tie-out chain around its neck.

Aria jumped back. Froth sprayed from the dog's mouth. Its body was thick and sturdy, all muscle. 'Shh,' she tried to say, but it came out barely more than a whisper. The dog growled viciously, no doubt smelling her paralyzing fear. She glanced desperately at the apartment on the garage's second floor. Jason would come down and help her, wouldn't he? But there weren't any lights on up there, either.

Aria splayed her hands out in front of her, trying to appear calm, but it only seemed to rile up the dog more, making it snort and plant its feet and bare its long, sharp teeth. Aria let out another helpless whimper and stepped back again. Her hip hit something hard, and she squawked, startled. She had bumped smack into the railing of the stairs to the apartment. With horror, she realized the dog had cornered her – the stone wall behind her that separated the garage from the main house was too high to scale quickly, and the dog was blocking the narrow path that led to the backyard as well as the rest of the driveway. The only possible route to safety was up the wooden garage steps to Jason's apartment.

Aria swallowed hard and dashed up, her heart beating like mad. The dog scurried up behind her, his paws slipping on the wet wood stairs. She pounded on the door. 'Jason!' she screamed. No answer. Frantic, Aria wiggled Jason's doorknob. It was locked.

'What the hell?' she cried, flattening herself against the door. The dog was only a few stairs away. Aria spied an open window next to the door. Slowly, she inched her fingers toward the windowsill, pushing the window open wider. Taking a deep breath, she whirled around and squeezed through. Her back hit something soft. A mattress. She pulled the window shut. The dog barked and scratched at Jason's door. Aria's chest heaved in and out as she listened to her heart pound. Then she looked around. The room was dark and empty. There was a coatrack near the door, but the hooks were bare.

Aria reached into her pocket for her phone and dialed Jason's number. It went immediately to voice mail. Aria hung

206

up, laid the phone on the bed, and stood. The dog was still barking; she didn't dare try to leave.

The apartment was basically a big studio divided into a bedroom, a dining area, and a small TV nook. There was a bathroom at the far end of the room, and a bunch of book-shelves off to the right. She walked around the room, inspecting the Hemingway, Burroughs, and Bukowski books on Jason's shelf. He had a little print of a drawing by Egon Schiele, one of Aria's favorite artists. She crouched down and ran her finger along the spines of his DVDs, noting the many foreign films. There were pictures on his little kitchen island, many of which looked like they'd been taken at Yale. Some were of a petite, smiling girl with dark hair and dark-framed glasses. In one of the photos, they both wore matching Yale T-shirts. In another, they were at what looked like a football game, holding red cups of beer. In another, she was kissing him on the cheek, her nose squished into his face.

Bile rose to Aria's throat. Maybe this was the secret A had told her about. But why had Jason asked her to come over? To make it clear that he only liked Aria as a friend? She shut her eyes, limp with disappointment.

As she returned to the bookshelf, she noticed a bunch of Rosewood Day yearbooks, lined up by year. One stuck out slightly more than the others, as if it had just been leafed through. Aria pulled it out and looked at the cover. It was from four years ago, the year Jason had graduated. The year Ali had gone missing.

She opened it slowly. The yearbook smelled like dust and old ink. She flipped through the senior pictures, hunting for Jason's photo. He wore a black suit, and gazed at a far-off point behind the photographer. His mouth was very straight and thoughtful, and his blond hair grazed his shoulders. She ran her fingers along Jason's nose and eyes. He looked so

207

young and innocent. It was hard to believe how much he'd gone through between then and now.

A few pages later, she found Melissa Hastings, Spencer's sister, who looked nearly the same as she did today. Someone had written something above her photo in red ink, but had then crossed it out so heavily Aria couldn't make out any of the words. Ian Thomas's picture was almost last. His wavy hair was longer, too, and his face was a little thinner. He was smiling his signature crinkly Ian Thomas smile, the one that used to assure all of Rosewood that he was the smartest, most handsome guy around – the one who would always have good luck. When this picture was taken, Ian had been fooling around with Ali. Aria shut her eyes, shuddering. The idea of them together was so wrong.

At the bottom of the page was another picture of Ian, a candid of him sitting in a classroom with his mouth slightly open and his hand raised. Someone had drawn a penis next to his mouth and devil horns on top of his curly head. There was a message written beneath the photo in black ink. The handwriting was small and lopsided.

Hey, dude. Cheers to beer bongs at the Kahns', the time we nearly wrecked Trevor's car, to four-wheeling on the weekends behind the property, and that time in Yvonne's basement … you know what I mean. There was another arrow drawn to Ian's head. *I can't believe what that asshole did. My offer still stands. Later, Darren.*

Aria held the book outstretched. *Darren?* As in Wilden? Licking her finger, she flipped a page and found his picture. His hair stood up in spikes, and he had the same leering look on his face as he had the day Aria caught him stealing twenty dollars from a girl's locker.

Were Wilden and Jason friends? Aria had never seen them

208

together in school. And what did Wilden mean, *I can't believe what that asshole did. My offer still stands*?

'What the hell?'

The yearbook slipped from Aria's fingers, making a dull thud as it hit the floor. Jason was standing in the doorway. He wore a bright red scarf and a black leather jacket. The dog was nowhere to be seen. Aria had been so intrigued by the yearbook, she hadn't even heard him walk up the stairs.

'Oh,' she breathed out.

Jason walked over to Aria jerkily, his nostrils flaring. 'How did you get in?'

'Y-you weren't here,' Aria squeaked, starting to tremble. 'Your dog broke free ... and he cornered me. I couldn't even go back to my car. The only way to get away from him was to run up the stairs and squeeze through the window.'

Jason's lips parted. '*What* dog?'

Aria pointed out the window. 'The ... the Rottweiler.'

'We don't have a Rottweiler.'

Aria stared at him. The dog had been dragging a heavy chain. She'd assumed he'd broken free from his tie-out post ... but maybe someone had cut his chain instead. Come to think of it, the dog hadn't barked once since she'd gotten inside. A horrible thought began to take shape in her mind.

'You didn't send me that e-mail this morning?' she said shakily. 'You didn't ask me to meet you here?'

Jason's eyes narrowed. 'I never would've told you to meet me here.'

The floorboards squeaked as Aria took a step back. How could she have been so stupid? Of course that e-mail she'd received this morning hadn't been from Jason. She'd been so relieved to hear from him, she hadn't remembered that he didn't have her e-mail address until this very moment. The note had been from ... someone else. Someone who had

209

known when Jason wouldn't be home. Someone who maybe even orchestrated sending a strange dog to chase her into his apartment. She gazed at Jason, her heart beginning to pound.

'Did you come in here only, or did you go into the main house, too?' Jason demanded.

'J-just here.'

Jason loomed over her, his jaw clenched. 'Are you telling me the truth?'

Aria bit her lip. Why did it matter? 'Of course.'

'Get out,' Jason barked. He stepped aside and pointed at the door.

Aria didn't move. 'Jason,' she stated. 'I'm sorry I came in here. It was a misunderstanding. Can we please talk?'

'Get. Out.' Jason whipped his arm to the side, knocking a bunch of books off the bookshelf. A glass plaque fell too, breaking into sharp, angry shards. 'Get out!' Jason roared again. Aria ducked and let out a trapped, terrified wail. Jason's face had transformed. His eyes were wide, the corners of his lips were pulled back, and even his voice sounded different. Lower. Meaner. Aria didn't recognize him at all.

She rushed out the door and bolted down the steps, slipping a few times on some of the wet treads. Her cheeks were streaked with tears. Her lungs burned with sobs. She fumbled for her car keys and threw herself into the front seat, as if something was chasing her.

When she looked in the rearview mirror, her breath caught in her throat. Far off in the distance, she saw two shadowy shapes of a person and a dog – a Rottweiler? – slipping safely into the woods.

24
Spencer, New Yorker

Spencer leaned back in her plushy seat aboard the Amtrak Acela train to New York, watching the conductor sway through the car taking tickets. Even though it was only Saturday, and even though Michael Hutchins, the Realtor, had said the landlord was using the weekend to clean out her brand-new Perry Street apartment, Spencer couldn't wait until Monday afternoon to see it. She might not be able to get inside the place today, but that didn't matter – merely sitting on the stoop, checking out the stores on her block, and getting a cappuccino at her soon-to-be-local Starbucks would be enough. She wanted to hit the furniture shops in Chelsea and on Fifth Avenue and put a few things on hold. She was eager to sit in a café and read *The New Yorker*, now that she would soon *be* one.

Perhaps this was what Ian felt once he'd escaped from Rosewood, free from his troubles, eager to start over. Where was Ian now? Rosewood? Or had he wised up and skipped town? She thought again about the person she'd seen in the woods outside the barn last night. It had definitely *looked* like Melissa ... but wasn't she in Philly? Perhaps Ian had left something behind after his dead-body stunt, something he'd asked Melissa to retrieve. But then, did that mean Melissa knew something about where he was and what he was doing? Maybe she knew who A was too. If only Melissa would call Spencer back – she wanted to ask her sister if she knew anything about the photos Emily had received. What did a photo of Ali, Naomi, and Jenna have to do with a photo of Wilden in church? And why hadn't Aria or Hanna received any missives from A, just Spencer and Emily? Was A focusing on them first? Were they in more danger than the others? And if Spencer moved to New York City, would she finally leave this A nightmare behind? She hoped so.

The train descended into a tunnel, and the passengers began to stand. 'Penn Station next,' a conductor's voice blared over the loudspeaker. Spencer grabbed her canvas shoulder bag and got in line with the others. When she emerged into the great hall, she looked around. The signs to the subways, the taxis, and the exits were a jumble. Pulling her purse close to her side, she followed the crowd up a long elevator to the street. Cabs jammed the broad avenue. Lights flashed in her face. The gray buildings rose into the sky.

Spencer flagged down a cab. 'Two twenty-three Perry Street,' she told the driver when she got in. The driver nodded, then veered into traffic, turning up the sports station on the radio. Spencer jiggled up and down giddily, wanting to tell him that she *lived* here, that she was going to her brand-new apartment, and that it was right around the corner from her mom's.

The cab driver ambled down Seventh Avenue and turned into the mazelike streets of the West Village. When he took a right onto Perry, Spencer sat up straighter. It *was* a beautiful street. Old, well-maintained brownstones lined each side. A girl about Spencer's age in a gorgeous winter white wool coat and a big fur hat passed, walking a labradoodle on a leash. The cab crept by a gourmet cheese shop, a store that sold musical instruments, and a quaint school, its tiny playground behind a polished iron fence. Spencer studied the printouts she'd made of the photos Michael Hutchins had sent the other day. Her future home might just be on the very next block. She scanned the street in anticipation.

'Miss?' The cab driver swiveled around, eyeing her. Spencer jumped. 'Did you say two twenty-three Perry?'

'Two twenty-three Perry, that's right.' Spencer had the address memorized.

The driver peered out the window. He wore thick glasses and had a pen tucked behind his ear. 'There is no two twenty-three Perry. It would be in the Hudson.'

Sure enough, they were at the very west end of Manhattan. Across the West Side Highway was a promenade, full of walkers and bikers. Beyond that was the Hudson River. Beyond *that* was New Jersey.

'Oh.' Spencer frowned. She rifled through her notes. Michael hadn't included the address in his e-mail, nor could she find the doodle from the other day. 'Well, maybe I got the address wrong. You can let me off here.'

She thrust a couple of bills at the driver and got out. The cab took a right at the light, and Spencer whirled around, puzzled. She started walking east, crossing Washington, then Greenwich. Michael had told her that the apartment was right around the corner from Marc Jacobs, which was at Perry and Bleecker. The numbers of the buildings around it were 92 Perry. Eighty-four Perry. Had the apartment's address been one of those?

She kept walking up Perry to make sure, but the numbers on the apartment buildings kept going down, not up. She made sure to look at each building carefully, trying to match

213

it with the building from the photos, but none looked quite right. Eventually, she hit the intersection of Perry Street and Greenwich Avenue. The street ended in a T. Across the street, Perry was nowhere to be seen – there was a restaurant called Fiddlesticks Pub & Grill instead.

Spencer's heart began to race. It felt as if she'd been plopped into a reccurring dream she'd had since second grade, the one where a teacher announced a surprise test, and while the other students eagerly began to fill in the answers, Spencer couldn't even decipher the questions.

She pulled out her cell phone, trying to keep calm, and dialed Michael's number. There was obviously an explanation for this.

A recording of an operator's voice blared through the receiver – the number she had dialed had been disconnected. Spencer dug around in her bag and found Michael's card. She keyed in his number again, repeating it back to herself to make sure she hadn't transposed any digits. There was the same recorded message. Spencer held the phone outstretched, pain radiating at her temples.

Maybe he changed phone numbers, she told herself.

Then, she dialed Olivia's number. But Olivia's phone just rang and rang. Spencer held her finger on the end button for a long time. This didn't necessarily mean anything, either – only that Olivia must not have an international calling plan.

A woman pushing a baby carriage veered out of her way, struggling to hold a bunch of grocery bags upright. When Spencer looked down the street, she noticed Olivia's new apartment building gleaming in the distance. She started walking for it, invigorated anew. Perhaps Olivia had another number for Michael somewhere. Perhaps the doorman would let Spencer upstairs for a little peek into Olivia's penthouse.

A woman in a bright blue wool coat exited the apartment building's revolving doors. Two more people went in, carrying gym bags. Spencer pushed through the door after them, walking into a marble atrium. At the far end of the room was a bank of three elevators. There was an old-school dial above each of them, telling which floor the cars were on. The room smelled like fresh flowers, and there was classical music playing quietly over a hidden speaker.

The concierge at the front desk wore a pristine gray suit and rimless eyeglasses. He gave Spencer a weary smile as she approached. 'Um, hi,' Spencer said, hoping her voice didn't sound too young and naïve. 'I'm looking for a woman who recently moved in here. Her name is Olivia. She's in Paris right now, but I'm wondering if I could get into her apartment for a moment.'

'Sorry,' the concierge said dryly, returning to his paperwork. 'I can't let you up unless I have the tenant's permission.'

Spencer frowned. 'But … she's my mom. Her name is Olivia Caldwell.'

The concierge shook his head. 'No one named Olivia Caldwell lives here.'

Spencer tried to ignore the sudden, gnawing pain in her stomach. 'Maybe she doesn't go by her maiden name. She might go by Olivia Frick. Her husband's name is Morgan Frick.'

The concierge gave her a withering look. 'No one named Olivia *anything* lives here. I know every resident in this building.'

Spencer stepped back, glancing at a line of gilded mailboxes on the far wall. There had to be two hundred units in this place. How could this guy honestly know every single person? 'She just moved in,' she pressed. 'Can you check?'

215

The concierge sighed, then reached for a spiral-bound black book. 'This is a list of the tenants in the building,' he explained. 'What did you say her last name was?'

'Caldwell. Or Frick.'

The concierge flipped to the C's, then to the F's. 'Nope. There's no one under either of those names. Look for yourself.'

He pushed the book across the desk. Spencer leaned over, looking. There was a Caldecott and a Caleb, but no Caldwell. There was a Frank and a Friel, but no Frick. Her whole body went hot, then cold. 'This can't be right.'

The concierge sniffed and returned the book to its shelf. A black phone on the front desk let out a bleat. 'Excuse me.' He picked up the receiver and spoke in a low, polite voice.

Spencer spun around, pressing her palm to her forehead. Two women toting Barneys shopping bags burst through the revolving doors, laughing loudly. A man walking a shaggy Bernese mountain dog came in and joined them at the elevator bank. Spencer was dying to slip in with them, ride the elevator up to the top floor and ... and what? Break into Olivia's penthouse to prove she really lived here?

Andrew's voice swirled in her head. *Don't you think you're moving a little fast? I don't want you to get hurt.*

No. The tenant book hadn't been recently updated – Olivia and Morgan had just moved in. And Olivia's phone wasn't ringing because she was out of the country. And Michael Hutchins's number was out of order because he'd unexpectedly changed it. Spencer's apartment *did* exist. She was going to move into an apartment on Perry Street, the best block in the Village, next week, to live happily ever after within a few blocks from her honest-to-God biological mom. This wasn't too good to be true.

Was it?

216

Spencer's skin felt braised. *Either give Long-Lost Mommy a rest and keep searching for what really happened . . . or pay my price*, A had said. Beyond halfheartedly telling the others that A had sent her a second note, Spencer hadn't searched for Ali's true killer at all. What if *this* was A's price? A knew she was looking for her birth mother. Perhaps A had a team of people under his or her control. A woman called Olivia. A man who posed as a Realtor, inventing an apartment at 223 Perry Street without looking at a map for accuracy. A had known Spencer wanted a family who loved her badly enough to risk everything, even her college education.

She turned away from the front desk in the lobby, fumbling for her Sidekick. In a few clicks, she was logging into the account she'd found on her dad's computer. It felt as if she couldn't get a deep breath. *Please*, she whispered under her breath. *This can't be happening*.

A statement popped onto the screen. There was Spencer's name, address, and account number. The balance was in red font at the bottom. When she saw it, Spencer's stomach heaved. Her vision narrowed until all she saw was the figure before her. It wasn't many zeros . . . just one.

The account had been cleared out, down to the very last penny.

25
And The Winner Is …

Saturday night, Hanna sat at her dressing table, sweeping the last touches of bronzer across her cheeks. The black, lace-lined Rachel Roy sheath dress she'd bought for the Radley party fit her perfectly, snug but not *too* snug around her waist and hips. She'd been way too busy competing for Mike this week to succumb to her usual Cheez-It binges. If only the Mike Montgomery diet came in a bottle.

There was a knock on her door, and Hanna jumped. Her dad stood in the doorway to her bedroom, dressed in a black V-neck sweater and jeans. 'Going somewhere?' he asked.

Hanna swallowed hard, gazing at her made-up reflection in the mirror. She doubted her dad would buy that she was spending a quiet night in. 'There's an opening for this big hotel outside town,' she admitted.

'Is that why Kate's door is shut too? You're both going together?'

Hanna set down her makeup brush, resisting the urge to smile. They weren't going together, because Hanna had won Mike all to herself. *Ha.* 'Not exactly,' she said instead, reining her feelings in.

Mr Marin perched on the edge of her bed. Dot tried to jump on his lap, but he swished him away. 'Hanna …'

Hanna looked at him pleadingly. He was going to enforce the punishment *now*? 'I have a date. It would be weird if she came with us. I've learned my lesson, I swear.'

Mr Marin cracked his knuckles, a habit Hanna had always hated. 'Who's the guy?'

'Just …' She sighed. 'Actually, he's Aria's younger brother.'

'Aria Montgomery?' Mr Marin squinted, thinking. The only time Hanna recalled her dad meeting Mike was when he'd taken Hanna, Aria, and the others to a music festival at Penn's Landing – Aria had had to drag Mike along because Mr and Mrs Montgomery were out of town. While they were watching one of the acts, Mike vanished. They frantically searched for him all over the grounds, finally tracking him down at the snack bar. He was hitting on one of the Pennsylvania Dutch girls who made the funnel cake.

'Does Kate have a date?' Mr Marin asked.

Hanna shrugged. Earlier today, she'd told Mike to get out of his date with Kate by telling her he'd promised to go with the lax boys in their rented Hummer. If he'd said he was going with Hanna, Kate would have immediately told Daddy and ruined the whole thing.

Her father sighed and stood up. 'Okay. You can go on your own.'

'*Thank* you.' Hanna breathed out.

He patted her back. 'I just want Kate to feel welcome here. She's having a really hard time at Rosewood Day. As I remember, you didn't always have it easy there either.'

Hanna felt her cheeks redden. Back in fifth and sixth grade, when Hanna and her dad used to be close, she used to moan to him about school. *I feel like a big nothing*, she confessed. Her dad always assured her that things would turn around. Hanna never believed him, but he'd ended up being right. Becoming friends with Ali had changed everything for good.

Hanna glanced at her dad suspiciously. 'Kate seems really happy at Rosewood Day. She's best friends with Naomi and Riley.'

Mr Marin stood up. 'If you talked to her, you'd know the truth. What she wants most is to be friends with you, Hanna. But you seem to be making that as difficult as possible.'

Then he left the room, padding softly down the hall. Hanna remained on her bed, feeling both puzzled and annoyed. As *if* all Kate really wanted was to be friends! She'd obviously told Hanna's dad that to get him even more on her side.

Hanna ground her fist into her mattress. It wasn't like too many people had broken down her doors desperately wanting to be her BFF. In fact, only two people came to mind: Ali, who had chosen Hanna among many other eligible sixth-grade girls, and Mona, who had sat down next to Hanna at eighth-grade cheerleading tryouts, struck up a conversation, and then invited Hanna to a sleepover at her house. At the time, Hanna had thought both girls chose her for specific reasons – Mona because Hanna had been Ali's friend and was therefore someone with a bit of status, and Ali because she saw a potential in Hanna that no one else had yet noticed. Now, Hanna knew different. From the very start, Mona had been probably plotting to bring Hanna down. Maybe Ali had had more sinister motives for choosing Hanna too – perhaps she saw how insecure Hanna was. Perhaps she realized how easily Hanna could be manipulated.

Deep down, a part of Hanna wanted to believe that what her dad said was true – that despite everything, Kate honestly wanted Hanna as a friend. But after all Hanna had suffered through, it was hard to trust that Kate's aims could be pure.

As she strode out of her bedroom, she heard water running in the hall bathroom. Kate was loudly belting out a recent song from *American Idol*, using up all the hot water. Hanna paused by the door, feeling wholly unsettled. Then, as a truck rumbled past outside, she turned away and marched down the stairs.

The Radley Hotel was bustling with guests, photographers, and staff. Hanna and Mike pulled into the driveway, parked, and handed the car over to the valet. As she got out, Hanna took in the charming brick walkways, the ice-crusted lake in the back meadow, and the grand stone steps leading to the stately wooden door.

When she and Mike walked into the main ballroom, Hanna's jaw dropped even farther. The party's theme was Palace of Versailles, and the Radley lobby was draped with silk tapestries and filled with crystal chandeliers, gold-framed paintings, and ornate chaises. There was a huge fresco of some mythological scene on the far wall, and Hanna could see a Hall of Mirrors at the back, just like in the real Versailles outside Paris. To her right was a throne room, complete with a tall, royal chair with a burgundy velvet cushion. A bunch of guests were gathered near the bar and standing in clumps near the tables. A complete orchestra was set up at the back, and off to the left were the lobby desk, the elevators, and a discreet sign to the spa and the bathrooms.

'Wow.' Hanna sighed. This was her kind of hotel.

'Yeah, it's okay,' Mike said, stifling a yawn.

Mike was dressed in a sleek black tux. He had his dark hair slicked off his face, showing off his prominent cheekbones. Whenever Hanna looked at him, her arms and legs felt noodly. Even more bizarrely, she kept getting vague twinges of sadness. It wasn't the way a winner was supposed to feel.

A caterer in a white suit swept past. 'I'm going to get a drink,' Hanna said airily, banishing the melancholy feelings from her head. She walked over to the bar and stood in line behind Mr and Mrs Kahn, who were whispering excitedly about which art on display they wanted to buy. Then a shock of blond hair across the room caught Hanna's attention. It was Mrs DiLaurentis, deep in conversation with a silver-haired man in a tuxedo. The man swept his arms around, pointing out the balcony, the fluted columns, the chandeliers, the hallway to the spa and the guest rooms. Mrs DiLaurentis nodded and grinned, but her expression seemed pasted on. Hanna shuddered, uneasy to see Ali's mom at a party. It was like seeing a ghost.

The bartender cleared his throat, and Hanna turned and ordered an extra-dirty Ketel One martini. As he mixed it up, she turned and stood on her tiptoes, searching for Mike. When she finally found him, he was in the corner near a gigantic abstract painting, next to Noel, Mason, and a few girls. Hanna narrowed her eyes at the pretty girl whispering in his ear. *Kate*.

Her stepsister was dressed in a floor-length navy gown and four-inch heels. Naomi and Riley flanked her on either side, both wearing ultrashort black dresses. Hanna grabbed her martini and shot across the room, the vodka sloshing over the lip of the glass. She reached Mike and tapped him hard on the shoulder.

'Hi,' Mike said, an I'm-not-doing-anything-wrong look on his face. Kate, Naomi, and Riley peered around him, snickering.

Hanna's skin felt scorched. Grabbing Mike's hand, Hanna

faced the others. 'Did you girls hear? Mike and I are going to prom together.'

Naomi and Riley looked confused. Kate's smile dimmed. 'Prom?'

'Uh-huh,' Hanna chirped, running her hands over her Time Capsule flag, which she'd tied to the gold chain of her Chanel purse.

Noel Kahn clapped Mike on the back. 'Sweet.'

Mike shrugged, as if he'd known from the start that Hanna would ask him. 'I need another Jäger shot,' he said, and he, Noel, and Mason ambled across the room to the bar, shoving one another every few steps.

The orchestra launched into a waltz, and a few of the dusty old partygoers who actually knew what that meant started to dance. Hanna locked her hands to her hips and shot Kate a smug smile. 'So! Who's the winner now?'

Kate lowered one shoulder. 'God, Hanna.' She burst out laughing. 'You seriously asked him to prom?'

Hanna rolled her eyes. 'Poor baby. You're not used to losing. But face it – you did.'

Kate shook her head vigorously. 'You don't understand. I never even *liked* him.'

Hanna let out a lip fart. 'You liked him as much as I did.'

Kate lowered her chin. 'Did I?' She crossed her arms over her chest. 'I wanted to see if you'd go after *anyone* if you thought I was going after him too. The joke's on you, Hanna. We *all* knew about it.'

Naomi made a nickering noise. Riley puckered her lips, trying hard not to erupt into giggles. Hanna blinked hard, knocked off balance. Could Kate be serious? Was *Hanna* the brunt of this joke?

Kate's face softened. 'Oh, chill. Think of this as payback for the herpes thing, and now we're even! Why don't you party with us? There are some gorgeous guys from Brentmont Prep in the Mirror Room.'

She looped her arm through Hanna's, but Hanna shook her away. How could Kate be so cavalier? How was this *payback* for the herpes thing? Hanna had *had* to tell everyone Kate had herpes. If she hadn't, Kate would have told everyone Hanna's binge-purge secret.

But suddenly, Hanna remembered how stunned Kate had seemed when Hanna broke the herpes news. She had looked at Hanna so helplessly, as though she'd been blindsided by the betrayal. Was it possible Kate never intended to tell Hanna's secret that night? Could what her dad said – that Kate just wanted to be friends – be the truth?

But no. *No.*

Hanna faced Kate. 'You wanted Mike, but *I* got him.'

It came out louder than she intended. A few people stopped and stared. A beefy-looking black man in a tux, presumably a bouncer, eyed Hanna warningly.

Kate lifted her hip. 'Are you really going to be like this?'

Hanna shook her head. 'I won!' she cried. 'You lost!'

Kate looked over Hanna's shoulder, her expression shifting. Hanna followed her gaze. Mike was holding two martinis outstretched – one for him, and a refill for her. His eyes looked extra-blue. By the way he was staring at Hanna, it seemed as if he understood perfectly what had just happened. Before Hanna could say a word, he gently set Hanna's drink next to her half-finished one and turned around, saying nothing. His back was ramrod straight as he disappeared into the crowd.

'Mike!' Hanna called after him, gathering her skirt and starting to run. Mike thought Hanna was only pretending to like him ... but maybe that wasn't the truth at all. Mike was funny and genuine. Maybe he was even more perfect for her than any guy she'd ever dated. It explained why she felt butterflies in her stomach whenever he was around, why she smiled giddily when he sent her texts, and why her heart pounded when they almost kissed on his front porch. It explained why Hanna had been feeling morose tonight, too – she didn't want this game with Mike to end.

She came to a stop at the other end of the ballroom, frantically searching around. Mike had disappeared.

26
Someone Has A Secret

Emily stood on the big stone porch outside the Radley entrance, watching the limos and town cars roll into the circular drive. The air smelled like a jumble of expensive perfumes, and a photographer was flitting around the party-goers, snapping pictures. Every time a flashbulb went off, Emily thought of the creepy photos from A. Ali, Jenna, and Naomi, gathered in Ali's backyard. Darren Wilden, emerging from confession. And then there was Jason DiLaurentis arguing with Jenna Cavanaugh in Jenna's living room. *What do you think* he's *so angry about?*

What did it mean? What was A trying to tell her?

She pulled her cell phone from her bag and checked the time once more. It was a quarter after eight, and Aria was supposed to meet her at the entrance fifteen minutes ago. About an hour after their uncomfortable phone conversation this morning, Aria called Emily back and asked if she wanted to go to the Radley party together. Emily figured it was Aria's way of apologizing for yelling at her, and although she hadn't really felt like going now that she and Isaac were through, she'd reluctantly agreed. They'd called Spencer and asked if she wanted to go too, but Spencer said she was spending the night in her sister's barn doing homework.

More people streamed through the Radley's doors, showing their invitations to a girl wearing a headset and holding a clipboard. Emily called Aria's phone, but she didn't pick up. She sighed. Maybe Aria had gone in without her.

The inside of the hotel was warm and smelled like peppermint. Emily slithered out of her coat and handed it to the girl at the coat-check window, smoothing down her strapless, dark red dress. After Isaac invited her to this, she'd rushed out to the mall, tried on this dress, and imagined Isaac swooning when he saw her in it. For once in her life, she'd bought it without even looking at the price tag. And for what? At 2 A.M. last night, Emily had rolled over in bed and looked at the little window of her phone, hoping Isaac had sent her an apology text. But there had been nothing.

She craned her neck, looking for him now. He was definitely here somewhere – and so were Mr and Mrs Colbert.

Her skin began to prickle. Maybe she shouldn't be here. It was one thing to accompany Aria – at least she'd have a buffer – but Emily didn't think she could deal with this place alone. She turned back toward the entrance, but tons of people had arrived at once, jamming the doors. She waited for the crowd to clear, praying she wouldn't see any of the Colberts. She couldn't bear the thought of seeing the hatred in their eyes.

On the wall next to her was a large bronze plaque describing the Radley's history. *G. C. Radley Retreat for Childhood Wellness began in 1897 as an orphanage, but eventually changed into a safe haven for troubled children. This plaque commemorates those children who have benefited from the Radley's unique facility and environment, and the doctors and staff who have dedicated years of their lives to the cause.*

Underneath were the names of various headmasters and deans of the facility. Emily scanned them, but they meant nothing to her.

'I heard some of the kids that stayed here were real lunatics.'

Emily looked over and gasped. Maya was standing right next to her, dressed in a hazelnut-colored tiered gown. Her hair was pulled back from her face, and she wore sparkly gold eye shadow. There was a teasing little smile on her face, not unlike the look Ali used to give Emily when she wanted to make Emily uncomfortable.

'H-hi,' Emily stammered. She thought about Maya standing in her bedroom window last night just as Emily pulled into the cul-de-sac, as if she'd anticipated Emily's arrival. Was that just a coincidence? And the other day at school, she'd seen Maya and Jenna talking. They lived right next to each other – had they struck up a friendship?

'See that balcony?' Maya pointed to the hotel mezzanine. People were leaning over the elaborate wrought-iron railing, peering down to the crowd below. 'I heard some kids killed themselves by jumping off that. They splattered right where the bar is. And I heard a patient *murdered* a nurse.'

Maya touched Emily's hand. Her fingers were stiff and deathly cold. And when she brought her face close to Emily's, her breath smelled hauntingly like banana gum. 'So where's your boyfriend?' Maya singsonged. 'Or did you two have a fight?'

Emily pulled her hand away, her heart slamming against her ribs. Did Maya somehow know ... or had she just guessed?

'I-I have to go,' she said. She faced the entrance again, but the crush of people was still there. She wheeled around, heading back through the ballroom. There was a staircase ahead of her, leading to the upper level. Gathering the hem of her dress, she ran for it, not even caring where it led.

At the top of the steps was a long dark hallway with several doors on either side. Emily tried a few, thinking they might be bathrooms, but the cold, slippery knobs wouldn't turn. Only one door at the end of the hall swung open. She fell inside, grateful for some quiet and privacy.

Emily's nose twitched. The room smelled like dust and mildew. Bulky shapes of what looked like a desk and a couch were in front of her. She fumbled for a light switch on the wall, snapping on an overhead lamp. The desk was covered in papers and books. An old scuffed leather love seat was heaped with books, too. There were bookcases along the back wall, piled with manila folders. Loose papers were scattered over the floor, along with an upended cup of pencils. It almost looked like the room had been deliberately trashed. Emily remembered Mr Colbert mentioning that parts of the hotel hadn't been renovated in time for the party. Maybe this was an office from when this place used to be a school ... or, as Maya put it, a house for lunatics.

A floorboard creaked. Emily turned toward the door and stared. Nothing. A shadow passed across the wall. Emily looked up at the cracked ceiling. A spider sat in the center of a large, sinuous web. There was a black mass of something caught in the silk, maybe a fly.

It was too spooky in here. Emily turned to go, carefully maneuvering around the stacks of books and journals spread out across the floor. Then something caught her eye. There was a book splayed open at her feet, a list of names written in dark blue ink. It seemed like a log. The page was divided into columns labeled *Name, Date, In, Out*. One of the names was ...

Emily knelt down, thinking – hoping – she'd imagined it. Her vision blurred. 'Oh my God,' she whispered.

One of the names in the book was *Jason DiLaurentis*.

His name appeared on the page three times, first on March 6, then on March 13, then on March 20. Seven days apart. Emily flipped a page. There was Jason's name again, on March 27, then April 3, then April 10. He'd logged into the book in the morning, and logged out in the evening. She turned the pages faster and faster. Jason's name kept cropping up. He'd logged in on April 24, Emily's birthday. The date was from eight years ago. Emily counted back – she'd been nine. It had been a Saturday. That year, her parents had taken Emily and her swim team friends out for a birthday dinner at All That Jazz!, her old favorite restaurant at the King James Mall. She'd been in third grade. Ali had started at Rosewood Day at the beginning of that year, her family moving here from Connecticut.

She grabbed the next book under it. Jason's name popped up through the summer between Emily's third- and fourth-grade years, to the winter of her fourth, to the fall of her fifth, to the summer between her fifth and sixth. He'd visited here the weekend after the first day of school when Emily, Ali, and the others started sixth grade. A few days after that, the school had announced the kickoff of the Time Capsule game. She flipped to the page that logged the next weekend, when she and her old friends sneaked into Ali's backyard to steal her flag. Jason's name wasn't there.

She flipped forward to the next weekend, about the time Ali had approached all of them at the Rosewood Day Prep Charity Drive, dubbing them her new BFFs. Still no Jason. She flipped ahead. His name didn't show up again. The weekend after the first day of school was the last time his name appeared in the log book.

Emily lowered the book to her lap, feeling woozy. What on earth was Jason DiLaurentis's name doing in a book in this dark, dank little office? She thought about the joke Ali had made years *ago – they should put him in the mental ward, where he belongs.* Had she been serious after all? Was Jason an outpatient here? Perhaps *this* was what Ali had meant when she told Jenna about sibling problems – maybe Ali told her Jason had issues, problems big enough that he needed to go to a *facility* for treatment. And maybe that was what Jenna and Jason were arguing about last night – he wanted to make sure that Jenna didn't tell a soul.

She thought of how Jason's face had twisted and reddened when he thought she'd bumped his car. He'd stepped so close to her, his fury palpable. What was Jason really capable of? What was Jason *hiding*?

There were footsteps in the hall. Emily froze. She heard someone breathing. Then a shadow appeared in the doorway. Emily started to tremble. 'H-hello?' she croaked.

Isaac emerged into the light. He wore a white caterer's suit and black shoes – Emily supposed his father was making him work tonight, now that he didn't have a date. She shrank back, her heart beating hard.

'I thought I saw you come up here,' he said.

Emily glanced at the ledger again – it was hard to switch gears, from Jason to Isaac. She lowered her head, unable to meet his gaze. Everything they'd said to each other the night before whooshed through her head, way too present.

'I don't think you're supposed to be up here,' Isaac said. 'My dad said this hall is for employees only.'

'I was just leaving,' Emily mumbled, starting for the door.

'Wait.' Isaac perched on the arm of the dusty leather couch. A few quiet seconds passed. He sighed. 'The picture you told me about, the one with your face cut out? I found it

231

last night. In the junk drawer in the kitchen. And ... and I confronted my mom. She lost it.'

Emily's mouth dropped open; she could barely believe her ears. Isaac leapt from the arm of the couch and knelt by Emily's side. 'I'm so sorry,' he whispered. 'I'm a jerk – and now I've probably lost you. Can you ever forgive me?'

Emily bit the inside of her cheek. She knew she should feel good right now – or at least justified – but instead, she felt even worse. It would be so easy to tell Isaac it was fine. *They* were fine. But what he'd done yesterday stung. He hadn't even considered believing her. He'd immediately jumped to conclusions, certain she was lying.

She moved away from him, bent down, and picked up the ledger. The cover of the book was thickly coated with dust and soot. 'I might forgive you someday,' she said, 'but not today.'

'W-what?' Isaac cried.

Emily shoved the book under her arm, biting back tears. Even though she hated telling Isaac something that would hurt him, she knew it was the right thing to do. 'I have to go,' she blurted out.

She ran down the stairs as fast as she could. At the landing, she heard a familiar giggle from the other side of the room. She sucked in her stomach, looking nervously around. The crowd shifted, and the laugh dissipated. The only person Emily recognized across the ballroom was Maya. She was standing against the wall, holding a martini, and staring fixedly at Emily, a whisper of a smile across her wide, glossy lips.

27
Déjà Vu ... Revealed

Hanna skidded across the slippery marble floor, coming to a stop. This hotel was a maze, and somehow, she'd managed to retrace her steps and was standing in front of the floor-to-ceiling tapestry of Napoleon yet *again*. She looked right and left, searching for Mike. The crowd of partiers was so thick, she didn't see him anywhere.

She passed the throne room and heard a familiar voice. Inside was Noel Kahn, draped over the large, velvet throne, his shoulders shaking with laughter. There was an upside-down champagne bucket on his head, a makeshift crown.

Hanna groaned. It was unbelievable what Noel could get away with at Rosewood parties, just because his parents bankrolled the town.

She marched up to him and poked his arm. Noel turned and brightened. 'Hanna!' He smelled as if he'd drunk a whole bathtub of tequila.

'Where's Mike?'

Noel threw his legs over the chair. His pant legs rose slightly, revealing blue-and-red argyle socks. 'Don't know. But I should kiss you.'

Ugh. 'Why?'

'Because,' he slurred. 'You won me five hundred bucks.'

She stepped back. 'Excuse me?'

Noel brought his cocktail, a reddish drink that looked a lot like Red Bull and vodka, to his lips. Liquid dribbled down his shirt and pooled on the seat of the chair. A few Quaker school girls sitting on paisley-upholstered footstools nudged one another, giggling. *How* could they think Noel was hot? If this were really Versailles, Noel wouldn't be the Louis XIV. He'd be the French version of the village idiot.

'The whole lax team had a bet going to see who Mike could get to take him to the prom,' Noel explained. 'You or your hottie stepsister. We made the bet after you started throwing yourselves at him. I'm going to give Mike half my winnings for being such a good sport.'

Hanna ran her hands along the piece of her Time Capsule flag, which she'd tied to the chain of her Chanel purse. She felt the color drain from her face.

Noel nudged his head toward the door. 'If you don't believe me, ask Mike yourself.'

Hanna turned. Mike was leaning against one of the Grecian-style columns, smiling at a girl from Tate Prep. Hanna let out a low growl and made a beeline to him. When Mike saw her, he grinned sheepishly.

'Your teammates *bet* on us?' Hanna screeched. The Tate girl quickly skittered away.

Mike sipped his wine, shrugging. 'It's no different than what you girls were doing. Except the other guys on the lax team were playing for money. What were you playing for? Tampons?'

Hanna ran her hand over her forehead. This wasn't how it was supposed to go. Mike was supposed to be vulnerable

234

and weak, a victim. And all along, he'd known they'd been competing. All along, he'd been playing her.

She sighed, weary. 'So I guess our prom date is off?'

Mike looked surprised. '*I* don't want it to be.'

Hanna searched his face. 'Really?' Mike shook his head. 'So then … you don't care that you were just some … bet?'

Mike glanced at her bashfully, then looked away. 'Not if you don't.'

Hanna tried her best to hide her smile – and her relief. She nudged him hard in the ribs. 'Well, you'd better give me half your winnings.'

'And *you'd* better give me half your …' Mike stopped, making a face. 'Never mind. I don't need half your tampons. We'll use the winnings for a bottle of Cristal for the prom, how's that?' And then, he brightened even more. '*And* for a motel room.'

'A *motel*?' Hanna glared at him. 'What kind of girl do you think I am?'

'Honey, with me, you won't care *where* we're at,' Mike said in the slimiest voice Hanna had ever heard. She stifled a groan, leaning into him. He leaned into her too, until their foreheads touched. 'Honestly?' Mike whispered, his voice softening and becoming almost tender. 'I always liked you better.'

Hanna's insides turned over. Giddy shivers scampered up her back. Their faces were very close, with only a small column of air hanging between them. Then Mike reached forward and pushed the hair out of Hanna's eyes. Hanna giggled nervously. Their lips met. Mike's mouth was warm, and he tasted like red wine. Tingles shot from Hanna's head to all ten toes.

'*Yeah!*' Noel Kahn bellowed from across the room, nearly tumbling off the throne. Hanna and Mike shot apart. Mike pumped his fist, his blazer sliding down his arm. He was still wearing his yellow rubber Rosewood Day lacrosse bracelet. Hanna sighed, resigned. There were all kinds of queer things she'd have to get used to, now that she was dating a lacrosse boy.

There was a loud crunch of static, and a fast, upbeat song blared over the loudspeakers. Hanna peeked into the ballroom. The orchestra section had vanished, and there was a DJ booth in its place. The DJ was dressed up in a long, Louis XIV-style curly wig, pantaloons, and a long robe. 'Shall we?' Mike asked, offering his hand.

Hanna stood up and followed him. Across the ballroom, Naomi, Riley, and Kate were lined up on a chaise, watching. Naomi looked annoyed, but Kate and Riley had little smiles on their faces, almost as if they were happy for Hanna. After a moment, Hanna shot Kate a small smile back. Who knew, maybe Kate really *did* want to be friends. Maybe Hanna could let bygones be bygones too.

Mike started writhing around her, practically humping her leg, and she kicked him away, laughing. When the song ended, the DJ leaned into the microphone. 'I'm taking requests,' he said in a smooth voice. 'Here's one right now.'

Everyone froze in anticipation. A few chords filled the air. The beat was slower, more subdued. Mike waved his hand. 'What loser requested *this*?' he scoffed, marching toward the DJ booth to find out.

A few notes filled the room. Hanna stopped, cocking her head. She recognized the singer, but she didn't know why.

Mike was back. 'It's someone called Elvis Costello,' he announced. 'Whoever *that* is.'

Elvis Costello. At the same time, the chorus began. *Alll-i-son, I know this world is killing you ...*

Hanna's mouth dropped open. She knew why this song

was familiar: A few months ago, someone had been singing it in her shower.

Al-i-son, my aim is true …

When Hanna emerged in the hall that day, she saw Wilden wrapped in her favorite white Pottery Barn towel. Wilden had looked startled. When Hanna asked why he was singing that song – only a crazy person would sing that within a hundred square miles of Rosewood these days – Wilden had reddened. 'Sometimes, I don't notice I'm singing.'

A spark caught fire in Hanna's brain. *Sometimes, I don't notice I'm singing!* Ali had said that in the dream this morning. She'd also said, *If you find it, I'll tell you all about it. The two of them.* Was Ali trying to say that Wilden was somehow linked with Ali's murder?

And then the déjà vu feeling she'd had when Wilden had backed out of the driveway slammed back to her. It was because of Wilden's car, the old black thing he was driving around while his cruiser was in the shop. She'd seen that car before, many years ago. It was the car parked at the DiLaurentises' the day Hanna and the others had tried to steal Ali's flag.

'Hanna?' Mike said, gazing at her curiously. 'You okay?'

Hanna shook her head faintly. Ali's dream looped through her mind. *Go fish*, Ali had said over and over again when Hanna asked who she was talking about. The words stood for Wilden … and Hanna understood that too. That sticker in the foot well, the one that had the fish logo on it. Hanna knew where she'd seen the sticker last: The DiLaurentises had one exactly like it. The pass granted them access to their gated community at the Poconos. But so what? Lots of people vacationed there; maybe Wilden's family had too. Why had Wilden tried to hide the sticker? Why had he been so secretive about it?

237

Unless Wilden needed it to be a secret.

Hanna staggered crookedly to the nearest chair and sank down. 'What is it?' Mike kept asking. She shook her head, unable to answer. Maybe Wilden *did* have a secret. He'd been acting so strange lately. Skulking around. Having hushed conversations on his cell phone. Not being where he said he would be. So quick to blame the girls for Ian's disappearance. Sneaking around Ali's old yard. Driving like a maniac to get Hanna home, practically killing her. Wearing that hood like the figure that had hovered over Hanna in the woods the night they'd discovered Ian's body. Maybe he *was* the figure.

What if I told you there's something you don't know? Ian had said to Spencer on her porch. *Something big. I think the cops know about it, too, but they're ignoring it. They're trying to frame me.* And then his IMs: *They found out I knew. I had to run.*

The ballroom whirled with people. There were security guards at each entrance and more than a few Rosewood cops, but Wilden wasn't among them. Then a reflection in one of the floor-to-ceiling mirrors caught Hanna's eye. She saw a familiar face, with blue eyes and blond hair. Hanna stiffened. It was the Ali from her dream. But when she looked again, the face had morphed. Kirsten Cullen stood there instead.

Mike was still staring at Hanna, his eyes wide and scared. 'I have to go find your sister,' she said, touching his hand. 'But I'll be back. I promise.'

And then she shot across the ballroom. Somebody was hiding something, all right. And this time, they couldn't turn to the cops for help.

28
Creepier And Creepier

By the time Aria finally fought through the snarl of traffic in line to park at the Radley opening, she was over an hour late. She tossed her keys to the valet and searched the crowd of bouncers, formally dressed partygoers, and photographers for Emily, but she wasn't anywhere.

After Jason had found Aria in his apartment earlier today and demanded she leave, Aria hadn't known what to do. Finally, she'd driven to St Basil's cemetery and walked up the hills to Ali's grave. The last time Aria was here, Ali's casket wasn't yet in the ground – Mr and Mrs DiLaurentis had held off on burying her, in denial that their daughter was truly dead. And although the DNA evidence still hadn't come in that it truly *was* Ali's body in the half-dug hole in the DiLaurentises' backyard, the family must have faced reality, because Aria had heard that they'd finally interred Ali quietly last month, without a ceremony.

Alison Lauren DiLaurentis, the headstone said. There was a new layer of freshly planted grass around her grave site, already stiff and frosty from the cold. Aria stared hard at the slab of marble, wishing Ali could talk. She wanted to tell Ali about the yearbook she'd found in Jason's apartment. She wanted to ask about the inscription Wilden had written over Ian's picture. *What did Ian do that was so awful? And what happened to you? What don't we know?*

A girl in a tight black tube dress stopped Aria at the Radley's grand, double-doored entrance. 'Do you have an invitation?' she asked, her voice nasal and condescending. Aria produced the invite Ella had sent her, and the girl nodded. Pulling her coat around her tight, Aria strode down the stone entrance and walked into the hotel. A bunch of Rosewood Day kids, including Noel Kahn, Mason Byers, Sean Ackard, and Naomi Zeigler, were on the dance floor, wriggling around to a remixed Seal song. After grabbing a flute of champagne and downing it in a few quick gulps, she started darting around the clusters of people, searching for Emily. She had to tell her about the yearbook.

When she felt a tap on her shoulder, she turned. 'You made it!' Ella cried, giving Aria a big hug.

'H-hi.' Aria tried to smile. Ella wore a lacy sea green wrap around her shoulders and a sleek black silk sheath. Xavier was right next to her. He wore a pin-striped suit over a blue button-down and held a glass of champagne.

'Nice to see you again, Aria.' Xavier's eyes moved from Aria's eyes to her boobs to her hips. Aria's insides curdled. 'How's life at your father's house?'

'Fine, thank you,' Aria said stiffly. She tried to shoot Ella a private, pleading look, but her mom's eyes were glassy. Aria wondered if she'd had a couple of drinks before they arrived. Ella often did that before a show.

Noel Kahn's father tapped Ella on her shoulder, and Aria's mother turned to talk to him. Xavier moved closer to Aria and placed his hand on her hip. 'I've missed you,' he said. His breath was hot and smelled like whiskey. 'Have you missed me?'

'I have to go now,' Aria said loudly, feeling color rise to her cheeks. She shot away from Xavier fast, ducking around a woman in a fluffy mink stole. She heard Ella call out, 'Aria?' There was hurt and disappointment in her voice. But Aria kept going.

She came to a stop in front of a large stained-glass window that featured a portrait of a pie-faced minstrel and his lute. When she felt a second tug on her arm, she cringed, worried Xavier had followed her. But it was only Emily. A few strands of her red-gold hair had loosened from her French twist, and her cheeks were flushed. 'I've been looking all over for you,' Emily exclaimed.

'I just got here,' Aria said. 'Traffic was horrible.'

Emily pulled a large, dusty green book from under her arm. Its pages were gilt-edged, and it reminded Aria of a volume of an encyclopedia. 'Look at this.' Emily opened it up and pointed to a name in cursive. *Jason DiLaurentis*. There was a date and time next to his name from seven years ago.

'I found it upstairs,' Emily explained. 'This must be a sign-in book from back when this place was a mental hospital.'

Aria blinked in disbelief. She raised her head, looking around. A handsome silver-haired man, presumably the hotel owner, glided through the crowd, looking pleased with his handiwork. There were displays throughout the ball-room describing the multimillion-dollar gym that had been built on the second floor, and the state-of-the-art spa facilities. She had heard something about this place once being a hospital for mentally ill children, but it was hard to believe that now.

'Look.' Emily leafed from page to page. 'Jason's name is

here, and then here, and then here. It goes on like this for *years*. It stops right before we staked out Ali for her flag.' Emily lowered the book to her hip, giving Aria a plaintive look. 'I know you have a thing for Jason. But this is *weird*. Do you think maybe he was … a patient?'

Aria ran her hands through her hair. *Is this some kind of joke?* Jason had asked when Aria had shown him the Radley invitation. Her heart sank. Maybe he'd once been a patient here. Maybe he thought Aria was taunting him with the invite, paranoid that Aria knew way more about him than she'd let on.

'Oh my God,' Aria croaked. 'A sent me a text a couple days ago. It said Jason was hiding something from me, and I didn't want to know what. I sort of … ignored it.' She lowered her eyes. 'I thought A was messing with me. But … I … I went out with Jason a couple times. On one of our dates, he got really uncomfortable when I told him I was coming to a party here. He also told me that he saw a psychiatrist at Rosewood Day. Maybe that was in *addition* to the doctor he saw … here.' She stared at the book again. Jason's name was written in achingly neat cursive, each letter looped and even.

Emily nodded. 'And I've been trying to tell you all day that A sent me a note last night telling me to go to Ali's old neighborhood. I saw Jason in Jenna's house. *Yelling* at her.'

Aria sank down into the velvet chair next to the stained-glass window, filled with even more dread. 'What were they saying?'

Emily shook her head. 'I don't know. But they seemed upset. Maybe he really *had* done something terrible to Ali – and that's why he was sent here.'

Aria stared down at the polished marble floor. She could see a haloed reflection of her peacock-blue dress in the tiles. This whole week, Aria had been so irritated with Emily, convinced she wasn't looking at the Ali and Jason situation objectively. But maybe Aria wasn't either.

Emily sighed. 'We should probably talk to Wilden about this.'

'We can't go to Wilden,' a voice interrupted.

They both turned. Hanna stood behind them, a frazzled look on her face. 'Wilden's the *last* person we should go to with anything.'

Emily leaned against the window. 'Why?'

Hanna settled onto the chaise. 'You remember when we met in Ali's backyard to steal her flag? After she went back inside, I saw this car sitting at her curb. It seemed like whoever was inside was casing the place. And the other day, I went running, and I saw Wilden standing in front of Ali's house again, even though the cops called off the search. He gave me a ride home ... but he wasn't driving his squad car. He was driving the same car I saw years ago in front of Ali's house. What if he was stalking her?'

Emily gazed at her quizzically. 'Are you sure it's the same car?'

Hanna nodded. 'It's this old vintage thing from the sixties. I can't believe I didn't make the connection before tonight. And *then*, when I was in Wilden's car, I saw this old sticker with a fish on it. It said *Day Pass*. You know the last time I saw that *exact* same sticker? On Ali's dad's SUV, when we used to go up to the Poconos. Remember?'

Aria rubbed her jaw, trying to keep up. Ali used to bring Aria and the others to her family's Poconos house a lot. Once, Aria had helped the family pack their belongings into the car. After Mrs DiLaurentis loaded the suitcases, she'd crouched down at the back bumper and pasted a new Poconos season pass right on top of the almost identical pass from the year before.

Aria nodded slowly. 'But what does that mean?'

Hanna's head bobbed feverishly. The DJ had turned on a strobe light, and Hanna's face went from light to shadow and back. It looked as though she were disappearing and reappearing. 'What if Wilden got hold of a pass a long time ago? What if he used to drive up to the Poconos to spy on Ali? What if ... what if he had some weird crush on her, a crush way weirder than Ian's? Don't you think he's behaved strangely lately? He was so quick to arrest Ian when Spencer came forward with – let's be honest – kind of shaky evidence. What if *he's* hiding something? What if *he's* the one who did it?'

Aria waved her hands, stopping Hanna. 'But Wilden could've gotten the pass from Jason. Did you know Jason and Wilden were friends?'

The corners of Hanna's mouth turned down. Emily pressed her hand to her bare collarbone.

'I know it sounds crazy,' Aria admitted. 'Today, I got an e-mail from Jason, telling me to meet him at his parents' house in Yarmouth. I got there, but he wasn't home. He didn't send me the text at all ... someone else did. Probably A. But while I was waiting in his apartment, I found an old Rosewood Day yearbook from Jason's senior year. Wilden signed right over Ian's picture. And he drew an arrow to Ian's head and wrote, *I can't believe what that asshole did. My offer still stands.*'

Emily clapped her hand over her mouth, her brown eyes wide.

Hanna sprang up on her toes, placing both hands on the top of her head. 'You're totally right. They *were* friends. That black car I was talking about? The old thing Wilden was driving around? I saw it one other time, too. Remember the day Time Capsule was announced? We were standing in the

244

courtyard, and Ian said he was going to kill Ali to get her Time Capsule piece? Jason came up, and he and Ian had that weird fight. And then Jason ...'

'Ran up to a black car,' Aria whispered, remembering that day.

'And he said, *Just drive*.' Emily's voice was soft. She pulled out her cell phone and scrolled through her photos. 'It works with this, too.' She showed them the photo they'd already seen, the one of Wilden leaving a confession booth, a guilty look on his face. *I guess we all have things to feel guilty about, huh?*

'It's so weird that A is sending stuff that actually ... makes sense,' Aria murmured.

'Yeah, that doesn't really seem like A,' Hanna agreed.

'What if A isn't malicious?' Emily hissed. 'What if A's trying to help?'

Hanna snorted. 'Yeah. We help A ... or A ruins our lives.'

The DJ shut off the strobe light and launched into another dance song. Partygoers staggered onto the dance floor. Parents clinked wineglasses, toasting another new hotel to escape to on weekends. Aria even noticed Mr and Mrs DiLaurentis across the ballroom, talking jovially to Mr and Mrs Byers as if nothing was wrong.

She glanced at the ledger in Emily's hands. The DiLaurentis parents could have been sending Jason to therapists for years, keeping it a well-guarded secret. Maybe they'd been hiding other things about Jason, too. Jason had been *so* angry today. Could he be one of those people who hid his anger expertly, seeming so sweet and mild until he suddenly ... erupted? Maybe Wilden was one of those people too.

'What if Jason found out Ali and Ian were dating?' Aria suggested. 'That day he came up to Ian and Ali in the courtyard, he was really protective of her, like he knew something was up. Maybe that's what Wilden meant by *I can't believe what that asshole did*. I would guess an older brother would want to kill the guy taking advantage of his sister.'

Hanna crossed her legs, her face crumpled in thought. 'Ian said in his IMs that *they* wanted to hurt him. What if *they* are Wilden and Jason?'

'But Ian implied that whoever drove him out of town were the ones who were really behind it,' Emily said. 'So that would mean ...'

'Jason and Wilden had something to do with Ali's murder,' Hanna whispered. 'Maybe it was an accident. Maybe something horrible happened that they hadn't planned.'

Aria felt sick. Was that *possible*? She looked at the others. 'The only person who knows the truth is Ian. Do you think we could talk to him on IM? Do you think he'd tell us?'

They exchanged uneasy glances, not sure what to do. The bass pumped on in the background. The scents of grilled shrimp and filet mignon filled the air, making Aria's vegetarian stomach turn. She breathed hard, her nerves standing on end. Her eyes landed on Hanna's piece of her Time Capsule flag, which she'd tied around the chain of her purse. She pointed to the black blob in the corner, remembering how Hanna had described it to Kate at Meredith's baby shower. 'Why did you draw a manga frog on your flag?'

Hanna blinked hard, as though confused at Aria's change of subject. Then she stretched the flag out and showed them the entire piece. Also on it was a Chanel logo, a field hockey girl, and the Louis Vuitton pattern. 'I decorated it in Ali's honor with the things she'd drawn on hers before it was stolen.'

Aria bit her thumbnail. 'Hanna, Ali didn't draw a manga frog on her flag.'

246

Hanna looked startled. 'Yes she did. I went home that afternoon and wrote down *everything* she said.'

A tingly feeling crept up Aria's back. 'She *didn't* draw a manga frog,' she protested. 'She didn't draw any animals at all.'

Hanna's eyes flickered back and forth, her face draining of color. Emily pushed a strand of hair behind her ears, looking worried. 'How do you know that?'

Aria's stomach churned. She had the same swooping feeling as the time when she was six years old and wanted to go on the big-kid roller coaster at Great Adventure. Her dad strapped her into the seat and pulled the big metal bar down over her chest, but as the ride was about to start, she was gripped with a searing panic. She'd screamed and screamed, making the amusement park technician stop the ride so she could get off.

Her friends blinked at her, waiting. As much as she didn't want to discuss this, she had to tell them the truth. She took a deep breath. 'That day we tried to take Ali's flag, I cut through the woods to go home. Someone was coming the other way. It was ... Jason. And ... well ... *he* had Ali's flag. Before I knew what was happening, he was shoving it at me. He didn't explain why. I knew I should've given it back to Ali, but I thought maybe Jason didn't want me to. I thought maybe there was a *reason* Jason took it from her. Like he thought it wasn't right that she'd found it so easily. Or that he was worried about what Ian said to her a few days before in the courtyard – that he'd kill her to get her piece. Or that maybe he liked me ...'

Emily snorted. She held up the ledger from the upstairs office. 'Or maybe he took it from her because he had *problems*.'

'I didn't know what to think at the time,' Aria protested.

'So you lied to Ali instead?' Emily shot back.

Aria groaned. She'd *known* Emily was going to react like this. 'Ali lied to us too!' she cried. 'We've *all* kept secrets from one another. How is this any different?'

Emily shrugged and turned away.

'I meant to give it back to Ali, I really did,' Aria said wearily. 'But then we became friends with her. The longer I didn't say something, the more awkward it would have been. I didn't know what to do.' She pointed again at Hanna's flag. 'I haven't looked at Ali's flag since the day I got it, but I swear there's no frog on it.'

Hanna raised her head. 'Wait. Aria – you still *have* her flag?'

Aria nodded. 'It's been in an old shoe box for years. When I moved my stuff to my dad's house, I saw the box again. But I didn't open it.'

Hanna's face paled. 'I had a dream this morning about the day we tried to steal Ali's flag. I need to see it.'

Aria began to protest when she felt a buzzing on her hip. Her cell phone was ringing. 'Hang on,' she mumbled, glancing at the screen. 'I have a new text.'

Emily's tiny clutch began to hum. 'Me too,' she whispered. They stared at each other. Hanna's iPhone was silent, but she leaned over Emily's Nokia. Aria looked at her own phone and pressed read.

Don't you girls hate it when your Manolos start to pinch? Me, I like to soak my toes in my backyard hot tub. Or sit in my cozy barn, snuggled under a blanket. It's so quiet there, now that the big, protective cops are gone. – A

Aria looked around at the others, puzzled.

'It sounds like A is talking about Spencer's barn,' Emily whispered. Her mouth fell open. 'I talked to Spencer earlier today. She's out in the barn ... all alone.' She pointed at the words *now that the big, protective cops are gone.* 'What if she's in danger? What if A is warning us that something awful is going to happen?'

Hanna put her iPhone on speaker and dialed Spencer's number. But the line rang and rang, finally going to voice mail. Aria's heart pounded hard. 'We should go make sure she's okay,' she whispered.

Then Aria felt someone's eyes on her from across the room. She looked around and noticed a dark-haired man in a Rosewood Day Police uniform by the door. *Wilden.* He was glaring at them, his piercing green eyes narrow slits, his mouth turned down. He looked as if he'd heard everything they said ... and all of it was true.

Aria grabbed Hanna's hand and started to pull her toward the side entrance. 'Guys, we have to get out of here,' she cried. '*Now.*'

29
They Were All So Wrong

It was 9 P.M., and Spencer had been rereading the same paragraph in *The House of Mirth* for an hour and a half. Lily Bart, the scrappy, eager New Yorker, was trying to make her way in high society at the turn of the twentieth century. Like Spencer, all Lily wanted was to find a way to escape from her dreary, uncertain life, but also like Spencer, Lily was getting nowhere fast. Spencer kept waiting for the part in the book where Lily finds out she's adopted, gets scammed by a wealthy woman claiming to be her mother, and loses the money in her dowry.

She laid the book down and gazed drearily around the barn apartment, which she'd retreated to as soon as she'd returned from New York. The fuchsia accent pillows splayed across the almond-colored couch looked washed-out and drab. The few bites of Asiago cheese Spencer had found in the fridge and eaten over the sink for dinner tasted like dust. In the shower, the water hadn't felt hot or cold, just lukewarm. All of Spencer's senses had been ripped away. The world was murky and joyless.

How could she have been so stupid? Andrew had *warned*

her. All the signs that Olivia was scamming her were there. When she'd visited, Olivia hadn't let them stop in the apartment, not even for a minute. And Olivia had struggled with that big file folder, conveniently forgetting it when she boarded the helicopter. She'd probably snickered once she was airborne, knowing exactly what Spencer would do. And to think Spencer had looked into Olivia's eyes and thought they looked alike! She'd hugged Olivia tight before she left, finally feeling like she was *connecting* with a member of her family! Olivia probably wasn't even her real name. And Morgan Frick, Olivia's so-called husband, was *definitely* a fake. How could she have missed that? Morgan Frick was just the names of two New York museums sloppily shoved together.

The barn creaked and buckled. Spencer flipped on the TV. There were tons of shows in her sister's TiVo, not yet watched. Earlier this evening, Spencer had heard a woman from the Fermata spa leave a message on Melissa's machine, saying Melissa had missed her appointment for an oxygen facial today, and did she want to reschedule. Why had her sister left in such a hurry? *Had* that been Melissa in the woods yesterday, searching for something?

Spencer turned the TV off again, not interested. Her gaze wandered to Melissa's bookshelves. They were piled with old textbooks from high school, among them the book she'd used for AP econ. Next to those was a leaf green Kate Spade boot box marked *High School Notes*. Spencer mustered up a small, sarcastic snort. Notes, as in the kind you passed back and forth in class? Prissy Melissa didn't seem the type.

She pulled out the boot box and opened the lid. A blue spiral-bound notebook that said *Calculus* was on top. Melissa must have meant note*books*. There were smiley faces on the cover, and Melissa's name and Ian's name doodled over and

251

over in flowery cursive. Spencer opened the notebook to the first page. It was filled with math problems, diagrams, and proofs. *Boring*, Spencer thought.

On the next page, a shock of green ink caught her eye. There were notes in the margin written in two different-colored inks. It looked like a conversation between two people, passed back and forth from desk to desk. Spencer recognized Melissa's handwriting in black, and someone else's in green.

Guess who I made out with at the party last weekend? said the first message in Melissa's telltale scrawl. Below that was a bubbly, green question mark. *JD*, was Melissa's answer. Then came a green exclamation point. And then, *Naughty, naughty! That boy is so in love with you ...*

Spencer held the page inches from her face, as if studying it closely would make it clear. *JD?* Her brain scrambled for a logical answer. Could that stand for Jason DiLaurentis? The day they tried to steal Ali's flag and Jason had stormed out of his house, he'd glowered at Melissa and Ian in Spencer's backyard. *He'll get over it*, Melissa had murmured to Ian later. Could Jason have been jealous that Melissa was dating Ian? Could he have secretly been in love with her?

She pressed her fingers to her temples. It didn't seem possible.

There was a forceful knock at the door, and the notebook slipped from Spencer's lap to the rug. Then, another knock. 'Spencer!' she heard someone call.

Emily and Hanna stood on the porch, Emily in a long red gown, Hanna in a short lacy black one.

'Are you okay?' Hanna rushed into the barn and clutched Spencer's forearms. Emily burst in behind her, carrying a large book with a dingy leather cover.

252

'Yeah,' Spencer said slowly. 'What's going on?'

Emily set the book on the kitchen island. 'We just got a note from A. We worried something happened to you. Have you heard any strange noises outside?'

Spencer blinked, stunned. 'No ...'

The girls looked at each other, breathing sighs of relief. Spencer's eyes landed on the leather book Emily was carrying. 'What's that?' she asked.

Emily bit her lip. She glanced at Hanna, and they both launched into the explanation of what they'd figured out earlier that day. They also said that Aria had run back to her house to retrieve Ali's long-lost flag – it might hold a vital clue – and would meet them here. When they finally went quiet, Spencer gaped at them, stunned.

'Jason and Wilden know something,' Hanna whispered. 'Something they're covering up. We need to reach Ian again. All that stuff he IM'ed you about – that he had to run, that they hated him, that they'd found out that he knew – we need to know *what* Ian knows.'

Spencer bunched up a throw pillow in her hands, feeling uneasy. 'What if it's dangerous? Ian was driven out of town because he knew too much. That could happen to us too.'

Hanna shook her head. 'A's begging us to do this. A might ruin us if we don't.'

Spencer shut her eyes, thinking of the big red *zero* on the balance line of her college savings account. A had *already* ruined her.

She shrugged and walked over to Melissa's laptop, not sure what else to do. Slowly, she swirled the mouse around, jolting the screen to life. The computer was still signed on to Melissa's IM account, and there were the online friends in her buddy window. When Spencer saw the familiar screen name, her heart began to pound.

'I can't believe it. That's him,' she said, pointing to *USCMidfielderRoxx*. This was the first time she'd seen him online in a week.

Hanna eyed Spencer. 'Talk to him,' she said.

Spencer clicked on Ian's icon and started to type. *Ian, it's Spencer. Don't sign off. I'm here with Hanna and Emily. We believe you. We know you're innocent. We want to help you figure this out. But you have to tell us about the conflicting evidence you hinted at when you were on my porch last week. What happened the night Ali was killed?*

The cursor blinked. Spencer's hands began to tremble.

And then, the IM screen flashed. They leaned forward. *Spencer?* the message said. The girls clasped hands. Another message popped up right after. *We shouldn't talk about this. If you know, you could be in danger.*

Spencer paled and looked at Emily and Hanna. 'See? Maybe he's right.'

Hanna pushed Spencer aside and typed. *We have to know.*

The IM window flashed again. *Ali and I were planning to meet up that night*, Ian wrote. *I was nervous to meet her, so I got drunk. I went to wait for her, but she didn't show. When I looked across the yard, I swear I saw two people with long blond hair in the woods. It looked like one of them was Ali.*

Spencer gasped. Ian had told her this when he met her on her porch last week. She and Ali had fought that night, but Ian said it might have been someone else. She shut her eyes, trying to imagine yet *another* person being out there that night ... someone they hadn't ever suspected. Her stomach started to ache.

Ian's messages kept coming. *It seemed like the two people were arguing, but they were too far away for me to tell. I figured Ali wasn't going to come over, which maybe was good, because I was pretty wasted. After Ali went missing, I didn't realize that the person she was fighting with that night could've hurt her – that's why I didn't say anything at first. She'd talked a lot about running away when we were together, and that's what I thought she did.*

Spencer looked at the others, puzzled. 'Ali never talked about running away, did she?'

'I used to talk about running away from my strict family,' Emily whispered. 'Ali said she'd come, too. I always thought she was just saying it to be nice ... but maybe not.'

The screen flashed again. *But after I was arrested, I figured out a lot of things. I found out who was really out there ... and why. They were coming for me, not for her. They found out what was going on, and they wanted to hurt me. But they got to Ali first. I don't know what happened. I don't know if it was an accident, but I'm pretty sure they did it. And they've been covering it up ever since.*

Spencer's vision narrowed. She thought about the figure in the woods last night, scrabbling for something in the dirt. Maybe there *was* something out there, some kind of proof.

Who are they? Spencer typed. *Who did it?* She had a feeling she knew Ian's answer, but she wanted him to confirm it.

Doesn't it seem weird that he went into law enforcement? said Ian's next message, ignoring Spencer's question. *He was the least likely guy to do something like that. But guilt is a crazy thing. He probably wanted to absolve himself of what happened any way he could. And they both had a solid alibi that night. They were supposed to be up at the Poconos house. No one knew they were really in Rosewood. That's why they were never questioned. They weren't there.*

Hanna pressed her hands to her cheeks. 'The Poconos house. Wilden's sticker.'

'And Jason *was* allowed to go up there by himself,' Spencer whispered.

255

She turned back to the keyboard. *Say who it is. Say their names.*

You could get hurt, Ian typed. *I've said too much already. They're going to know that you know. They probably know already. They'll stop at nothing to keep this secret.*

SAY IT, she typed.

The cursor flickered. Finally, the next message arrived with a loud *bloop*.

Jason DiLaurentis, Ian wrote. *And Darren Wilden.*

Spencer pressed her hand to her clammy cheeks, a fault opening in her head. She remembered the photo that had been on her dad's screen saver, the one of all of them at the DiLaurentises' house in the Poconos. Jason's wet hair had stretched down past his shoulders, as long as a girl's. She widened her eyes at Emily and Hanna. 'Jason's hair used to be long back then, remember? So if Ian saw two people with long, blond hair ...'

'It could've been him,' Emily whispered. 'And Ali.'

Spencer shut her eyes. It fit the memory she had of that night, too. After she'd fought with Ali and fallen, Ali had run down the path. Spencer had looked across the yard and had seen Ali talking to someone. Of course she'd assumed it was Ian – so many signs pointed to him. But as she squeezed her eyes shut and thought hard, the picture began to change. The person no longer had Ian's chiseled jaw and short, wavy hair. His hair was straighter and blonder, his features more delicate. He leaned into Ali intimately, but also protectively. The way a brother would, not a boy-friend.

How could it have happened? Was it a twisted accident? Was Jason overcome with disturbing rage over what his sister was doing with Ian? Had they fought, and had Ali accidentally fallen into the hole? Had Jason and Wilden run off

256

into the woods, petrified by what had happened? Ian wouldn't have told the cops about seeing anyone in the woods with Ali, because that would've put him at the scene – and he'd also have had to explain his and Ali's secret relationship. But when he came forward with what he really knew after his arrest, the person who'd most likely taken his statement was Wilden ... and Wilden obviously wouldn't pass on Ian's story to a higher authority. Once Ian got a lawyer and started ranting about how he wasn't the killer and the truth was still out there, perhaps Wilden threatened him. Which was why Ian had to flee.

Everyone was silent for a long time. There was a neigh of a horse, far off in Spencer's stables. A swish of wind, rattling the tree branches. Then Emily raised her chin, sniffing the air. A disturbed look crossed her face.

'What?' Hanna asked, concerned.

'I ... smell something,' Emily whispered.

They breathed in deeply. There *was* a strange smell in the air, one Spencer couldn't immediately identify. As it grew stronger and more concentrated, Spencer's head began to pound. Her eyes fell to one of Ian's last IMs. *You could get hurt. They probably know already.*

Spencer's heart leapt to her throat. 'Oh my God. It's ... gasoline.'

And then they heard the telltale sound of a match being struck.

30
Hell On Earth

Aria clambered down the spiral staircase from her loft bedroom in her new house, twice stumbling and clutching the
wrought-iron railing for support. She burst out of the front
door, sprinted to the Subaru, and turned the ignition.
Nothing happened. She gritted her teeth and tried it again.
No engine. 'Please don't do this,' Aria begged the car, banging her head on the steering wheel. The horn honked weakly.

Defeated, she climbed out of the car and looked right and
left. She'd left her bike at Ella's, which meant she had to walk
to Spencer's barn. The quickest way was through the thick,
coffin-black woods. But Aria hadn't gone in there at night by
herself ... well, ever.

A crescent-shaped moon hung in the sky. The night was
very still and quiet, without a hint of wind. Aria could see the
golden porch light of Spencer's barn through the trees.
Before she started through the woods, she pulled Ali's flag
out of her jacket pocket. The flag was where she'd known it
would be, nestled deep in the shoe box. She'd grabbed it
without looking at it, frantic to get back to Spencer and the
others.

The fabric was still shiny and thick, almost perfectly preserved. It even smelled a little bit like Ali's vanilla hand soap. Aria beamed the flashlight she'd grabbed from the kitchen, examining the designs Ali had drawn. There was the Chanel logo and the Louis Vuitton design, same as the drawings on Hanna's flag. There was also a cluster of stars and comets and a doodle of a wishing well. But there wasn't an anime frog anywhere. Nor was there a cartoon girl playing field hockey. So had Hanna remembered incorrectly ... or had Ali?

Aria spread the piece out to its very corners. Off to the left, Ali had drawn a strange symbol she hadn't noticed before. It looked like a NO PARKING sign, the kind that had a letter *P* with a big red line through the center. Only, instead of *P*, Ali had written another initial instead. Aria brought the flag close to her face. At first glance, the letter looked like an *I*. But as she looked closer, she realized it wasn't. It was a *J*.

For ... *Jason*?

Heart hammering, Aria shoved the flag back into her pocket and ran into the woods. The snow had melted, and the ground was slick. Aria sprinted over wet leaves and soggy puddles, splashing mud everywhere. When she came to the bottom of a ravine, her boots went out from under her. She hit the ground with a *thwack*, landing hard on her hip. The pain was white and hot, and Aria let out a muffled shriek.

A few quiet seconds passed. The only sound she heard was her own breathing. Slowly, she got up, wiped mud off the side of her face, and looked around.

Across the clearing was a familiar, twisted tree. Aria frowned, realizing. This was where they'd found Ian's body last week – she was sure of it. Something glinted from underneath a patch of logs and dry leaves. Aria carefully walked over to it and crouched down. It was a platinum class ring, half-caked in mud. She pulled her shirtsleeve over her hand and wiped the ring clean. A blue stone glinted. Around the base of the stone were the words *Rosewood Day*. She shut her eyes, remembering Ian's body lying among the leaves just one week ago. Her gaze had gone straight to the class ring around his bloated finger. That ring had a blue stone in it too.

She shined the flashlight on the name inscribed on the inside of the band. *Ian Thomas*. Had this fallen off Ian when he escaped? Had someone pried it off him? She looked again at the pile of wet leaves. The ring had been sitting on top of them, barely hidden. How could the cops not have found it?

A twig snapped. Aria whipped her head up. The noise sounded close. More twigs broke. Leaves crunched. Then a figure slithered through the trees. Aria crouched down. The figure took a few steps and stopped. It was too dark to see who was there. Something made a sloshing noise, like liquid hitting the sides of a container. Aria's eyes watered, an odd smell filling her nose. It was the odor of a gas station, one of her most-hated smells in the world.

When she saw the figure bend down and heard the liquid glugging out of the container and splattering on the muddy ground, Aria realized what was happening. She stood up fast, a scream frozen in her throat. Slowly, the person reached into his pocket and pulled out an object. Aria heard a *flick*.

'No,' she whispered.

Time slowed down. The air felt thick and still. Then the forest turned orange. Everything lit up. Aria screamed and sprinted back up the ravine. She careened into trees and stepped in a small ditch, twisting her ankle. For the first few seconds, all she heard was the hideous crackle of the fire building and building, eating everything in its path. But as she rounded a corner, she heard another sound. It was small and pitiful and desperate. A tiny whimper.

Aria stopped. The flames were at the ravine, where she'd been moments ago. To the right was a huddled figure. This person seemed smaller and weaker-looking than the figure that had traipsed through the woods moments before, lighting everything on fire. The person's leg was caught underneath a heavy tree branch that had fallen, and tiny, fingerlike flames were climbing up the branch, closer and closer to the person's foot.

'Help!' whoever it was screamed. 'Please!'

Aria sprinted up. The person's face was covered by a huge hood. She assessed the log. It was big and bulky, and she hoped she could move it.

'You're going to be okay,' she shouted, her face beginning to warm from the flames. Mustering her strength, Aria shoved the log down the hill. It rolled into a pool of gas and exploded. The person shrieked and collapsed against the tree. There was another deafening *crack* behind them, and Aria turned and screamed. The woods were a wall of orange. The fire was climbing the trees now, felling more branches. In seconds, they would be surrounded.

The person was still pressed against the tree trunk, staring at Aria with a shell-shocked look on his or her sooty face. 'Come on,' Aria wailed, starting to run. 'We have to get out of here before we're dead!'

31
Rising From The Ashes

Emily, Spencer, and Hanna sprinted out of the barn, running as fast as they could away from the flames that had erupted around them. The air smelled thickly of smoke and burning trees. Emily's lungs burned as she ran.

They waded through a bunch of thick shrubs, ignoring the burrs that were affixed to their sweaters, skin, and hair. Then Hanna abruptly stopped and pressed her hands to the top of her head. 'Oh my God,' she wailed. '*Wilden*. I saw him the other day at Home Depot, loading a bunch of drums of something into his car. It was *propane*.'

Emily felt nauseated and dizzy. She thought of how Jason had stared right at her the other night, after he'd left Jenna's house. How Wilden had glared at them at the party. They *knew*.

'Come *on*,' Spencer urged, pointing through the trees. They could see the outline of Spencer's windmill ahead. Safety was close.

The wind kicked up, blowing ashes everywhere. Something flat and square fluttered past Emily, coming to a stop at the foot of a small, knobby tree. It was the picture from the Ali shrine, the one of Ali wearing a Von Dutch T-shirt and the four of them surrounding her, laughing. The corners of the photo were charred from the flames, and half of Spencer's head had been burnt away. Emily gazed into Ali's joyful, bright blue eyes. Here they were, running through the very woods where she'd died, with quite possibly the same people who had killed her trying to kill them, too.

They burst into Spencer's backyard, coughing the noxious smoke out of their lungs. The Hastingses' windmill was on fire, too. Each of the old, wooden blades broke off and clattered to the ground. The bottom part, which had *LIAR* written across it in bloodred spray paint, was lying flat on the grass, seemingly burning the brightest.

A thin scream emerged from the woods. At first Emily thought it was a fire engine siren – surely they were on their way. Then, she heard another scream, shrill and terrified. She grabbed Spencer's hand. 'What if that's Aria? Her new house is one neighborhood over. She could've cut through the woods to get here.'

Before Spencer could answer, two figures tumbled out from the thick, burning trees. *Aria*. Someone else was behind her, someone dressed in a bulky hooded sweatshirt and jeans.

The girls surrounded Aria. 'I'm okay,' she said quickly. She gestured to the person next to her. Whoever it was had curled in the fetal position on the dead grass. 'He was trapped under a big branch,' Aria explained. 'I had to push it off.'

'Are you hurt?' Emily asked the person. He shook his head, whimpering again. Far off in the distance, a fire engine wailed. Hopefully they'd send an ambulance, too.

'What were you doing in the woods, anyway?' Spencer asked him.

The person let out a violent, hacking cough. 'I got a note.'

Emily paused. The person's voice was barely more than a whisper, but it sounded like a girl's, not a boy's. 'A ... note?' Emily repeated.

The girl covered her face with her hands, shuddering with sobs. 'I was told to come into these woods. It was really important. But I think they were trying to kill me.'

'*They?*' Spencer asked. She gaped at the others. The flames from the woods danced across her face.

The girl coughed again. 'I was sure I was going to die.'

A slithery feeling crawled over Emily's skin. The girl's voice was still muffled and scratchy, but it had a tonal quality Emily hadn't heard for a long, long time. *I've inhaled too much smoke*, she told herself. *I'm hearing what I want to hear*. But when she looked at the others, they had startled expressions on their faces too.

'It's okay. You're safe now,' Spencer murmured.

The girl tried to nod. When she took her hands away from her face, they were covered in black soot. Then she lifted her head. The soot and smoke had streaked down her cheeks, revealing clear, pink skin. When she looked at the girls for the first time and smiled gratefully, Emily's heart stopped. The girl had bright blue eyes. A perfect, slightly upturned nose. Bow-shaped lips. As she wiped away more soot, there was her angular, heart-shaped face.

She peered at them blankly, appearing not to recognize them. But they recognized her. Hanna let out a small, pained squeak. Spencer stood very still. Emily felt so dizzy she sank to the muddy grass, clutching her head.

Here was the girl in the pictures on the news. The girl on the screen saver of Emily's phone. The girl in the photo that had blown through the woods just moments before. The one

264

who'd been wearing the Von Dutch T-shirt in that photo, laughing as if nothing bad would ever happen to her.

This can't be happening, Emily thought. *There is no way this can be happening.*

It was … *Ali.*

What Happens Next...

Ha! Betcha didn't see that one coming. But you know how it is in Rosewood – one minute you see something, and the next ... poof! It's gone. Which makes it kind of impossible to figure out what's really going on. Soooooo frustrating, right?

The questions are probably killing you: Is Ian actually dead ... or is he sipping mojitos in Mexico, plotting his revenge? Did Spencer's faux-mommy really steal her cash ... or did she simply pay my price? Is Aria's crush a psychotic murderer ... or did my notes just make her think so? Did Emily uncover a dark DiLaurentis family secret ... or did yours truly leave the sign book for her to find? Did Hanna's favorite cop just try to burn her to a crisp ... or does someone else want these bitches dead? And what about me? Am I on these girls' sides, or am I pulling all the strings?

But here's the million-dollar question: Who – or *what* – did they just see rise from the ashes? Could Ali be *alive*? Or is it all just smoke and mirrors?

It's enough to make *anyone* crazy. The Radley may be closed for business, but there are other loony bins nearby. By the time I'm done with Hanna, Aria, Spencer, and Emily, four pretty new patients might just be checking in.

Sleep tight, girlies. While you still can.

Kisses,

– A

Acknowledgments

Words cannot express how grateful and fortunate I am to have such a smart, driven, and creative editorial team behind me, helping to make *Killer* as twisted, riveting, and tight as it possibly could be. Enormous thanks goes to Josh Bank and Les Morgenstein, for their spot-on sense of what makes a great plot; to Kristin Marang, for all her help on the wonderful Pretty Little Liars Web site; to Sara Shandler, creative genius extraordinaire and lover of dogs; and especially to Lanie Davis, for being a pleasure to work with, for sitting through many a long phone call struggling to piece exactly how this book hinged together, and for having so many ideas that really pushed *Killer* to the next level. Huge thanks to Farrin Jacobs, Gretchen Hirsch, and Elise Howard at HarperCollins for all their skillful input, fastidious attention, and unrelenting support. I am forever indebted.

Thanks to the readers of these books, many of whom I have had the pleasure of meeting and talking with. Thanks to my husband, Joel; my sister, Alison; my parents, Shep and Mindy; and my parents-in-law, Fran and Doug, for allowing me to write this novel in their living room. And finally, this book is for Riley, a wonderful bear of a dog. We will miss you so.

The mystery continues in . . .

Pretty Little Liars

HEARTLESS

1
Don't Breathe In

Emily Fields opened her eyes and looked around. She was lying in the middle of Spencer Hastings's backyard, surrounded by a wall of smoke and flames. Gnarled tree branches snapped and dropped to the ground with deafening thuds. Heat radiated from the woods, making it feel like it was the middle of July, not the end of January.

Emily's other old best friends, Aria Montgomery and Hanna Marin, were nearby, dressed in soiled silk and sequined party dresses, coughing hysterically. Sirens roared behind them. Fire truck lights whirled in the distance. Four ambulances barreled onto the Hastingses' lawn, giving no heed to the perfectly shaped shrubs and flower beds.

A paramedic in a white uniform burst through the billowing smoke. 'Are you all right?' he cried, kneeling down at Emily's side.

Emily felt as if she'd awakened from a yearlong sleep. Something huge had just happened ... but *what*?

The paramedic caught her arm before she collapsed to the ground again. 'You've inhaled a lot of smoke,' he yelled. 'Your brain isn't getting enough oxygen. You're lapsing in and out of consciousness.' He placed an oxygen mask over her face.

A second person swam into view. It was a Rosewood cop Emily didn't recognize, a man with silvery hair and kind green eyes. 'Is there anyone else in the woods besides the four of you?' he shouted over the din.

Emily's lips parted, scrambling for an answer that felt just beyond her reach. And then, like a light switching on, everything that had happened in the last few hours flooded back to her.

All those texts from A, the torturous new text messages insisting that Ian Thomas hadn't killed Alison DiLaurentis. The sign-in book Emily had found at the Radley hotel party with Jason DiLaurentis's name all through it, indicating he might have been a patient back when the Radley was a mental hospital. Ian confirming on IM that Jason and Darren Wilden, the cop working on Ali's murder case, had been the ones to kill Ali – and warning them that Jason and Wilden would stop at nothing to keep them quiet.

And then the flicker. The horrible sulfuric smell. The ten acres of woods bursting into flames.

They'd run blindly to Spencer's yard, catching up with Aria, who'd cut through the woods from her new house one street over. Aria had a girl with her, someone who'd been trapped in the fiery woods. Someone Emily thought she'd never see again.

Emily pulled the oxygen mask away from her face. '*Alison*,' she shouted. 'Don't forget Alison!'

The cop cocked his head. The paramedic cupped his hand to his ear. 'Who?'

Emily turned around, gesturing to where Ali had just been lying on the grass. She took a big step back. Ali was gone.

'*No*,' she whispered. She wheeled around. The paramedics were loading her friends into ambulances. 'Aria!' Emily screamed. 'Spencer! Hanna!

Her friends turned. 'Ali!' Emily screeched, waving at the now-empty spot where Ali had been. 'Did you see where Ali went?'

Aria shook her head. Hanna held her oxygen mask to her face, her eyes darting back and forth. Spencer's skin paled with terror, but then a bunch of EMTs surrounded her, helping her into the back of an ambulance.

Emily turned desperately to the paramedic. His face was backlit by the Hastingses' burning windmill. 'Alison's *here*. We just saw her!'

The paramedic looked at her uncertainly. 'You mean Alison DiLaurentis, the girl who ... died?'

'She's not dead!' Emily wailed, nearly tripping over a tree root as she backed up. She gestured toward the flames. 'She's hurt! She said someone was trying to kill her!'

'Miss.' The cop placed a hand on her shoulder. 'You need to settle down.'

There was a snap a few feet away, and Emily pivoted. Four news reporters stood near the Hastingses' deck, gaping. 'Miss Fields?' a journalist called, running toward Emily and jabbing her microphone in Emily's face. A man with a camera and another guy holding a boom raced forward too. 'What did you say? *Who* did you just see?'

Emily's heart pounded. 'We've got to help Alison!' She looked around again. Spencer's yard was crawling with cops and EMTs. By contrast, Ali's old yard was dark and empty. When Emily saw a shape dart behind the wrought-iron fence that separated the Hastingses' yard from the DiLaurentises', her heart leapt. *Ali?* But it was only a shadow made by the flashing lights of a police car.

More journalists gathered, spilling from the Hastingses' front and side yards. A fire truck screamed up too, the firefighters leaping from the vehicle and pointing a huge hose at the woods. A bald, middle-aged reporter touched Emily's arm. 'What did Alison look like?' he demanded. 'Where has she been?'

'That's enough.' The cop brushed everyone away. 'Give her some space.'

The reporter shoved the microphone at him. 'Are you going to investigate her claim? Are you going to search for Alison?'

'Who set the fire? Did you see?' another voice screamed over the sound of the fire hoses.

The paramedic maneuvered Emily away from them. 'We need to get you out of here.'

Emily let out a fevered whimper, desperately staring at the empty patch of grass. The very same thing had happened when they saw Ian's dead body in the woods last week – one minute he was lying there, bloated and pale on the grass, and the next he was … *gone*. But it couldn't be happening again. It *couldn't*. Emily had spent years pining over Ali, obsessing over every contour of her face, memorizing every hair on her head. And that girl from the woods looked *exactly* like Ali. She had Ali's raspy, sexy voice, and when she wiped the soot from her face, it had been with Ali's small, delicate hands.

They were at the ambulance now. Another EMT clapped the oxygen mask back over Emily's mouth and nose and helped her onto a small cot inside. The paramedics buckled themselves in beside her. Sirens whooped, and the vehicle rolled slowly off the lawn. As they turned onto the street, Emily noticed a police car through the ambulance's back window, its sirens silenced, the headlights off. It wasn't driving toward the Hastingses' house, though.

She turned her attention back to Spencer's house, looking once more for Ali, but all she saw were curious bystanders. There was Mrs McClellan, a neighbor from down the street. Hovering by the mailbox were Mr and Mrs Vanderwaal, whose daughter, Mona, had been the original A. Emily hadn't seen them since Mona's funeral a few months ago. Even the Cavanaughs were there, gazing at the flames in horror. Mrs Cavanaugh had a hand resting protectively on her daughter Jenna's shoulder. Even though Jenna's sightless eyes were obscured by her dark Gucci sunglasses, it seemed like she was staring straight at Emily.

But Ali wasn't anywhere in the chaos. She'd vanished – again.

2
Up In Smoke

About six hours later, a perky nurse with a long brown ponytail pushed back the curtain to Aria's little cordoned-off nook in the Rosewood Memorial emergency room. She handed Aria's dad, Byron, a clipboard and told him to sign at the bottom. 'Besides the bruises on her legs and all the smoke she inhaled, I think she's going to be fine,' the nurse said.

'Thank God.' Byron sighed, penning his name with a flourish. He and Aria's brother, Mike, had shown up at the hospital shortly after the ambulance deposited Aria here. Aria's mom, Ella, was in Vermont for the night with her vile boyfriend, Xavier, and Byron had told her that there was no reason for her to rush home.

The nurse looked at Aria. 'Your friend Spencer wants to see you before you go. She's on the second floor. Room two-oh-six.'

'Okay,' Aria said shakily, shifting her legs underneath the scratchy, standard-issue hospital linens.

Byron rose from the white plastic chair beside the bed and met Aria's gaze. 'I'll wait for you in the lobby. Take your time.'

Aria slowly got up. She raked her hands through her blue-black hair, little flakes of soot and ash raining onto the sheets. When she leaned down to pull on her jeans and put on her shoes, her muscles ached like she'd climbed Mount Everest. She'd been up all night, freaking out over what had just happened in the woods. Even though her old friends had been brought to the ER, too, they'd all been taken to separate corners of the ward, so Aria hadn't been able to speak to any of them. Every time she'd tried to get up, the nurses had swept into her room and told her that she needed to relax and get some sleep. *Right*. Like that was going to happen again.

Aria had no idea what to think about the ordeal she'd just been through. One minute, she was sprinting through the forest to Spencer's barn, the piece of Time Capsule flag she'd stolen from Ali in sixth grade tucked in her back pocket. She hadn't looked at the shiny blue fabric in four long years, but Hanna was convinced the drawings on it contained a clue about Ali's killer. And then, just as Aria had slipped on a patch of wet leaves, the acrid smell of gas had filled her nostrils and she'd heard the papery rasp of a match igniting. All around her, the woods exploded into flames, burning hot and bright and searing her skin. Moments later, she came upon someone in the woods screaming desperately for help. Someone whose body they'd all thought was in that half-dug hole in the DiLaurentises' old backyard. *Ali*.

Or so Aria had thought at the time. But now ... well, now she didn't know. She looked at her reflection in the mirror hanging on the door. Her cheeks were gaunt, her eyes rimmed with red. The ER doctor who'd treated Aria explained that it was common to see crazy things after inhaling a bunch of noxious smoke –when deprived of oxygen, the brain went haywire. The forest *had* been really suffocating. And Ali had seemed so hazy and surreal, definitely like a dream. Aria hadn't known that group hallucinations were possible, but they'd all had Ali on their minds last night. Maybe it was obvious why Ali was the first thing each of them thought of when their brains began to shut down.

After Aria finished changing into the jeans and sweater Byron had brought her from home, she made her way to Spencer's room on the second floor. Mr and Mrs Hastings were slumped on chairs in the waiting area across the hall, checking their BlackBerrys. Hanna and Emily were already inside the room, dressed in jeans and sweaters, but Spencer was still in bed in her hospital gown. IV tubes fed into her arms, her skin was sallow, and there were dark purple circles under her blue eyes and a bruise on her square jaw.

'Are you all right?' Aria exclaimed. No one had told her Spencer was hurt.

Spencer nodded weakly, using the little remote on the side of the bed to sit up straighten 'I'm much better now. They say smoke inhalation can sometimes affect people really differently.'

Aria looked around. The room smelled of sickness and

bleach. There was a monitor in the corner tracking Spencer's vital signs, and a small chrome sink with stacks of boxes of surgical gloves in the corner. The walls were wasabi green, and next to the floral-curtained window was a big poster explaining how to self-administer the monthly breast exam. Predictably, some kid had drawn a penis next to the woman's boob.

Emily was perched on a child-size chair near the window, her reddish-blond hair tangled, her thin lips cracked. She shifted uncomfortably, her broad swimmer's body too big for the seat. Hanna was by the door, leaning against a sign proclaiming that all hospital employees must wear gloves. Her hazel eyes were glazed and vacant. She looked even frailer than usual, her skinny, dark-denim jeans hanging loosely on her hips.

Wordlessly, Aria pulled Ali's flag from her yak-fur bag and spread it on Spencer's bed. Everyone moved in and stared. Shiny silver doodles covered the fabric. There was a Chanel logo, a Louis Vuitton luggage pattern, and Ali's name in big bubble letters. A stone wishing well, complete with an A-frame roof and crank, was in the corner. Aria traced the outline of the well with her finger. She didn't see any glaring, vital clues here about what might have happened to Ali the night she was killed. This was the same kind of stuff everyone drew on their Time Capsule flags.

Spencer touched the edge of the fabric. 'I forgot Ali made bubble letters like that.'

Hanna shivered. 'Just seeing Ali's writing makes me think she's here with us.'

Everyone raised their heads, exchanging a spooked glance. It was obvious they were all thinking the same thing. *Just like she was with us in the woods a few hours ago.*

At that, they all spoke at once. 'We've got to—' Aria blurted.

'What did we—' Hanna whispered.

'The doctor said—' Spencer hissed a half-second later. They all stopped and looked at one another, their cheeks as pale as the pillowcases behind Spencer's head.

It was Emily who spoke next. 'We've got to do something, guys. Ali is *out there*. We need to figure out where she went. Has anyone heard anything about people looking for her in the woods? I told the cops we saw her, but they just stood there!'

Aria's heart flipped. Spencer looked incredulous. 'You told the cops?' she repeated, pushing a strand of dirty blond hair out of her eyes.

'Of course I did!' Emily whispered.

'But ... Emily ...'

'What?' Emily snapped. She glared at Spencer crazily, as if there was a unicorn horn growing out of her forehead.

'Em, it was just a hallucination. The doctors said so. Ali's *dead.*'

Emily's eyes boggled. 'But we *all* saw her, didn't we? Are you saying we all had the exact same hallucination?'

Spencer stared unblinking at Emily. A few tense seconds passed. Outside the room, a beeper went off. A hospital bed with a squeaky wheel rolled down the hall.

Emily let out a whimper. Her cheeks had turned bright pink. She turned to Hanna and Aria. 'You guys think Ali was real, right?'

'It *could* have been Ali, I guess,' Aria said, sinking into a spare wheelchair by the tiny bathroom. 'But, Em, the doctor told me it was smoke inhalation. It makes sense. How else could she have just vanished after the fire?'

'Yeah,' Hanna said weakly. 'And where would she have been hiding all this time?'

Emily slapped her arms to her sides violently. The IV pole next to her rattled. 'Hanna, you said you saw Ali standing over you in your hospital bed the last time you were here. Maybe it really *was* her!'

Hanna fiddled with the high heel of her suede boot, looking uncomfortable.

'Hanna was in a coma when she saw Ali,' Spencer jumped in. 'It was obviously a dream.'

Undaunted, Emily pointed at Aria. 'You pulled someone out of the woods last night. If it wasn't Ali, then who was it?'

Aria shrugged, running her hands along the spokes on one of the wheelchair's wheels. Out the big window, the sun was just coming up. There was a line of shiny BMWs, Mercedes, and Audis in the hospital parking lot. It was amazing how normal everything looked after such a crazy night. 'I don't know,' she admitted. 'The woods were so dark. And ... oh *shit*.' She dug in the inner pocket of her bag. 'I found this last night.'

She opened her palm and showed them the familiar-looking Rosewood Day class ring with a bright blue stone. The inscription on the inside of the band said IAN THOMAS. When they'd discovered Ian's supposedly dead body in the woods last week, the ring had been on Ian's finger. 'It was just lying there in the dirt,' she explained. 'I don't know how the cops didn't find it.'

Emily gasped. Spencer looked confused. Hanna snatched the ring from Aria's palm and held it to the light above Spencer's bed. 'Maybe it fell off Ian's finger when he escaped?'

'What should we do with it?' Emily asked. 'Turn it in to the cops?'

'Definitely not,' Spencer said. 'It seems a little convenient that we see Ian's body in the woods, make the cops search the place, they find nothing, and then *voilà*! We find a ring just like that. It makes us look suspicious. You probably shouldn't have picked it up at all. It's evidence.'

Aria crossed her arms over her Fair Isle sweater. 'How was *I* supposed to know that? So what should I do? Put it back where I found it?'

'No,' Spencer instructed. 'The cops will be mobbing those woods again because of the fire. They might notice you putting it back and ask questions. Just hold on to it for now, I guess.'

Emily shifted impatiently in the little chair. 'You saw Ali after you found the ring. Right, Aria?'

'I'm not sure,' Aria admitted. She tried to think about those frantic minutes in the woods. They were growing blurrier and blurrier. 'I never actually *touched* her . . .'

Emily stood up. 'What is wrong with you guys? Why do you suddenly not believe what we saw?'

'Em,' Spencer said gently. 'You're getting really emotional.'

'I am not!' Emily cried. Her cheeks flushed bright pink, making her freckles stand out.

They were interrupted by a loud, squawking alarm in an adjacent room. Nurses yelled. There were frantic footsteps. A sick feeling welled in Aria's stomach. She wondered if it was the alarm warning that someone was dying.

A few moments later, the wing fell silent again. Spencer cleared her throat. 'The most important thing is figuring out who set that fire. *That's* what the cops need to concentrate on right now. Someone tried to kill us last night.'

'Not just someone,' Hanna whispered. '*Them.*'

Spencer looked at Aria. 'We got in touch with Ian in the barn. He told us everything. He's sure Jason and Wilden did it. Everything we talked about last night is true, and they're definitely out to keep us quiet.'

Aria's chest heaved, remembering something else. 'When I was in the woods, I saw someone set the fire.'

Spencer sat up even more, her eyes saucers. '*What?*'

'Did you see their face?' Hanna exclaimed,

'I don't know.' Aria shut her eyes, calling back the horrible memory. Moments after she'd found Ian's ring, she'd seen someone skulking through the woods only a few paces ahead of her, his hood pulled tight and his face in the shadows. Instantly, she felt in her bones that it was someone she knew. When she realized what he was doing, her limbs froze. She felt powerless to stop him. In seconds, the flames were speeding along the forest floor, making a hungry beeline for her feet.

She felt her friends' stares, waiting for her answer. 'Whoever it was had a hood on,' Aria admitted. 'But I'm pretty sure it was ...'

Then she trailed off at the sound of a loud, long creak. Slowly, the door to Spencer's hospital room swung open. A figure emerged in the doorway, his body backlit in the bright hall. When Aria saw his face, her heart jumped to her throat. *Don't pass out*, she told herself, instantly feeling woozy. It was one of the people A had warned them about. The person Aria was almost certain she'd seen in the woods. One of Ali's killers.

Officer Darren Wilden.

'Hello, girls.' Wilden strutted through the door. His green eyes were bright, and his handsome, angular face was chapped from the cold. His Rosewood police uniform fit him snugly, showing off how in shape he was.

Then he paused at the edge of Spencer's bed, finally noticing the girls' unwelcoming expressions. 'What?'

They exchanged terrified glances. Finally, Spencer cleared her throat. 'We know what you did.'

Wilden leaned against the bed frame, careful not to bump into Spencer's IV fluids. 'Excuse me?'

'I just called for the nurse,' Spencer said in a louder, more projected voice, the one she often used when she was on stage for the Rosewood Day drama club. 'She'll call security before you can hurt us. We know you set that fire. And we know *why*.'

Deep creases etched Wilden's forehead. A vein bulged in his neck. Aria's heart beat so loudly it drowned out all the other sounds in the room. No one moved. The longer Wilden glared at them, the tenser Aria felt.

Finally, Wilden shifted his weight. 'The fire in the *woods*?' He let out a dubious sniff. 'Are you serious?'

'I saw you buying propane at Home Depot,' Hanna said shakily, her shoulders rigid. 'You were putting three jugs into the car, easily enough to burn those woods. And why weren't you on the scene after the fire? Every other Rosewood cop was.'

'I saw your car speeding *away* from Spencer's house,' Emily piped up, curling her knees into her chest. 'Like you were fleeing the scene of the crime.'

Aria sneaked a peek at Emily, uncertain. She hadn't noticed a cop car leaving Spencer's house last night.

Wilden leaned against the little metal sink in the corner. 'Girls. *Why* would I set fire to those woods?'

'You were covering up what you did to Ali,' Spencer said. 'You and Jason.'

Emily turned to Spencer. 'He didn't *do* anything to Ali. Ali's alive.'

Wilden jerked and glanced at Emily for a moment. Then he appraised the other girls, a look of betrayal on his face. 'You really believe *I* tried to hurt you?' he asked them. The girls nodded almost imperceptibly. Wilden shook his head. 'But I'm trying to *help* you!' When there was still no response, he sighed. 'Jesus. Fine. I was with my uncle last night when the fire broke out. I lived with him in high school, and he's really sick.' He shoved his hands into his jacket pockets and whipped out a piece of paper. 'Here.'

Aria and the others leaned over. It was a receipt from CVS. 'I was picking up a prescription for my uncle at nine fifty-seven, and I heard the fire started around ten,' Wilden said. 'I'm probably even on the drugstore's security camera. How could I be in two places at once?'

The room suddenly smelled pungently of Wilden's musky cologne, making Aria woozy. Was it possible Wilden *wasn't* the guy she'd seen in the woods lighting the fire?

'And as for the propane,' Wilden went on, touching the large bouquet of flowers that sat on Spencer's nightstand, 'Jason DiLaurentis asked me to buy it for his lake house in the Poconos. He's been busy, and we're old friends, so I said I'd do it for him.'

Aria glanced at the others, taken aback by Wilden's nonchalance. Last night, finding out that Jason and Wilden were friends had seemed like a huge breakthrough, a secret busted open. Now, in the light of day, with his open admission, it didn't seem to matter very much at all.

'And as for what Jason and I did to Alison . . .' Wilden trailed off, stopping by a little tray on wheels that held a small pitcher of water and two foam cups. He looked dumbstruck. 'It's crazy to think I'd hurt her. And Jason's her brother! You really think he's capable of that?'

Aria opened her mouth to protest. Last night, Emily had found a sign-in ledger from when the Radley was a mental hospital with Jason DiLaurentis's name all through it. New A had also teased Aria that Jason was hiding something – possibly about issues with Ali – and tipped off Emily that Jenna and Jason were fighting in Jenna's window. Aria hadn't wanted to believe that Jason was guilty – she'd gone on a few dates with him the week before, fulfilling a longtime crush – but Jason had flown off the handle when Aria had gone to his apartment in Yarmouth on Friday.

Wilden was shaking his head with utter disbelief. He seemed so blindsided by all this, which made Aria wonder if anything A had led them to believe was even remotely true. She gazed questioningly at her friends. Their faces were laced with doubt, too.

Wilden shut Spencer's door, then turned around and glared at them. 'Let me guess,' he said in a low voice. 'Did your New A plant these ideas in your heads?'

'A is *real*,' Emily insisted. Time and again, Wilden had insisted that New A was nothing more than a copycat. 'A took pictures of you, too,' she went on. She rifled through her pocket, pulled out her phone, and scrolled to the picture message of Wilden going to confession. Aria caught sight of A's accompanying note: *What's he so guilty about?* 'See?' Emily dangled it under his nose.

Wilden stared at the screen. His expression didn't change. 'I didn't know it was a crime to go to church.'

Scowling, Emily stuffed her phone back into her swim bag. A long pause followed. Wilden pinched the flap of skin at the bridge of his long, sloped nose. It seemed like all the air in the room had seeped out the windows. 'Look. I need to tell you what I *really* came in here for.'

His irises were so dark they looked black. 'You girls have to stop saying you saw Alison.'

Everyone exchanged a startled glance. Spencer looked a bit vindicated, raising a perfectly arched eyebrow as if to say, *I told you so*. Predictably, Emily was the first to speak. 'You want us to *lie}*'

'You *didn't* see her.' Wilden's voice was gruff. 'If you keep saying you did, it's going to bring a lot of unwanted attention on you. You think the backlash was bad when you said you saw Ian's body? This will be ten times worse.

Aria shifted her weight, fiddling with the cuff of her hooded sweater. Wilden was speaking to them like he was a South Philly cop and they were meth dealers. But what had they done that was so wrong?

'This isn't fair,' Emily protested. 'She needs our help.'

Wilden raised his hands to the white popcorn ceiling in defeat. His sleeves were rolled to his elbows, revealing a tattoo of an eight-pointed star. Emily was glancing at the star too. From her narrowed eyes and wrinkled nose, Aria guessed she wasn't a fan.

'I'm going to tell you something that's supposed to be top secret,' Wilden said, lowering his voice. 'The DNA results for the body the workers found in the hole are at the station. It's a perfect match for Alison, girls. She's dead. So do what I say, okay? I really *am* looking out for your best interest.'

At that, he flipped open his phone, strode out of the room, and slammed the door hard. The foam cups on the food tray wobbled precariously. Aria turned back to her friends. Spencer's lips were pressed together fretfully. Hanna chewed anxiously on a thumbnail. Emily blinked her round, green eyes, stunned into speechlessness.

'So now what?' Aria whispered.

Emily whimpered, Spencer fiddled with her IV, and Hanna looked like she was going to keel over. All their perfectly crafted theories had gone up in smoke – literally. Maybe Wilden hadn't set the fire – but Aria had seen *someone* out there in the woods. Which unfortunately meant only one thing.

Whoever had lit that match was still out there. Whoever had tried to kill them was still on the loose, maybe waiting for a chance to try it again.

Sara Shepard graduated from New York University and has an MFA from Brooklyn College. She currently lives in Tuscon, Arizona, with her husband. Sara's Pretty Little Liar novels were inspired by her upbringing in Philadelphia's Main Line.